The Dreamer in Fire and Other Stories

THE DREAMER IN FIRE
and Other Stories

Sam Gafford

Hippocampus Press

New York

Published by Hippocampus Press
P.O. Box 641, New York, NY 10156.
http://www.hippocampuspress.com

Cover artwork © 2017 by Jared Boggess.
Cover design by Jared Boggess.
Hippocampus Press logo designed by Anastasia Damianakos.

First Edition
1 3 5 7 9 8 6 4 2

ISBN 978-1-61498-195-4

Contents

Casting Fractals

"Ever read much H. P. Lovecraft, kid?" asked Carl Eckhardt.

We were sitting in Mulligan's Bar down in the Lower East Side of Manhattan. It was June 1962, and it had taken me the better part of the year to find Eckhardt. Now I'd begun to wonder why I bothered.

He was well into his third drunken stupor according to the bartender. These were the years when you could drink all night in New York City as long as you knew where to go and your money held out long enough. Near as I could tell, Eckhardt had run out of both.

"Can't say as I recall the name," I answered and took a full swig of my beer. "What is it? Some kind of porn?"

Eckhardt chuckled and scratched his chest harshly.

"Nah. Horror stories. Back when I was a little squirt, I was nuts for the pulps, you know? I read them all. *The Shadow. Doc Savage. G8 and His Battle Aces.* But some of my favorites were the horror pulps. *Weird Tales. Shudder Stories.* I'd buy every one that came out. Drove my father nuts! He really hated those things.

"Anyway, Lovecraft was one of the big writers for *Weird Tales* and one of my favorites. He was . . ."—Eckhardt waved his hand, nearly spilling his whiskey—"ten times better than most of the other hacks. Not that it made much of a difference. Not many people remember him today and even fewer people read him. That's something we reporters can relate to, eh?"

Eckhardt motioned for another round.

"Carl, so what? What's this got to do with anything? No one's seen or heard from you since you got fired from the *Daily Mirror*. Now you're sitting here sprouting some garbage about a pulp writer from thirty years ago? What does it matter?"

The bartender served out another glass of whiskey, and Eckhardt took a hard swallow. He made the kind of hiss between his teeth that only comes with hard liquor.

"And that, my young friend Richard, is the exact point. Everything is connected. In one of his stories, Lovecraft wrote something that I've never forgotten. It's stayed with me all these years. He said, 'The most merciful thing in the world, I think, is the inability of the human mind to correlate all its contents.' I memorized it. What do you think that means, Richard?"

I shrugged. I truly didn't see the point to any of this. "I don't know. I guess that we forget a lot of stuff?"

"Nah. It means that there are things going on all around us. Stuff we don't even think is important, but it is. Everything is connected and if, *if,* we could put it all together, we'd go mad at what we saw."

"And what would we see, Carl?"

He sat there for a moment, staring at his glass before emptying it then said, "Our insignificance."

With an agility I didn't think he was capable of, Eckhardt got off his stool and stumbled toward the door. "Leave me alone, kid. Just go away, will ya?"

*　　*　　*

Carl Eckhardt had been one of the leading reporters of the 1950s in New York City. He hit all the big stories and had front-page bylines on the *New York Herald Tribune* back when that was a "newspaperman's newspaper." Carl was the kind of reporter you'd expect to see in movies like *The Front Page,* shirt sleeves rolled up, cigarette clenched in his teeth, and pounding out a breaking story on an old typewriter. He was exactly the kind of reporter I wanted to be.

When I started as a stringer back in 1959, I was in awe of the man. He walked through the newsroom like a giant. People got out of his way, and the only one who ever challenged him was his editor, Lou Kluger. Their screaming matches were legendary. Eckhardt fought for his stories hard, maybe too hard.

Then, something happened to him in 1961. It wasn't as if the fight had gone out of him, but now there was a despondency that seeped into his work. And he began to drink. Eckhardt had never been married and had no kids or family. That meant that there was nothing there to keep him from falling off the rails—which he did . . . spectacularly so.

I happened to be in the newsroom that day. One of the other reporters was working on an article about Sputnik, and I'd brought him some of the details from the paper's morgue. It wasn't a particularly interesting article and I could have written it myself, but there was a hierarchy to be maintained.

Eckhardt was in Kluger's office but, for once, he was on the receiving end of the yelling. I couldn't hear much, but Kluger was howling mad. Something about an article that Eckhardt had written about some dead Russian kids. The issue was that Eckhardt had made some implications regarding their deaths that Kluger, or someone else, strongly objected to.

Soon, almost everyone in the newsroom stopped and watched. We knew there was something epic happening even if we didn't know exactly what it was. Words like "jackass" and "joke" could be heard as well as "drunk" and "washed-up." One thing that everyone heard loud and clear was "you're FIRED!"

Eckhardt didn't even bother to clear out his desk. He just walked out of the newsroom as if this was just some play he had already seen and whose outcome he knew. He never came back to the *Herald Tribune* again.

After about a month, they were going to throw out all the stuff from Eckhardt's desk, but I put it all in a box and kept it in my apartment. I didn't know why at the time. It just seemed like the right thing to do.

For the next year, I heard rumors about Eckhardt. He stumbled from paper to paper, writing ever stranger articles. Soon, those who knew him referred to him as the 'monster of the week' reporter. Then came word that he got fired from the *Daily Mirror*. And when the *Daily Mirror* fired you, you didn't have much lower to go. He had become the reporter's cautionary tale—the kind we tell to each other in that sort of 'there but for the grace of God' type of thing. Some thought that he had broken under the stress of his work, that the big stories had simply beaten him. Others thought he just decided to crawl inside a bottle, but the result was still the same.

I'd tried to find him, but there were only rumors and gossip everywhere I went. When I got my first article published in the *Herald Tribune* (a minor piece about a murder victim), I tried to find him to show him what he had inspired me to do. But, wherever he was, he didn't want to be found.

After that brief meeting in the bar in 1962, I didn't look for him anymore. I didn't get what I wanted from him and probably never would. Besides, after the events in Texas in 1963, we all had more important things to worry about. Eckhardt slipped from my mind and from the pages of the newspapers as if he had never existed. But that was the nature of newspaper work. The only thing that mattered was today's edition. Yesterday's paper, and the men who wrote them, were forgotten.

After the New York newspaper strike of '62–'63, we all went back to work and I finally found myself writing regular articles for the *Herald Tribune*. I was one of the youngest reporters; in a rare sense of foresight, Kluger wanted someone to try and speak to the new generation. Things were happening in the country and the world, and it was an exciting time to be a reporter.

Until I got the message from Eckhardt that day at the end of July 1965.

It had been left for me at the front desk, and the secretary gave it to me as I was returning from lunch. I'd asked who had left the note and she just replied, "some bum." She hadn't been at the paper when Eckhardt was there, so she didn't recognize him; but the note was in his characteristic scrawl. It said to meet him at a certain apartment at 5 P.M. and to "bring booze." The signature was Eckhardt's usual unrecognizable jumble, but I knew it well.

I debated if I should just ignore it. Eckhardt belonged to my past and I didn't feel I owed him anything. Whatever his problem, he'd created it himself. But, like a good reporter, I smelled a story; so, at 5 P.M., I found myself climbing the stairs of a tenement in the Red Hook section of Brooklyn with a bag containing a bottle of Jack Daniel's.

The building was old, probably one of the oldest in the neighborhood. This had been a slum in the '20s and '30s and not much had changed since then. The hallways smelled of piss and vomit and there were sounds of foreign words and music spilling through the thin walls. I knocked at the appropriate door and waited. There was movement from the other side of the door as if it was taking something a great deal of effort to get to the door. Eventually, the door opened a creak and a single eye looked at me.

"Did you bring the booze?" Eckhardt asked.

I showed him the bag, and the eye relaxed and smiled at me. The door opened slowly. At first I thought it was because it wasn't used to being opened; but when it did, I saw that it was because there was so much garbage behind it.

Some people would have called Eckhardt a packrat. In 1965, he was just a nut.

"I wasn't sure you'd come," Eckhardt said as he eagerly took the bag from me and started walking down a narrow path carved through the debris in his hallway. "But I shouldn't have worried. You've got the gift, sonny Jim! Always knew you did."

"What gift is that?" I asked as I carefully navigated piles of newspapers and books and magazines that looked as if they would fall on me at any minute and crush me to death.

"The worst gift of all—*curiosity!*"

I followed him down the hall, looking in the rooms we passed on the way. They were similarly filled with newspapers and books. I noticed that not a few of the volumes had library markings on them and wondered if they'd been stolen. Eckhardt kept scratching at his chest, but I don't think he realized he was doing it. For some reason, it had become some sort of reflex action.

We squeezed around a corner and into a larger room. The tumult was only slightly lessened here. There was an easy chair near the wall by windows that had been blocked with yet more overstuffed bookcases. The chair faced a furniture contraption upon which perched three televisions. All three of them were on different channels.

There was another, wooden chair that was covered in a pile of papers. I went to move them off and make room for myself when Eckhardt shouted, "No! Don't do that. Everything is carefully ordered and arranged."

He quickly picked up the pile of papers and placed it on top of yet another pile that seemed to have no connection to the original pile. If there was any sort of order to the place, it was only in Eckhardt's mind. He scratched his chest again. Bedbugs maybe?

"What do you mean 'ordered,' Carl? This place is a dung-heap. I'm surprised you don't have rats or roaches."

He was insulted by this. "This place is clean, Richard! I'll have no filth here. Look around! Do you see decaying plates of food or garbage?"

It was true. Aside from the papers, books, and magazines, there was no evidence of food. I did notice several empty whiskey bottles that were neatly placed in the corner.

Eckhardt settled into his seat and opened the bag. He took a glass from the floor near his chair and offered it to me. I nodded a polite refusal, and he scoffed.

"Still no taste for the hard stuff, eh? You'll never be a true newspaperman if you don't learn how to drink like us."

Even if I had learned how to drink, I wasn't fond of the idea of using Eckhardt's glass.

"Why are you watching three TVs at the same time?" I asked.

"Got to keep current. You never know when something important will come on."

One of the televisions was showing a Huckleberry Hound cartoon.

I sighed. "OK, Carl, what am I doing here? What do you want?"

He looked hurt. "Ooo, such hostility from a man who used to guzzle my beer!"

"Fine," I said and looked at my wristwatch, "you've got ten minutes."

He shook his head. "Ten minutes, he gives me. How can I explain the universe in ten minutes?"

I sat down on the wooden chair and finally got a chance to look at some of the books and papers that littered the room. Most were history textbooks, while some were science and mythology and still others were newspapers from places around the world. It was as if all the information in the world had come to this place to die.

"You ever hear of a guy named Charles Fort?" he asked abruptly.

I nodded. "Sure. He was a quack. A poor man's 'Ripley's Believe It or Not.'"

Eckhardt got excited and leaned closer. "No, that's where you're wrong. Fort was an archivist of the weird. He charted those strange things that no one could explain and spent his life looking for a connection, a pattern that he never found."

"And you did?"

He shook his head. "Not all of it. Just a part, a tiny piece."

Eckhardt leaned back in his chair and closed his eyes. He looked tired and old.

"It started," he said, scratching his chest, "back in 1958 with Van Allen. You may remember that he was the guy who discovered that the earth was surrounded by radiation belts. This was big news back then and impacted a lot of the space plans. I interviewed Van Allen in '58, but I wasn't a big 'science' guy. To be honest, it was the kind of story that made all the scientists excited but didn't really have an impact on the 'man in the street.' It wasn't until I interviewed Van Allen again in '59 that I learned about what really happened.

"You see, the military brains behind our government decided that they wanted to explode an atomic bomb in outer space."

I nodded. "Yeah, I remember that. It set off one of those 'electromagnetic pulses,' didn't it?"

"It did—but it was the other bomb, the one they didn't tell anyone about, that did more."

"What are you talking about? There was no other bomb."

Eckhardt smiled. "You still believe in the government, don't you? Do you know that when the bombs were exploded, Van Allen thought it would start an atomic 'chain reaction' that would wipe out all life on this planet? He warned them not to do it, and they did it anyway! The 'electromagnetic pulse' bomb was the cover for the other bomb that was ten times more powerful. Van Allen told me he aged a lifetime that day.

"But the 'chain reaction' Van Allen feared never happened, so everyone relaxed and continued with their space radiation research and set off a few more bombs in outer space to make the Russians nervous. Except that something did happen, something unexpected."

Eckhardt opened his eyes and looked at me intently.

"Haven't you ever wondered, Richard, why everything is going to hell? Since 1958, the world keeps getting worse and worse. I could give you a list of all the crap that's happened in the last seven years and it's going to get worse."

I just shook my head.

"The world's going through changes, Carl. You can't have change without pain."

"*PAIN?* You call this pain?" He threw a pile of papers at me. There were pictures and statements in folders. I could see photos of JFK's assassination mixed with pictures of bodies frozen in snow and Asian villages being torched while flaming children ran down the streets. "The world's going mad, Richard."

"Carl, this doesn't prove anything. You know that there have been disasters like this throughout history. Are you going to blame Lincoln's assassination on this now?"

"No! You're not getting it! You remember what I told you once? 'Everything is connected!' It didn't start in 1958; it just got worse. Because of the bombs."

I started to get out of my chair. "You know, you're starting to sound like one of those conspiracy nuts who believe that JFK was killed by the mob. Why did you want me to come here anyway? I haven't seen or heard from you in years, and now you want to meet and you start sprouting all these insane theories. Why am I here?"

Eckhardt took a big swig of whiskey from his glass and glared at me.

"OK, here it is." He wiped his mouth with his hand. "When they kicked me out of the *Herald Tribune,* I left some stuff there in my desk. I need it back now. Do you have any idea what happened to it? Did they throw it out?" His voice was that of a pleading man; a drunk begging for one more drink.

Until that moment, I had completely forgotten about the box buried in my closet. I looked at him and wondered if I should tell him the truth and eventually decided to because, if for no other reason, it would get me out of there faster. "I have it. I put all the stuff from your desk in a box and kept it."

His face lightened up. It was like seeing a kid when he wakes up and realizes it's Christmas morning.

"You have it? THANK GOD! You've got to bring me the box. Right away. TONIGHT!"

I shook my head. "No, I'm not doing that, Carl. I'll bring it over in a couple of days when I have a chance, or I'll send it over by some courier. You've waited for it for a few years, you can wait a few more days."

He wanted to hit me then. I could see it in his eyes, but then they relaxed except that the hate was replaced with a steely glare. "Sure, no problem, Richard. You send it over when you get a chance. Why don't you sit down and have a drink with me? Talk about old times."

"No thanks," I said as I started walking down the path back to the front door. "I'll get that stuff to you but, Carl, don't call me again. You understand?"

"Sure, sure, I understand. But listen, Richard, don't take too long, OK? I'm running out of time. 'The center cannot hold!'"

I was out the door and away before he could say any more. Carl Eckhardt had become a fungus and I was intent upon scraping him off my shoe as quickly as possible.

*   *   *

I forgot about Eckhardt almost immediately.

There were other things that were going on in the world and I truly didn't care that much about a washed-up reporter who was festering in an apartment full of junk. The world was moving forward in ways that no one could have predicted before. Martin Luther King Jr. had led his successful four-day march to Montgomery, Alabama, with 25,000 civil rights activists earlier in the year. President Johnson had announced his plan for a 'perfect society' and we all felt that we were building a better world.

Except then things started to fall apart.

Malcolm X, a radical civil rights activist, had been assassinated that February. Johnson escalated the 'police action' in Viet Nam by bringing the number of troops overseas to 125,000 in July, which was the same month he announced his "War on Poverty" by creating Medicare and Medicaid. More than one of us in the newsroom wondered about

Johnson's schizophrenic nature. And then, three days after I had left Eckhardt's apartment in a huff, the Watts neighborhood of Los Angeles exploded in a race riot.

It began as a typical traffic stop with the white California Highway Patrol officer stopping a black driver he believed to be intoxicated. It escalated quickly from there and would last for four days. What made it so horrifying and frightening to everyone was that it was televised. The violence was right there in your living room. There were frequent bulletins on the TV and updates coming over the wires. Most of us slept in the newsroom for those four days, deathly afraid that we would miss the latest news. Through it all, Walter Cronkite was there on CBS News.

When it was all over, there were 34 deaths, 1,032 injuries, 3,438 arrests, and more than $40 million in property damage. It was the worst riot in American history and, even more than the sight of 25,000 people marching for equal rights, it seared the racial experience into our minds.

It had been the kind of four days that you couldn't forget if you tried. I had put the last words down on an article about local reaction to the riots and had given it to the stringer when my phone rang. It was the Police Department and they wanted to verify my name and address. I was then told that I needed to get to my apartment quickly. The implication was that if I did not show up, they would come and get me.

The cab got me home fast but couldn't get me through the police barricade. I gave my name to the first cop I saw, and he rushed me through into the building. I didn't live in a really expensive neighborhood, but it wasn't a slum either. As I walked inside, the janitor gave me an evil look. It was likely that I'd have to be looking for a new home after this.

My place was on the third floor, and I passed several cops going up and down the stairs. A couple of medical-looking people were talking among themselves outside my door and just shaking their heads. I caught the words "from the inside" before I was hustled away from them. No matter how much I asked, no one would tell me why I was there, but that became obvious once I walked through my front door.

The place had been ransacked. All my books and records and stuff had been tossed across the room. "This is it?" I asked the cop who'd escorted me upstairs. "You called me here because my place got robbed?"

"Nah," said the detective in a cheap but clean suit who walked over to me. "We called you because of him."

He pointed behind my couch, and there was Eckhardt. He was not only dead but quite spectacularly dead. Something had ripped a bloody hole in his chest.

"I'm Detective Cardy. This is your apartment, right?"

I was stunned. Even though I had covered murder trials, I had never seen a dead body myself. Especially not one I knew.

"Yeah, yeah, this is my place. What the hell happened here?"

Cardy guided me away from the body, but I couldn't keep from looking at it. "That's what we're hoping you can tell us. Did you know him?"

"What? Yeah, that's . . . that's Carl Eckhardt. I used to work with him at the paper. He was a reporter."

"Uh-huh. And when's the last time you saw him?"

I stopped to think. "Ah, I guess about a week or so ago. I visited him at his apartment. How did he know where I lived? Who the hell did this to him?"

We walked into my small kitchen and I sat down dumbly on a chair. Part of me was horrified at seeing my friend lying dead in my living room, but the other part of me was taking notes and analyzing everything for the article I was already itching to write.

"That's a good question. We got a call from your janitor last night saying that there was a lot of noise coming from your place. When the responding officers got here, they found the door open and your friend on the floor. Any idea who might want to do something like this to him?"

I shook my head. "No, none of us had even heard from him in years. He'd dropped off the face of the earth."

"And yet you saw him a week ago? How was that?"

I explained how Eckhardt had left me a message and I had visited him at his place.

"Why did he want to see you? I mean, you hadn't heard from this mook in years, right? Then out of the blue he says 'come on over' and you come running? What's the deal?"

"I think," I said hesitantly, "that he just wanted free booze. He started going on about how there was some giant conspiracy and that the world was going to hell." For some reason, I didn't mention the box that I hoped was still in my closet.

Cardy snickered at that. "Yeah, ain't it though? And where were you last night?"

I lit a cigarette and took a deep breath, feeling the nicotine hit my system. "At the paper. I've been there for the last four or five days. I never left the newsroom except for coffee or to take a piss. We were covering the Watts Race Riot. You hear of it?"

Cardy looked disgusted, which told me a lot about the man. "Yeah, seen it on the TV. Guess we get what we deserve, huh? Anyone at the paper can verify this?"

I nodded. "Just about everyone. Go ahead and ask."

Flipping his notebook closed, Cardy grinned at me. "Oh, we will. Trust me. Thing is, this is a weird one. I mean, there's very little blood. Wounds like that, we should be swimming in blood, but there's barely enough to wet a sponge. Of course, he must have put up quite a fight, right? I mean, this place is a mess. And why would he be here anyway? He wouldn't be looking for anything, would he?"

I shrugged. "I don't know. More booze? Stuff to sell? The guy had fallen pretty far, you know. He was living like a bum."

"Uh-huh. Well, they're clearing out the body now, so we'll be out of your way in a minute. Anything else you can think of that we might need to know?"

"Not that I can think of."

"Right, well, here's my card. I'll be in touch. And you might want to invest in some new locks."

Cardy left the room and I sat there, listening and waiting. I called the night desk and quickly gave them the details. The editor was suitably unimpressed, which meant that it might get a mention in the obits and maybe in the back section. The cops took lots of pictures, made measurements, and eventually took Eckhardt away and I waited. The last cop left and still I waited until the barricades were removed and the last patrol cars drove away. There was no one left in the street when I finally allowed myself to go to the closet. There, buried beneath a pile of old clothes and bags of stuff my mother had sent me, was Eckhardt's box. I don't know how he could have missed it.

I pulled it out of the closet and brought it to the kitchen table, taking care not to look at where the body had been only an hour or so ago. Opening the box, I saw a few personal items like his nameplate and mug and desk crap. Below them was a pile of papers that I only vaguely remembered taking out of the bottom drawer of Eckhardt's desk. I sat down at the table, poured myself a glass of beer, and started to look through them.

By the time I had finished, it was late morning and I could barely breathe. It was too much for me to deal with and I was close to just burning all the files. But, like Eckhardt, I couldn't bring myself to do it. I needed to learn *more*.

After that, I began keeping records of my own and, once I knew what to look for, it wasn't hard to find. There was Albert DeSalvo, the 'Boston Strangler,' who confessed to the rapes and murder of thirteen women, although others have said he was not in it alone. Kitty Genovese, in 1963, was raped and stabbed to death outside her apartment building in Queens. Reportedly thirty-seven people in neighboring apartments saw or heard the attack and did nothing. In 1965, Hurricane Betsy (a Category 4 storm) struck Florida and the Gulf Coast resulting in eighty-one deaths and more than $1 billion in damages. In 1965, the Compton Cafeteria Riots in San Francisco began when police were called to arrest transgender customers who were picketing the cafeteria. The plate-glass windows of the cafeteria were broken and a police car's windows and doors were smashed. It is impossible to determine the injuries or deaths resulting from the riots because newspapers agreed not to cover it. To them, it never happened. Also in 1966, Charles Joseph Whitman climbed a tower at the University of Texas at Austin where, using a rifle, he shot and killed sixteen people and wounded thirty-two. His motives were unknown because Whitman was shot and killed by an Austin police officer.

The list goes on and on throughout the '60s. The Six Day War in the Middle East. The Apollo 1 test launch fire that killed three astronauts trapped in their missile. The Tlatelolco Massacre where as many as 300 students were executed by Mexican military and police ten days before the opening of the 1968 Summer Olympics in Mexico City. A leak of nerve gas in Utah kills 6,000 sheep. The My Lai Massacre where between 347 to 504 unarmed civilians in South Vietnam were murdered by U.S. troops. Victims included men, women, children, and infants, with some of the women being gang-raped and their bodies mutilated.

Then there were the assassinations of Martin Luther King Jr. and Robert F. Kennedy in 1968. The best chances for peace and guidance in the coming decades died with them. The Manson Family murders in 1969 where a pregnant Sharon Tate and others were brutally killed. 1969 also ushered in the Presidency of Richard M. Nixon. Every time I saw his face on television, I felt an itching deep within my chest.

I have made my files and my notes. Some days I wonder if Eckhardt would have made the same connections. Once you know, it becomes absurdly easy to spot it. With time, you can even spot the ones that have been influenced the most. My head hurts most of the time now. Drinking helps a bit but doesn't take it all away.

Eckhardt's original files have become the core of my collection of misery. I have them memorized in case someday my apartment is 'robbed' even though, eventually, they will find me with a suspicious hole in my chest. But I remember every word in those files.

There were eight files in the box. Most were on specific cases or events, but the last one was filled with Eckhardt's notes. He had been working on an article that would have tied all these cases, and more, together. My mind flew back to that day all those years ago when Eckhardt had gotten fired. I'm sure now that it was because of this article he tried to write.

One of the files was labeled "VA belt" and had pictures of scientists posing happily for the camera. Under one of them was the name "Van Allen." Another, later picture of him showed a man who looked haunted, as if he jumped at every sound around him. There were government reports with large blocks of text blacked out to the point where they made no sense, but there were also handwritten statements that Eckhardt had gathered from Van Allen and some of the men in the photograph. They were trying to warn about what had really happened when those bombs exploded. The words 'fractured reality' were used more than once.

Another file was even more disturbing. It was labeled "Dyatlov Pass" and had gruesome pictures of frozen bodies. It looked as if it had been the result of a failed rescue attempt, but even more disturbing were autopsy photos of some of the bodies. One had the eyes gouged out and another was posed to show that the victim's tongue was missing. Some of the papers in the file were in Russian, which I couldn't understand. A crude map showed the progress of a party through a mountainous region close to Siberia.

The third file said simply, "Space." It was a list of space missions, but I didn't recognize any of them. Most of them were Soviet launches, but there were several American ones listed as well. None of them were on any official list of space missions. Eckhardt, again, had pictures of the missiles and crew, but these were no public relations events staged for photographers. These were frightened men climbing into rocket cans for secret purposes. Eckhardt had notes next to each that read either "lost," "abandoned," or "dead on recovery." One particularly disturbing photo showed a Soviet woman standing next to a Russian general. Neither one looked eager to discover new horizons. There was a report that had a detailed translation of a transmission from one lone cosmonaut whom I believed to be that woman. She had been pleading for help, pleading for them to send someone to rescue her from something. In the end she begged them to destroy the capsule, but they refused. They demanded to know what was happening, and all she could say was that something was walking on the outside of the capsule, tapping and making *rhyming* sounds. Her last words were screams and the final lines of the translation simply said, "sounds of metal collapsing and being ripped." Eckhardt's note next to her mission said only, "sacrificed."

There were more. Many cases of unbelievable horror and brutality that, on the surface, had no connection whatsoever. But the more I looked, the more I thought I could see something there behind it all. Just when I thought I had a grip on it, though, it would slip away and leave me with only pieces of the puzzle.

That's when I read Eckhardt's notes. Like most reporters, his handwriting was terrible, but I could read most of it. At first it was like the ravings of some lunatic, but by the time I reached the end I felt entirely differently.

"ITEM: 1958. Despite warnings to the contrary by Van Allen and other scientists, America proceeds with plans to explode an atomic device in the upper atmosphere to counter Russian tests. The resultant blast knocks out electronic devices over ¼ of the hemisphere. What only Van Allen knew was that a second bomb was exploded at the same time. The first was a decoy. It was the second that was the real test. After the detonation, the Aurora Borealis reached the brightest intensity it had ever known before or since. Van Allen had been afraid that the bombs would ignite the atmosphere and set off a deadly 'cascade effect' that would destroy all life on this planet. The second bomb opened a crack in space and something came through. Van Allen is haunted by the thought of what that 'something' could have been.

"ITEM: 1959. Nine experienced hikers enter the Ural Mountains in Russia. None return. A search party finds their abandoned tent, which looks perfectly normal. There are slits in the back of the tent that later study shows were cut *from the inside*. When the bodies are found later, they were all barefoot and several were not wearing their coats. Something had compelled them to leave their tent in the middle of the night, unclothed and unprepared, to go into the snow in -22 degree temperatures. None of the corpses showed any signs of struggle, but two had fractured skulls, another two had broken ribs, and one was missing parts of her face. Her tongue had been ripped out. Photo graphic evidence found at the scene (along with personal journals of the hikers) described how the night before they had seen mysterious orbs of light above the mountains. The records of the investigation were quickly sealed and the bodies quietly buried. The official cause of death is listed as a *'compelling natural force.'* What 'natural force' found them camped alone in the mountain?

"ITEM: 1960. Largest earthquake ever recorded hits Chile. Measures 9.5 on the Richter scale. The resulting tsunami affected southern Chile, Hawaii, Japan, the Philippines, eastern New Zealand, southeast Australia, and the Aleutian Islands. Some reports list as many as 6,000 dead.

"ITEM: 1961. The Bay of Pigs invasion. The CIA launches an attempt to overthrow Castro and fails miserably and publicly. America has shown its weakness. What compelled the CIA to do this?

"ITEM: 1961. The U.S. sends 900 'military advisors' to Viet Nam. This begins a new type of war that America is not equipped morally or militarily to fight. What inspired this aggression?

"ITEM: 1962. The Cuban Missile Crisis. Russia parks atomic warheads in Cuba, sparking a confrontation that brings the world to the brink of nuclear war. The madness is spreading and quickly.

"ITEM: 1963. The 'Age of Assassination' begins with JFK and Medgar Evers. Television brings the JFK murder into everyone's home. The idea spreads that anyone can be killed anywhere at any time. JFK's assassin is himself killed on television. Murder is no longer a vague concept. No one is safe.

"Something came through.

"There is a pattern to reality lying underneath our perceptions. Sometimes, there are those who can recognize the pattern. People like Rasputin or Nostradamus. Most of us are blissfully unaware and go about our lives like ignorant ants, but—and this is the important thing—it is not just a pattern, it is a noose. A noose that is tightening around us and this world ever harder with each new completion of the circle.

"'By their fruit you will recognize them. Do people pick grapes from thorn bushes, or figs from thistles?'—Matthew 7:16."

"It's getting worse. Ever since 1958, it has escalated. The intervals between events are getting shorter and shorter. Something is making us act this way. People are easily influenced, especially when they think that they aren't. There will be no big event. There will be no apocalypse. There are no monsters. 'Cthulhu' does not exist, but the *concept* of Cthulhu does. The world will end because we contribute to it every day. One step forward, two steps back. Subtly, we are moved, shaped in the proper directions. What we think are our decisions have been made for us. Seeds have been planted that are carefully cultivated and will soon bear fruit. Those who see the pattern are removed, sacrificed like pawns on the chessboard.

"There is a deep scratching in my chest that will not go away. The more I learn, the worse it gets. 'This evil worm that gnaws the world,' said Dante.

"It is the force behind us, driving our actions, and it will not end until it is finished. I don't know what it is but I know it gets more powerful every year and there is no fighting it. This thing is in our blood now, it is in our minds, it drives us relentlessly, but it is patient. Give it ten years, twenty, even fifty, and our world will be a bloodbath of wars and violence. Massacres will become commonplace and not just in war zones but in our schools and hometowns.

"'Things fall apart; the centre cannot hold,' said Yeats. We are rushing toward oblivion but are driven there by some obscene swine-herd. The truth within me will come out of its own accord.

"God help me. I have seen the thing behind the curtain and it has seen me."

Showtime

"Hey kids! It's Captain Billy time!"

For more than ten years, that was the phrase that kids in the New England area woke up to every weekday morning. In the world of regional children's television, Captain Billy (William Turner) was approaching the big time. He had already brought the show to prominence in the New England market, far eclipsing any other show in recent memory and was approaching record numbers that hadn't been seen since the heady days of *Salty's Shack*. Within days, a new contract would be signed and Captain Billy would be on his way to national syndication. Everyone was poised for the kind of market penetration that hadn't been seen since Mr. Rogers retired, except for one thing: no one could find Captain Billy.

The rotund funnyman, loved by thousands of youngsters, had been missing for more than two weeks. The local Rhode Island network, which aired the show, filled the space with repeats and had managed, through a great deal of pressure, blackmail, and cash, to keep the events from reaching the newspapers or evening news; but I knew more than they had realized. Although I had only been working in the *Captain Billy Show* production department for the past six months, I knew panic when I saw it—and everyone was in full panic mode. Even the producer, Mr. Banks—a small, beady man who looked the part of a middle-aged accountant turned producer—acted worried, and no one could ever recall Banks being rattled by anything. Not by the lawsuits from certain children's parents, not by the rumors of sponsor kickbacks, not even by the mysterious late night 'trips' that Captain Billy would take. But this rattled him. This shook him to the core. He didn't show it around the set, but I could sense it and each day made it worse. Of course, it was strange how Banks was even more upset when Captain Billy returned.

The executives were thrilled, naturally, as Billy Turner came back just in time to sign on the dotted line and make everyone's dreams of money and syndication come true. "I just needed to take some time by myself," Billy said. "I never thought it would be such a big deal! Didn't you get my memo?" Everyone laughed and said how Billy was such a kidder and bottles of champagne flowed and various other substances were ingested and fun and laughter was had by all. Except for Mr. Banks. Not many noticed that he didn't stay around for the after-signing party or for the after-signing party "party" that was invitation only. Being only a production assistant, I wasn't included in that last celebration, but that was okay. A few of the other "non-included" office workers and I stopped at a local bar afterwards and continued with our own party. When I had finished my fourth beer or so, I staggered my way to the men's room—and that's when I saw Banks. He was sitting alone in a booth in the back, away from the lights and the noise and the people. When I got closer, I saw something that I never thought I would see. Mr. Ryan Banks, terror of the network, the man with ice water in his veins, was sobbing.

Not the kind of crying you see most people doing with little tears falling from their eyes. This man was sobbing with his entire body. He shook as he cried; so badly that you would have thought he had palsy. Unbelieving, I went up to him. "Mr. Banks, you OK?" I asked tentatively.

He recognized my voice and looked up sheepishly. "Ah, Kevin," he said, "I was just having a few drinks. Been a long few weeks, you know. Why . . . uh, why don't you join me for a few, eh?"

Now, even drunk, I knew the politics involved. When your boss asks you join him for a drink, you don't refuse. Not if you want to get anywhere, that is, and I *really* wanted to get somewhere. Banks motioned for the waitress and ordered a double shot of whiskey. I ordered the same and he chuckled at that. "You've got a way to go if you want to catch up to me, Kevin." The drinks came; he gulped his down quickly and ordered another. I tried to do the same but ended up coughing a bit and needed a few tries to get it down. Banks smiled at that and ordered another.

"So," he finally said, "everyone's still celebrating, eh? Big payday for all of us now. National syndication, big-time ratings, lots of money flowing in. Everybody's happy. Are you happy, Kevin?"

I told him I was.

He snorted into his empty glass. "I was happy once. Seems like a long time ago, though. I remember being happy when I met Bill Turner. I remember being happy when the show started climbing in the ratings. I remember being happy the first time I went to one of the 'elite' parties he throws. I don't remember being happy again after that."

I asked why he wasn't at the after-party party tonight.

"I will be, soon enough. Have to fortify myself privately first." He raised his glass. "But I'm expected and I will have to put in my appearance." He sniffed and wiped his eyes. "Did you know ... " He stopped for a moment to compose himself. "Did you know that they used to do it all through books? It's true. Once upon a time, the world communicated through books. Imagine that. No instant communication. No faxes. No phones." He chuckled to himself and then sang, "'Not a single luxury'!"

I could feel the room spinning around me and could barely hear what he was saying, but he wouldn't have made much sense even if I had been sober.

"In those days, ideas were communicated over long distance through books. Especially *dangerous* ideas. The kind of ideas you could get killed for having. Books were easily disguised and hidden if need be, but it wasn't enough. You still couldn't reach enough people because not enough of them could READ! Not to mention the fact that a lot of the books became 'forbidden' so people couldn't even find the damn things!"

Another round of drinks came and Banks downed his again. I had no idea he was such a prodigious drinker. I could barely touch mine.

"The thing that everyone kept missing was that communication was essential. Even at the right time, even when the 'stars were right,' if there weren't enough people who believed, *truly believed,* then it still wouldn't work. So things went underground for quite a while. You going to drink that?"

I shook my head, and he downed my drink as well.

"But then, at the beginning of the last century, things started to change. Faster communication of ideas was a lot easier with the invention of wireless, and they almost got it right. But only part of it got through. Still, that was enough to result in World War I and the 1918 flu epidemic. Millions died and Europe was devastated, but there still weren't enough *believers*. You have to believe to make it work. So then came radio. It helped spread the word but, primarily due to the efforts of one small scribbler from Rhode Island, a lot of people didn't take it seriously. So that resulted in World War II. Still not enough power.

"Then came television.

"Now *that* started to work. But there were problems. Sometimes the message didn't convey correctly, and that resulted in such debacles as McCarthy and Southeast Asia. But then they hit on the right formula and connection. It's taken a while to get it all together and coordinate the astronomical factors, but they're nearly ready to try it again."

Banks leaned forward and whispered to me.

"Kevin, have you ever seen what happens to kids when they watch TV? They're mesmerized. They become totally absorbed in whatever is on and they soak it all in. To top it off, they'll believe anything they see. Want to sell a piece-of-crap toy? Tell them how great it is and you won't be able to make enough of them. Packaging a new cereal or candy? Make them believe how delicious it is and it'll fly off the shelves. Their friend in Germany knew this. Capture the young and you can determine the future. And that's what Bill Turner was for. Start small. Make sure it works and then go big time. Well, it's the big time now. They're gonna spread it electronically and spread it nationally."

Banks grabbed my hand.

"Do you want to know, Kevin? Do you really want to know what goes on at the 'after-party' parties? What really walks the earth in the guise of Bill Turner? Then I'll show you!"

Banks looked into my eyes and I saw, for the briefest instant, what he had seen. It was the future. The earth had been wiped clean, and huge, hideous things slid and climbed over the wreckage of humanity.

Dark horrors swam through the air and reached through the clouds. They had been waiting for centuries to reclaim this world and now, finally, through the miracle of television, they would succeed. Cthulhu roared through the abyss. Nyarlathotep gloated over his huge camps of human slaves and pain. Hastur, in his golden lake, luxuriated in his horror. And over it all, orchestrating the terror, was Azathoth. The Lord of Chaos ululated grotesquely over the cosmos.

I fell off my chair as if an electric shock had gone through me.

"So now you see. When Bill disappeared a few days ago, I knew what was about to happen. He was getting ready for his big debut. Except . . . except when he came back, it wasn't Billy. The man was gone. In his place was something *wearing* Billy like a cheap suit. Yog-Sothoth had claimed him. It was in his eyes. God help me, I could see it and I did nothing. Nothing!"

Banks started sobbing again.

"And now I'm going to go to that 'party' and do nothing again. I'll sit there and do nothing as they gather believers and open the door. I'll do nothing when they come through and I'll do nothing when they wipe the earth clean in their image."

Banks got up to leave as two well-dressed men appeared.

"And you'll do nothing either, Kevin. You can't, you see? It's the power of television. It convinces you that it is the best thing in the world to sit there and do nothing."

I tried to get up, but my legs wouldn't work and I fell forward. I remember something very hard hitting my head and then nothing for a while.

When I woke up, it was two days later and I was in the hospital. It was explained to me that I had passed out from intoxication and hit my head on a table. A minor concussion, they said, nothing to be too worried about. As I left the hospital, I walked by the pediatric ward and saw something that happens every day, but which I had never noticed before. The children were all gathered around the television, watching.

None of them moved.

None of them blinked.

None of them did anything.

They just watched with an intensity I had never seen before.

I didn't even have to see their eyes to know that they were also looking at me and *it* was looking at me through them.

I bought a bottle of whiskey on the way home and drank it all within an hour.

Later, I put my television outside and listened to the news reports on the radio as they described strange happenings around the country.

The Captain Billy Show was number one in the ratings and Mr. Banks was nowhere to be seen.

I sat there and drank and did nothing. Because nothing was all any one man can do. Because you just can't beat good TV.

The Adventure of the Prometheus Calculation

Over the past few weeks, I had seen little of Holmes in our rooms at 221B Baker Street in London. It was not an especially alarming situation, as he would frequently be absent from our shared apartment whenever he was especially embroiled in a new case. Still, I could not help but be a little concerned, since there was always the possibility that he might be in need of repair or calibration of his internal engines.

The view from our sitting-room window was obscured by a particularly thick fog this morning. The many steam-horses and bicycles had increased the normal London fog to the point where it was practically impenetrable. The constant, steady hum of the airships that had virtually replaced the underground trains told me that they were still up there whether I could see them or not.

I was beginning to wonder if I should venture out in search of my friend myself or contact Inspector Lestrade when I head the downstairs door slam violently and Holmes's heavy, metallic footsteps on the seventeen stairs.

"Mrs. Hudson!" he cried out. "Hot water!"

When he stepped through the door, I was once again amazed at the sight of Holmes, the world's only living, functional robot. Even after years of chronicling his cases, I can barely find the words to describe him. Standing roughly three inches over six feet, Sherlock Holmes, the most brilliant detective on Earth, was a combination of cylinders, tubes, and vents. His head was an oddly shaped oval with two lenses for eyes and a round speaker screen for a mouth. His body was a large circular cylinder, not unlike a flattened barrel. His arms and legs were thin tubes with circular knobs for shoulder, elbow, hip, and knee joints. His feet were flat pads, in the shape of a turtle, while his hands were square blocks with even thinner tubes and knobs for fingers. His voice, while not unpleasant, was slightly mechanical as was to be expected.

As a doctor, I found his internal workings to be particularly interesting. The bulk of his torso was taken up by an internal combustion engine that ran on a derivative of oil. Inside was a series of pistons and gears that were more suited for diagnosis by an engineer than by a physician. The engine, or so we deduced it to be, sat in the cavity where a normal man's heart would be and ran all Holmes's other systems. Not only did it provide his locomotion but it generated the electricity that kept his remarkable brain running.

That was the vital point of Holmes's construction. All other pieces could be replaced if needed, but if his mechanical brain was deprived of its electrical fuel, everything he was and had ever seen, thought, or been would be lost. He was so like us in so many ways, and yet so different as well.

Normally Holmes took great care with his appearance. Although his existence was well known by virtually everyone in England, he did not like to call attention to himself. So he took pains to dress like a typical Englishman with clothes from head to toe. Shoes, especially made for him to give the illusion of normal boots, pants, shirt, coat, long coat, gloves, and hat were his uniform whenever he left our rooms. Today, however, all his clothes were ripped and torn. His gloves, hat, and long coat were all missing and his shirt and pants were in tatters. There was dirt and mud all over him and his hands showed signs of deep scratches and scuff-marks. I had never seen him in such disarray.

"Holmes!" I cried. "What the devil has happened to you?"

"My dear Watson, I cannot express how happy I am to see you. There have been many times this past fortnight when I was convinced that my functions would permanently cease!"

I rushed to help him to his favorite chair as Mrs. Hudson came into the room with a bucket of steaming water and we got to work cleaning off all the mud and filth. "Holmes, where have you been?"

"For the last two weeks, Watson, I have been running for my life."

"What do you mean? What case have you been working on?"

"The biggest case of my career, Watson. Everything else pales before this. It is my most important case, the only one that has ever mattered: *Who built me?*"

An hour later and Holmes was restored to his normal state of composure, although there was now a nasty dent on the back of his head which I know irritated him but which he tried desperately to ignore. And yet, he was filled with an intensity I had never seen in him before.

"We have no time to spare, Watson; we must be off to follow the thread of my current investigations. That is, of course, if you are willing to join me. I must warn you that this will be extraordinarily dangerous for us both."

"I shall stand by your side as always, Holmes."

"Excellent!" he almost shouted. "I knew my 'Boswell' would say nothing less. Bring your revolver, though; it may have no effect on me, but our opponents do not share my natural armor!"

With that he was out the door and down the steps, nearly knocking Mrs. Hudson down in the process. I rushed after him, mumbling my usual apologies to our landlady, and followed him into a steam-carriage that had appeared almost on command.

As the cab pushed through the overcrowded streets toward the West End, past the newspaper dispensers and automated restaurants, Holmes briefly brought me up to date.

"You're well aware that the details of my construction and early life are lost to me. Those memories were erased at some point. All I can recall is awakening in my parents' home where it was explained to me that my name was Sherlock Holmes and that Mycroft was my older brother, even though he was but ten years of age and I was already twice his height. I had been 'adopted,' apparently."

I nodded respectfully. All this was well known to me, but I allowed Holmes to continue.

"I was told simply that I had been found wandering the underground of the East End by Mycroft's father and brought home as a curiosity. It was determined that my brain was an actual working version of Babbage's Analytical Engine, capable of making calculations and conclusions faster than the normal man. A remarkable achievement, as Babbage himself was unable to make his own invention work. Someone had taken his designs and expanded them, giving me life, so to speak.

"As time went on, I pressed my own independence and eventually left my parents' home to make my own way in the world. Shortly after, both of my parents died when their house burned down. Mycroft blamed me and has not spoken to me since.

"It is he whom we are going to see now."

"Holmes," I said, "something has happened. There's no other reason you'd speak to your brother after so long. So what has changed?"

He sat quietly, looking out the window at our newly mechanized world. "I believe he has been trying to kill me."

Holmes opened the cab window and thrust his hand out from the cab. "Forgive me, Watson. My anger has increased my consumption."

A thin line of black smoke trailed out from under his sleeve and added to the general pollution of the city as he expelled some of his exhaust.

"I had been aware for some time that there was a force working against me. An evil counterpart to myself, if you will, and I have worked diligently toward his capture. Unfortunately, all I have been able to achieve is the arrest of his henchmen. But, as my attention focused on him, so has he focused upon me.

"Two weeks ago I was waylaid after leaving the British Museum, where I had needed to consult material relating to the Parkinson case. I was able to fight them off but not without cost. I had to hide myself while affecting repairs and, almost like clockwork, every time I would emerge, I would be attacked again. I knew then that my opponent wanted me at my peak condition. My death when weak was a meaningless victory."

"And you think that this mastermind is your brother?"

"None other. He blames me for our parents' death and seeks my destruction."

"Why now? He has known your location for years. You've not kept it a secret!"

"That is a question I long to put to him face to face."

We rode in silence to the Diogenes Club.

Mycroft had risen in society since his parents' death, eventually becoming a consultant to the highest officials of the British government.

However, he was a thoroughly disagreeable person who preferred to spend his life between two places—his home and the Diogenes Club.

This, Holmes once told me, was a private men's club for the type of man unsuited for any other men's club in London. Not just rich or powerful but rude, arrogant, and contemptuous. This was the type of man we had come to confront.

To his credit, the doorman did not flinch at the sight of a mechanical man handing him a calling card. "Ah, yes," he said slowly, "I believe you are expected, sir. Mr. *Holmes* will meet you in the private 'discussion' room."

We followed the servant through the club, which was filled with men swallowed by large, mahogany chairs who refused to acknowledge our presence despite Holmes's insistence on walking loudly.

After a few minutes in the 'discussion room,' which was a bare affair, Mycroft entered. He was an extremely large man of considerable girth. His hair was salt and pepper while his face was flush with red splotches. My medical training told me that he was suffering from a heart condition and, most likely, did not have long to live.

With a wheeze, he settled into the nearest chair and glared at both of us.

"You are nine point five minutes late," he admonished. "My calculations led me to expect you earlier!"

"Traffic," I offered, and he nodded dismissively at me.

"I see you've brought your pet along, *brother*," Mycroft said with loathing. "I've been amused by his . . . *tales* of you. All in an attempt to humanize a tin man."

Holmes turned on Mycroft. If his face were able to present emotion, I am sure it would have been one of intense hatred and loathing.

"The sight of you is equally disgusting to me, Mycroft. Shall we dispense with the pleasantries?"

Mycroft nodded.

"I have come to arrest you for the murder of our parents."

Laughing, Mycroft replied, "Once again, your deductions are faulty. Yes, I am behind the recent attempts on your 'life,' but I was working under the instructions of another—a man who seeks your destruction as fervently as do I!"

"You are seeking to distract me. I have evidence that it was you who set the fire that killed our parents."

Mycroft looked at me and pointed toward Holmes with a snide movement of his head. "Like a parrot, he keeps on repeating the same phrase over and over again."

He turned back to Holmes. "No, you abomination, that 'evidence' was left for you to find. We knew that nothing other than that would bring you here to me. I *know* that it was you who burned down the house because I *saw* you do it!

"Lost within a frenzy of hate, you destroyed the laboratory in which you were created. Simply because you sought to kill the man who gave you life."

"That is not logical," Holmes responded. "Our father was not capable of constructing—"

"Do *not* speak of him!" Mycroft shouted as his body shook with rage. "He was a good man, though somewhat simple. No, the man you wanted to kill, your *creator,* was my math tutor, Professor James Moriarty!"

The revelation shook Holmes, and I actually saw him step backward. "Impossible! I have no memory of such events."

"Because you deleted them! Erased them like some uncomfortable truth. But it *was* you, and I shall see you ripped asunder while I yet live."

Before I could move, Holmes leapt over and grasped Mycroft by his throat, lifting him off the chair.

"Where is he? Where is Moriarty?"

"Closer than you think," replied the man in the doorway. He was a thin man with an air of knowledge and learning about him.

"Moriarty!" Holmes screamed, his tin voice shrill in the room. With a movement, he snapped Mycroft's neck and reached for Moriarty, who pulled goggles over his eyes and tossed something into the room.

Suddenly, a white flash blinded me and a screeching noise filled my ears. As I lost consciousness, I saw Holmes standing as if frozen, and then I was gone.

When I awoke, Inspector Lestrade was standing over me. I tried to move, but a crippling pain seized my head.

"Slowly, Doctor. You've taken quite the blow."

I looked around and could see a few others around me, most notably Inspector Gregson. There was a sheet covering a large body on the floor; I could only assume it was Mycroft.

"What's happened here, Doctor?" Gregson asked.

I quickly filled them in on the events and saw them look at each other.

"We've reports of a man fitting your description leaving the club with a large crate."

My heart fell. "Then he has Holmes! Quickly! Where did he go?"

I struggled to my feet with Lestrade's assistance. "The doorman got him a steam-cab and heard him ask for Waterloo Station," said Gregson.

"There's no time to waste," I said. "Moriarty means to kill Holmes, and he already has a head start!"

We nearly flew to Waterloo Station, where we learned that Moriarty had had a private train waiting for him. Thankfully, a stoker had been pressed into service filling the train's boiler and had been told by the engineer to make sure there was enough coal for a non-stop trip to Essex.

That's when I knew.

"Home, Inspectors—they've gone home."

It took the better part of an hour to get Scotland Yard's airship diverted to us, and by the time we were underway I feared the worst. As we set down on the great lawn of Holmes's ancestral home, I could see the ruins. Even though the fire had occurred well over a decade before, there had been no rebuilding. The burnt shell still stood there—a silent reminder of the tragedy of that night.

The three of us leapt from the airship and began running toward the ruined pile. I was shouting out Holmes's name when the rest of the building exploded.

We were thrown off our feet and backwards by the concussion. There was nothing left of the mansion. I tried to run into the debris, but Lestrade and Gregson stopped me. I crumpled on the lawn and wept.

Shifting through the pieces, Gregson found Holmes's recording device. He'd use it when making notes for me to use. I took it home and there, the four of us (Lestrade, Gregson, Mrs. Hudson, and I) listened to Holmes's last words.

There was a conversation between Holmes and Moriarty.

"For years I tried to forget you, forget the *thing* I created."

"Why did you?"

"You were an experiment—an attempt to create mechanical life. When I saw you move and talk, when you came into my bedroom the night of your creation, I knew what I had done and could not bear it. I fled. But they took you in and cared for you."

"You deserted me. A new creation and you abandoned me."

"Yes. I should have destroyed you then, but I was willing to forget your existence."

"Then things changed."

"Mycroft came to me and revealed that he had been the one opposing you. Your 'Napoleon of Crime.' I played along until he told me what had really happened that night."

"The fire."

"You had gone back home because of what you'd discovered. Somehow you'd learned that your mother and I had had an affair and I was Mycroft's true father. You confronted them and, berserk at your mother's betrayal, went mad and started the fire. Until that moment, I did not know you had killed them, had killed *her*. I vowed to destroy you then. For her sake. Because I had loved her and she had loved me and my creation had been the cause of her death. Because you could not inspire love, you inspired fear."

Holmes's voice was cold with hate. "I have tried to give my life meaning, to be the sword of justice. Now I understand why."

"It will not help. I've wired this room. It will explode in three minutes even as your friends arrive to try and save you. 'From Hell's heart, I stab at thee . . .'"

"'For hate's sake, I spit my last breath at thee . . .'"

There was the sound of them struggling against each other and then the explosion. Finally, there was silence.

We found no trace of either man. I am sure that Holmes left the recorder for me to find. But there is still a part of me that wonders if he survived after all. At night, I find myself listening for the heavy sounds of his metal footsteps on the seventeen stairs of 221B Baker Street. Perhaps, one day, I will hear them again.

Homecoming

Ruth Frye had been missing for five days. As one would expect, the town of Dunwich had gone a little crazy because of it. The news media from Arkham and Boston came down with all their cameras and reporters, and Ruth's mother and I spent a lot of time begging her to come home or for any news. The cops spent hours searching our house, looking in every corner for clues, tearing apart her room for secret messages from boys or men, but they found nothing. They impounded her laptop and had the phone company print out every text she'd ever received or sent. They even took me in and sweated me for a very long night because, after all, I was her stepdad and she was a pretty teenager, so maybe I had something to do with it. In the end, the police had to confess that they had no clue what had happened to Ruth. She'd gone out jogging one night and, just like that, the sixteen-year-old pride of Dunwich's high school track team had vanished without a clue. No one knew where she was or what had happened to her.

Until, that is, she showed up on our doorstep on the fifth night. She was dirty, her clothes were a torn mess, and her blond hair was spotted and matted with mud. She looked as if she'd dragged herself through several miles of hell, but she was smiling as she stumbled through the door. My wife, Crystal, screamed and caught her before she fell down. Crying, Crystal asked where Ruth had been for five days, why hadn't she called? "I got lost," she said. "I've been lost in the woods. I couldn't find my way home." Together, they hugged and cried and held each other as the photographers snapped picture after picture. Stunned, I stepped forward and hugged them both, knowing that I had to make it look good. The cops would be suspicious if I didn't. But I couldn't think. My mind was blank. Because I knew, beyond a doubt, that I had killed Ruth five days earlier.

I'd held her lifeless body in my arms. I'd seen the light go out of her eyes. It wasn't like anything I'd ever expected or seen on TV or in the movies. It was as if she was just there one minute and then gone the next. I didn't feel any different either. I'd just raped and killed my stepdaughter and nothing had happened. God didn't strike me dead. The earth didn't swallow me whole and drag me to hell. Nothing was different. Well, nothing other than the fact that Ruth was dead, that is.

It's important to me that you know that I did not start out evil. I'd had a good enough childhood, I suppose. There was nothing in my youth to suggest anything like this. I didn't wet the bed. I didn't kill small animals or start fires. Sure, my father beat me up when I was a kid, but only if I misbehaved, so I learned quickly to do what was expected of me. I was just a quiet, unassuming kid who read comic books and watched a lot of TV. I wasn't the brightest kid around, but I'd always been good at fixing things, so when I grew up I got a job as a mechanic. Soon after that, I'd worked myself up to the point where I owned three garages. Even in the midst of recessions and bad economies, I managed to keep things running. I suppose, in a manner of speaking, that I was something of a success.

I'm not trying to excuse what I did or what I did afterward. I just want you to know that I wasn't always like this.

When I met Crystal, Ruth's mom, I wasn't looking for a relationship. I'd had them before and they'd never really worked out. To be honest, I knew I was ugly. My own mother said I had a face like roadkill. So I pretty much kept my head down and focused on working. Occasionally I'd go out with a few of the boys to the bars or stripclubs and, yeah, I'd had my share of lap dances and nights in sweaty hotels, but they'd never been anything special or important.

Then Crystal started coming to the garage. It seemed her car was always breaking down or needing some repair or other. Then she began coming by for no reason at all. Before I knew what was happening, we were dating, then engaged, then married. I suppose that most people considered her the dominant one in our relationship, but that didn't matter much to me. I moved into her house with her fourteen-year-old daughter and six-year-old son and, just like that, I had a ready-made family and a wife in my bed. It was a good arrangement, I guess, for a while at least. After all, for a thirty-eight-year-old woman, she still looked damn good and I enjoyed her bleached blond hair and large boobs.

I went about my business, working in the garages, keeping them going. Crystal kept the house running and was a good mom to her kids. I tried to be a good dad but didn't really know how. After all, my own father ran off when I was about twelve and Mom never remarried. There were lots of guys around, but none that she stayed with. My stepson, Kyle, was a pretty good kid, I guess. Didn't get into too many fights and had the coordination of a one-legged frog, but good enough kid.

But when Ruth turned sixteen, things changed. I didn't notice her at first, but suddenly I couldn't stop looking at her. I'd wake up thinking about her and noticed how skimpy her clothing was. I thought that she was acting nicer to me, putting her hand on my arm or bending over in front of me, but now I wonder if I was just seeing what I wanted to see. She was a pretty girl, all the folks around could see that, and she'd come from an old Dunwich family, unlike myself. I came from Marlborough and never really spent much time in Dunwich before opening my garage there. All the folks seemed to know Crystal and her kids; it was just me they weren't too sure about.

Well, I won't go into the details. After all, you don't really want to know about that, do you? Let's just say that I couldn't take it anymore. I knew where Ruth ran and I knew where the woods around Cold Spring Glen were. I found her there, jogging, and offered her a ride home. More eager than I expected, she got in my truck and we drove away. By the time she realized what was going on, it was too late. She didn't even fight me all that much. Soon she was dead and I made sure not to leave any evidence. I'd seen enough true-crime shows to know what not to do. I still can't say why I did it. No more than I can really say why I married Crystal in the first place. It just seemed that, once I set my foot on that path, it pulled me along. It's like when you get on a roller coaster. Once you're in that seat you have no choice—you just have to grit your teeth and try and make it through to the end of the ride.

But I knew one thing. Certainly and without any doubt, I knew this one thing to be true . . . Ruth was dead when I left her. Now her lifeless body was standing in the doorway and I was hugging her and trying to make myself cry. Sure, I was shaking, but it wasn't from tears.

Her flesh was warm to the touch. She smelled of trees and leaves, not death at all. When I pulled back and looked in her eyes, something looked back. It wasn't Ruth. It was something old, evil, and *hungry*. I backed away as the Ruth-thing smiled at me. For a moment, I thought I caught a glimpse of the thing behind her face but, just as quickly, it was gone and she was hugging her brother, who was crying so much that I thought he would vomit.

I looked over and saw that Detective Armitage, who had been in charge of the case and had been the one who grilled me the worst, staring at me. I felt his eyes boring into me and struggled to smile and pat Ruth on the back. Crystal wouldn't stop crying and tugging at her daughter, "Is it true? Did it really happen?" To which Ruth responded by caressing her hair and softly saying, "Yes, Mom. It really happened. I'm home now."

The TV reporters lapped it up. I think we made all the major news programs that night. They got their shots of the happy family reunited and took off. For them, the story was over. I'd be seeing them again soon enough. Detective Armitage pushed his way forward and, placing a fatherly hand on both Crystal and Ruth's shoulders, requested a few minutes with Ruth . . . alone.

I lightly pulled Crystal away and told her to go to the kitchen and fix Ruth something to eat. "She's been lost in the woods for five days. She must be hungry."

"Oh, yeah, Dad," Ruth seductively replied, "you've no idea *how* hungry I am!"

I cringed but tried not to show it.

Armitage and Ruth went into the dining room while I helped Crystal in the kitchen. She was prattling on to me about Ruth's 'miraculous' return, but I wasn't listening to her. I kept straining to hear the voices in the dining room. My hearing had never been the best, so I couldn't make out everything they were saying. I could hear Armitage's voice being forceful, but not anything Ruth said. I tried to keep my hands still, but they were shaking so hard. Frightened, I put them under the tap and ran hot water on them for as long as I could stand it.

Finally, they came out of the dining room and Crystal pushed a plate of meatloaf, mashed potatoes, and corn in front of her daughter. It was one of the meals that the neighbors had brought over for us in our time of distress. "Right," Armitage said, "I guess everything's turned out for the best. Maybe next time, little girl, you'll think twice about running out in the dark by Sentinel Hill?"

Ruth smiled and stuffed her face with food. "Walk me out, Walt?" Armitage said to me. Reluctantly, I followed him out of the kitchen.

"Remarkable story," Armitage said, "running through the woods for five days. Never catching sight of another soul or the road or the lights of town. Never even hearing the search party we had out looking for her. Truly remarkable."

"I know," I said. "I can't believe it myself."

"Yeah," Armitage replied. "I bet you can't. All right, look, Mr. Rice, I'm going to be blunt with you. Until that girl walked through that door, I thought you'd killed her. I was working hard to find enough evidence to arrest you and sweat you until you gave up her body. Your alibi was shaky—"

"I told you I'd been at the garage, working on the books."

"Yep, yep, you did. No one to verify it, though. No calls made. None received."

"But you impounded my truck! You didn't find any hair or fibers, nothing."

Armitage nodded. "True, all very true. But, you know, that was strange too. I mean, family vehicle and all. I'd expect to find *lots* of hairs and fibers and DNA all over it. But there was nothing. Odd, don't you think?"

I stumbled for words. "Well, I don't know what to tell you, Detective. Ruth's here. She's alive. What more could we want?"

"Oh, I agree! We always hope for this type of result in these cases. You know how often that happens though, Mr. Rice?" I must have looked puzzled. "Not at all. Be seeing you, Walt! Count on it!"

Armitage walked out to his car and left. I hadn't been this nervous and scared when I killed Ruth. I turned and looked back at the house, Crystal's house. I wanted to get in my truck and drive off, but I couldn't. Not just yet. I'd have to get together some cash, and that would take a few days; and I'd have to make sure that Armitage didn't suspect anything and stop me. Until then, I had to just keep it together. I had to keep away from whatever it was in that house that was calling itself Ruth.

I walked inside and went to the kitchen. They were all laughing and talking at the same time. A happy little family out of some old Norman Rockwell painting. I didn't know what to do next.

"Walt! Isn't it wonderful?? Our baby's back!" Crystal laughed and cried.

I smiled and agreed. What could I do? I couldn't yell out, "This isn't Ruth! I killed her! This is something wearing her like a hat or coat!"

So I started drinking.

By the time I'd gotten through about a case of Narragansett beer, I was well and truly drunk. I staggered off to bed and tried to get some sleep. At some point I woke up, and Ruth was staring me in the face.

"Ruth? What are you doing? Where's your mother?"

Ruth smiled. I expected snakes to curl out of her mouth. "She's asleep right next to you. Can't you feel her?"

She put her hand under the covers and touched my leg. I could feel Crystal's weight in the bed next to me.

"Wh-what do you want?"

"I want to know how you feel, Walt. Aren't you happy I'm home?"

I tried to smile, but I was starting to sweat.

"Of course I am, sweetie. I—we were all worried about you."

Ruth's face moved closer to mine. "No, you weren't, Walt. You knew exactly where I was and I know exactly what you did to me. Or, rather, what you did to 'Ruth.' But maybe I do owe you something. I mean, I wouldn't be here otherwise."

She kissed me, hard. There was nothing loving or sexy in the kiss. It was hard and mean. Her hand moved up under the covers and grabbed my penis and squeezed. My eyes teared from the pain.

"I could rip it off, Walt." Ruth whispered. "Then watch it flop around like a dead fish. Would you like that?"

I whimpered and muttered, "No . . ."

She smirked. "I bet you wouldn't." She moved away so quickly that I almost fell off the bed. "I changed my mind, Walt, I'm not going to kill you right now. I'm gonna make you watch. I'm gonna make sure you know every little thing I do in this piece-of-shit town. And as you watch me open the way for the others, you'll know that it's all your fault and you couldn't do a fucking damn thing about it."

She slinked out of the room, actually *slinked!* I never thought anyone could really do that. As she left she blew me a kiss and licked her lips. If I didn't know any better, I'd think I was in a bad horror movie.

I've never liked phones. I always thought they were an incredibly rude device. That might be because I've never liked talking on the phone. I'd always get nervous and try to rush through the call as quickly as possible even if I knew the person on the other end. But I had to accept the phone as part of my life because of my business. At any point, I could get a call from AAA to go tow someone. If I didn't have a phone, I'd lose money. But in the days after "Ruth's" return, I hated my phone even more.

I had tried to get out of the house early the next day so I could avoid seeing her, but Ruth was already gone. For the next several hours I got an endless series of texts and videos from Ruth on the phone. They started out calmly enough—"Enjoying the sunshine on this wonderful September day, aren't you?"—but they didn't stay that way.

They got worse as the day went on. Some were sexual, talking about what she wanted to do with this new body. Some taunted me, goading me about not being able to stop her. Others I couldn't understand.

"Yog-Sothoth is the gate. Yog-Sothoth is the key and guardian of the gate. Past, present, and future all are one in Yog-Sothoth. I am he as you are me and we are all together, goo goo g'joob."

There were others like that that I couldn't understand at all. It was as if she were texting gibberish or some little kid had gotten hold of her phone and was just pressing buttons at random.

Then there was a pic and text that chilled me to the bone. It was a picture of a little baby, cute and babbling in a crib. The text simply said, "Feeling hungry, time for lunch?"

I stared at the picture. I didn't know what to do. There was no way to identify the baby. I didn't recognize it and Ruth was careful enough not to show anything that would tell her location. I couldn't do anything and she knew it. I sent her texts telling her not to do anything, but she never answered. I sat and stared at my cell phone, trying to think of a way to find her. I knew that the police could run a trace on her phone, track it through their GPS system or whatever. But I'd have to tell them why and they wouldn't believe me. Short of driving aimlessly around town, I couldn't do a damn thing. So that's what I did.

As it got dark, I was still driving around in the garage's tow truck looking for Ruth. I hoped that people would figure I was just trolling for business. I couldn't find her. Ruth had an old car—a POS Honda Civic which I fixed up for her. But I couldn't find it anywhere. I called Crystal and told her I was working late. She was used to that. Then I started driving through the back roads through the woods.

Around 8 P.M., I got a message from Ruth. I was still driving and nearly ran off the road. When I opened it, it was the sound of a baby crying and Ruth laughing and chanting. I couldn't make out what she was saying, but it sounded like "N'gai n'gha'ghaa, bugg-shoggog, y'hah; Yog-Sothoth, Yog-Sothoth!"

I shut it off. I couldn't listen to any more.

The next message was a picture. I debated opening it because I wasn't sure I wanted to see it. But, eventually, I couldn't resist and pressed the button. Ruth had held the phone up and took a picture with her phone. She was naked. Her mouth was bloody and she was smiling. The text read simply, "Wanna kiss me now, Walt?"

I pulled over to the side of the road and puked.

When I got back home, Ruth was already there. She and her mother were sitting in the kitchen, laughing and talking. Ruth looked as if nothing had happened to her at all in the last week. She was smiling and happy. Truthfully, I'd never really seen her so happy before.

"Did you use the Voorish Sign?" Crystal asked her and Ruth sheepishly shook her head. "Well, that's why it didn't work." I grabbed a beer and went into the living room to watch TV. If I was hungry before, I certainly wasn't after seeing the news. I'd half expected it, of course, but to see that baby's face on the news and the parents crying over their lost child made it all too real.

"Isn't that terrible?" Crystal said behind me. "Thank God our baby is home safe and sound, right, Walt?"

I nodded as Ruth sat down on the couch next to me. My skin began to crawl as she cuddled up to me. "I know Daddy Walt's happy, Mom, I can see it in his eyes."

I tried not to vomit.

Crystal smiled and went to bed. I could feel all the blood draining out of my body.

"What did you do to that kid?" I asked.

Ruth sat up and looked at me. The air between us grew cold.

"What do you think I did?" she purred. She tossed her blond hair back as if she was posing for a photo shoot.

"I think you killed him."

She looked at me as if I was dumb. "And that's *all* you think I did? You have no imagination, Walt. None at all."

She ran a finger down the front of my shirt. "I killed him, sure. But I did other things too. There were certain . . ."—she pouted her lips—"certain *rituals* or rites that had to be done in the right order. I kinda . . ."—she flipped her head back and rolled her eyes—"kinda messed that up a bit. I'll do better next time. Just takes practice, you know?"

I shuddered. "No, no, you won't! I'm not gonna let you . . ."

Ruth lunged forward and grabbed me by the throat. "You? What the fuck do you think you can do about it? I *own* you! You go to the cops and I'll tell them you took me up by Cold Spring Glen and kept me prisoner there for five days. I'll tell them you raped me over and over again and how I barely escaped with my life. They'll love that story, especially in prison. I *know* that Detective Armitage would just love to hear me say that."

"What the hell *are* you?" I gasped.

She smirked and pulled her hand away. "Like you would know or even begin to understand what a *dhole* is. You're just like all these other *people*. Thinking that what you see is all that matters. There are other spheres of existence, ones you couldn't possibly comprehend. All this you see is just an illusion, a dream from which this world will awaken soon enough. You truly have no idea how little you all matter. Before long, I will open the way and they will break this reality apart. It's not like before." She laughed. "You humans make it all so easy for us now. Worried about your economies and money and sex. Like any of that matters. You'll learn what really matters, what this world *really* is."

Ruth leaned forward and kissed me. I tried to pull away, but she grabbed my head and held it tight. I could feel her tongue pressing against my mouth. Although I tried to keep my lips closed, she twisted my hair and her tongue darted inside my mouth. I could feel it searching, probing . . . then it split in two.

I tried to pull away, but she held my head in tight. Without wanting to, my tongue touched hers and I could feel that it was thick and scaly. Each part moved by itself, and it felt as if the parts had turned into some kind of tentacles with suckers and teeth. I grabbed Ruth by her shoulders and pushed as hard as I could. She landed on the floor with a thud and just grinned as she pulled her tongue back into her mouth. I could see that I was right and her tongue was now a pair of octopus-like tentacles. She opened her mouth and her tongue was back to normal.

"Keep your phone on tomorrow. I've got something special planned for you."

I sat in the dark and drank until I passed out.

The next morning I had a change of plans. I was going to watch Ruth all day, no matter what it took. It was a Saturday and Crystal left early with her son, Kyle, leaving me alone in the house with Ruth.

"Gonna be a busy day, Walt. Lots to do! I'll text you!" Ruth ran out the door and I was close behind her. Her white Honda headed toward the downtown area, and I followed closely in my old truck. I didn't care if she saw me. In fact, I hoped that she did see me so she'd know I was there and maybe she'd not do anything.

Ruth parked the white Honda outside of Osborn's Department Store, so I stopped further up the street and watched her walk into the store. There wasn't much in the way of stores in Dunwich. Most folks bought their food at the old IGA up on Aylesbury Pike. There was a Walmart outside Arkham, but most people didn't bother to drive that far. I waited, but Ruth didn't come out.

Cautiously, I got out of my truck and walked down the street, looking around for her. I stopped at her car and looked inside. There was nothing unusual there. I stopped and turned around, but she was nowhere in sight. As I walked up to the front door of Osborn's, I heard tires screeching and someone shouting. I turned around and saw Ruth riding in a white Mustang convertible and hooting and hollering as if she was riding a bull.

"Hey, Walt! Missed me?" she yelled as the car tore by me. I could see young Bill Osborn in the driver's seat. She'd never even spoken to the guy before last week. He was one of the town's young punks. His family owned the town store ever since there was a town, I guess, and he liked to spend that money on booze and drugs. I was getting a real bad feeling.

Even though I rushed back to my truck, it wasn't fast enough. I couldn't see the white Mustang anywhere. I felt stupid. I should have known that just following her wouldn't make a difference. If I really wanted to stop Ruth, I'd have to take more drastic steps.

I stopped at the hardware store and bought an axe. I used my hands the last time, but I knew that wouldn't be enough now. A gun would be good, but I didn't have one and didn't have the time to get one. I was going to have to move fast if I had any hope of succeeding. I didn't know what the hell she was now, but I figured that anything will die if you chop it into enough pieces.

The rest of the day was spent driving around. I never saw her and her car never moved. Around 3 P.M., my phone rang. It was Ruth. I gripped the wheel tighter and clicked the button.

"Wallllltttt! Where you been, baby? You know, you could've just come with me. All you hadda do was ask!"

"Where are you?"

"Aw, ain't that sweet? You miss your baby, Daddy Walt? You're gonna make me cry. Well, I'm having a little party, sweetie. You wanna join in? I've got me a nice, quiet cabin at Morgan's Motor Lodge out on the Pike. I'm in number twenty-one. I'm waiting for you."

She hung up the phone and I turned the truck around. Morgan's Motor Lodge was one of those old places with separate cabins. I don't really know why it was ever even built. Dunwich was never much of a tourist place. The place was mostly used by junkies and prostitutes out of Arkham.

I thought that there was someone following me, but I was probably just nervous.

Pulling into the back of the motor lodge, I could see the Osborn kid's convertible in front of cabin 21. There was another SUV that I didn't recognize. The cabins consisted of nothing more than a bedroom and a bathroom, usually in really ugly colors. I used to come here before I met Crystal. As I walked up to the cabin, I could see that the window was open and the shade was up. I knew that meant that Ruth wanted me to see. The closer I got, I could hear the sounds of three different men and Ruth . . . all moaning.

Telling myself that I needed to look so I'd know what I was getting into, I peeked through the window. I wish I had never done that.

They were all naked and thrashing on the bed. Ruth was gyrating on top of the Osborn kid while some other guy was behind her working like a piston engine. A third guy was standing next to her, thrusting himself into her mouth. My hand tightened around the axe handle. I hadn't expected this. I couldn't take on all of them.

I figured I might have to fight off the Osborn kid, but there was no way I could get through three of them before getting to Ruth. I was turning away from the window when Ruth saw me. She spit the guy out and squealed, "Walt! You made it, baby! C'mon in and join us!"

I started to back away when I noticed that there was something wrong with the guys. They were moving, but only in the same way that a machine will keep running if you leave it on too long. Their eyes were completely white. Their pupils had risen up into their heads. They were already dead; they just didn't know it yet.

"Hey, Walt!" Ruth yelled. "Pay attention! You wanna see something really special?"

She started laughing again—that hideous, high-pitched laugh that sounded more like a screech. As I watched, her flesh started to ripple. It wasn't from the rough sex. It was like when you look at the street on a really hot day and the heat just makes the air pulse.

Suddenly, her head flattened and caved in. Tentacles popped out, including what was once her tongue. They moved and flexed about as they attached themselves to the third man next to the bed and began sucking.

Her chest bulged and a milky eye burst through the skin, blinking and looking around. Her hips and waist exploded outward, but what came out had never been inside a human before. There were snakelike appendages with mouths and tongues whipping about. They crawled over the Osborn kid like leeches, attaching and sucking. Her legs became scaly and clawlike, looking like a wet lizard. The men never stopped thrusting, but I didn't want to know what they were touching. I couldn't get the image of a dead cow being milked out of my mind.

I started screaming and backing away when the tentacle mouth reached through the window at me and spoke.

"What's the matter, Walt? Don't I turn you on anymore? Doesn't the *real* me make you hot?"

I screamed and ran for the truck. I could hear her laughing behind me and the sounds of something sucking and licking.

As quick as I could, I got to Abe's Bar. Abe saw me come in and didn't say a word. He just put a bottle of whiskey in front of me and walked away. I couldn't decide what to do. A part of me really wanted to just get in the truck and run away, even though I hadn't been able to pull together enough money. And then there was the issue of Crystal and her son. I couldn't just leave them there. Ruth would get them. I had to get them out. Then we'd all get the hell out of here and just deal with whatever happened.

Staggering, I threw some money on the bar and left. When I got outside, I was surprised to find that it was already dark. I'd been drinking for over five hours. The birds were loud, louder than I'd ever heard before, and they were everywhere in the sky. I climbed into my truck and started to drive home.

About halfway there, I was sure there was a car following me. The lights moved the same way I did. It was Ruth. It had to be. My hands were sweating and shaking and I reached for the axe on the seat next to me. But, when I turned a corner under a street light, I could tell it was just some old black Ford.

Relieved, I turned down my street. I could see that Ruth's car wasn't at home, but neither was Crystal's. I already got a bad feeling. I pulled into the driveway and walked up to the door.

Inside, everything was dark but, before I even put on the light, I could tell something was wrong. I flipped the switch and saw that the living room had been torn apart. It looked as if there had been a huge fight in the room. Furniture was turned over; pictures were smashed on the floor; and over everything was a kind of slime. It was like some thick spit. I was already too late. While I sat at the bar getting drunk, Ruth took them.

I slumped down into the corner and cried.

Sometime later, my phone rang again. It was Ruth.

"Hey, baby! I guess I just missed you before." I could hear Crystal and Kyle screaming in the background.

"Where are you? I'll kill you, you *fucking* bitch!"

Ruth laughed. "You wanna try, Walt? Bring it on! We're having a big party here. Everyone's having fun, especially Kyle. Remember I told you that all I needed was a little practice?"

I heard Kyle screaming louder now and begging.

"You leave him out of this! It's between you and me!"

"Then come and get me, big boy. You know where I am." She hung up the phone and, just like that, I *did* know where she was. She was in the woods by Cold Spring Glen—where I killed her the first time.

I looked around the house quickly. I still had the axe in my truck, but I knew I'd need something more, especially if she had those three zombie-things with her. So I grabbed a big carving knife from the kitchen and Kyle's old baseball bat. It was all I had, so I'd have to make do.

The drive there took longer than I ever would have thought it could. The birds in the sky were going crazy, screeching and hollering, but I tried not to pay attention to them and the traffic around me. I just had to get there as quickly as possible. I didn't think she'd kill them before I got there; she'd want me to watch first. But maybe I could throw her off if I got there quicker than she expected.

I pulled off the road in the same place I did before. I thought I saw headlights somewhere behind me, but when I turned to look, they were gone. I tucked the knife into my belt and walked into the woods; axe in one hand and baseball bat in the other.

It was as if I was following a path. I was on some trail made a long time ago by something so monstrous that nothing would grow there afterwards.

As I walked, I could feel myself climbing higher. I was already beyond the point where I had killed Ruth before, and I kept walking. It was as if I was in a trance. I must have been because, not only were the birds screeching and howling, but I could swear that I heard voices coming from below the ground as well. Shortly, I could see points of light ahead of me. Moving closer, I could see that they were small fires. As I crested the hill, there was a clearing before me. There were large stones set in the ground in odd places. In the middle of the clearing was a large, flat stone almost like a table. On that stone, tied down, were Crystal and Kyle.

Ruth and the three zombies were dancing around the table. They were naked and gyrating and chanting something that I couldn't even say for sure was any kind of language. It sounded like a bunch of grunting and barking, but every time Ruth made a noise, the men answered. She was back in her regular form, her body naked and wet from sweat. I didn't have any time to waste.

Leaping forward, I rammed the axe into the back of the Osborn boy and he fell like a sack of wet sand. At the same time I swung the baseball bat and sent the second guy's lower jaw flying outside the clearing. The third man rushed me, but I had time to take my batter's stance and swing for the bleachers. His head came clean off his shoulders and I felt the impact run up my arms. As soon as they hit the ground, their bodies started to bubble and melt. Within seconds, they were only piles of green slime.

I jumped toward the table and started cutting Crystal free. I took a second to look at Ruth, who was just standing there, giggling. She wasn't even trying to stop me. I turned back to look at Crystal, just about to say that we had to get moving fast, when she brought her hand up and smashed me in the head with a rock.

Everything was dark, but I tried to swim through it as hard as I could. I must have woken up faster than they thought, because they were still trying to tie me to the stone. They'd stripped all my clothes off and there were these strange symbols carved on my chest and down my legs.

Crystal was trying to hold my arm down while Kyle was failing to tie me up.

"What the hell are you doing?" I yelled.

"Shut the *fuck* up, you stupid hick! You're going to ruin every-thing!" Crystal screamed. "Kyle, tie him down, *now!*"

Kyle tried to loop the rope around my leg, but I reared up and kicked him square in the head. He fell back hard and didn't get up again.

"Kyle!" Crystal screamed. She looked squarely at me. "You're not going to *fuck* this all up, Walt! I've worked too hard for this."

"What the hell are you talking about?" I was trying to get off the table, but she had a grip on me such as I'd never felt from her before. My chest and legs burned and blood was dripping from a hundred plac-es. Out of the corner of my eye, I could see Ruth down by the bottom of the stone table. She was covered in blood. Probably my blood from all the cuts she'd made. Her eyes were white and she was chanting.

"You think this just happened? I've planned it! All of it! I looked years for a dumb *fuck* like you. Someone who could be influenced so easily. Do you think any woman would want you, you ugly piece of shit? I used you!"

I could see the axe lying on the ground. It was in the middle of a pile of green slime that used to be the Osborn kid.

"Did you think it was your idea? You haven't had an original thought your whole fucking life! I put it in your head! I made you want Ruth. I told you where she ran because *I* sent her there! And you did the job all right. But that's all a dog like you is good for."

Ruth continued to chant. Her flesh started to ripple again. I knew what that meant.

"I needed someone to rape and kill her so that the *dhole* could en-ter her body. Then it was just a matter of getting you back up here for the last part—the Scarlet Ceremony. It would give her the power she needed to open the gate. But you were too stupid to do it right!"

She lunged to push me back down on the stone and I moved out of her way. Her head made a really satisfying smack with the stone. I punched her in the face, hard, and jumped off the stone.

I didn't have much time. I grabbed the axe and brought it down on Crystal's head. You hear about people's heads splitting like ripe melons, but it doesn't happen like that. It's more like cracking open a coconut. She screamed and fell forward onto the stone. Her blood fell into the grooves of the stone, making patterns and symbols like the ones on my chest.

"Ooooo, Walt, you like it rough, huh?" I turned and looked at Ruth. Her whole body was shaking. "Mom or you. Don't really matter. It's all good."

I wanted to ask what the hell she really was and what she was trying to do. I wanted to understand what all this meant and why it had happened to me, but I didn't have the time. I swung the axe with all my might and felt it thud into her throat.

"You gotta try harder than that, Walt," Ruth laughed, blood foaming out of her mouth. She drew back her hand and smacked me hard. I fell back on my ass. "So simple. Speak the right words at the right time and open the way. Like computer instructions."

She turned away from me and went back to the table. Her body was shifting again but not as much as last time. The tentacles came out of her waist and started feasting on Crystal's body. Ruth turned her head to the sky and chanted.

"N'gai n'gha'ghaa, bugg-shoggog, y'hah; Yog-Sothoth, Yog-Sothoth!"

Ruth raised her hands to the sky and the stars started to shimmer and blink. The birds grew quiet.

"Ygnaiih . . . ygnaiih . . . thfthkh'ngha . . . Yog-Sothoth . . . Yog-Sothoth! Y'bthnk . . . h'ehye-n'grkdl'lh!"

Crystal's body began to shrink, like a balloon with all the air let out. I staggered to my feet, axe in my hand. Without a word, I brought it down on the stone, splitting her tentacles in two. She screamed and grabbed my head. She started to squeeze and pull my head toward the hole that had been her stomach. I swung the axe blindly and felt it hit her leg. Her blood sprayed on my face.

The birds were screeching again, their cries getting louder and louder, almost like a symphony that had spiraled out of control.

Ruth stepped backward, and that was all the break I needed. I lifted the axe high above my head and brought it down on her with all my strength. It split her head in two. Some sort of liquid steam oozed out and she began to melt. I tugged the axe out and was getting ready for another swing when I heard someone shouting behind me.

"RICE! Put it down! Put it down right now or I'll shoot!"

I swung around and saw it was Detective Armitage with a couple of cops. I smiled. They'd understand. They'd know that I had to do it; that Ruth was some sort of thing from outside. She had to die. But before I could tell them anything, Armitage fired.

Three days later, I woke up in the hospital in Arkham. I was hand-cuffed to the bed. My head hurt as if several mules had taken turns kicking it. I lay there, laughing and crying until the doctor came in. He shone that light in my eyes, took my pulse, and left. No matter what I asked, he wouldn't answer.

I couldn't even turn on the TV.

I fell asleep again and, when I woke up this time, Armitage was there. He just glared at me. "Did you see it?" I asked. "Did you see her?"

"Oh, yeah, I saw her all right, Walt. I saw all of them. Your wife. The boy. And the girl. All hacked to death. By you. With the very axe we have videotape of you buying. I knew there was something hinky with you. That's why I've been following you since Ruth came home, but there's just one thing I don't understand, Walt. Why'd you do it? Why?"

"What are you talking about? Didn't you see her? The tentacles? The . . . the mouths and suckers? She was a *thing*. A thing from outside. She was going to . . . to . . . (what the hell did she say?) . . . open the way! She was going to let something in that would've taken over the world."

Armitage just gritted his teeth and stared at me. "So that's how it's going to be, eh? Going with the insanity defense? Gonna say you sacri-ficed them to some 'voice' in your head? That's why you cut yourself on your chest and legs with the knife we know you took from your kitchen? Thought you were a man, Walt. Thought you'd stand up and take responsibility for what you did."

"I am! I killed a *thing!* I don't know what she was, but she wasn't human!"

"Not human. Right. Here, Walt, take a look at this."

Armitage dropped a file in my lap. I opened it up and there were full-color pictures of my dead family. But something wasn't right. Crystal looked fine. Well, except for being dead from an axe to the head. But she didn't look as if she'd had the life sucked out of her. And Ruth . . . well, Ruth looked like any other sixteen-year-old dead girl. No tentacles. No big eye in the middle of her chest. No scaly legs. She looked perfectly normal . . . and perfectly dead.

I didn't understand any of it, but it didn't make any difference. As Ruth had said, none of this really mattered. All our laws and morals are nothing more than the chattering of insects. So I let them go through the motions. I refused the insanity defense. I pleaded guilty and got a life sentence three times over for it. They shipped me to Walpole Prison where I sit in my cell, pressed against the farthest corner from the door. No one comes near me and that's the way I like it. I'm safe here; safer than most people because they don't know what I know. Those *things* are all around out there . . . just waiting for their chance to come through. They don't care about us. We're nothing more than tools to be used and discarded—when they bother to think of us at all. As soon as they come through, they'll wipe the earth clean and they will reign supreme. I know it's true because, at night, while I listen to the birds screech along with my breathing, I finger the scars on my chest and remember.

The Gathering Daemonica

Inside the main lobby of the Biltmore Hotel, groups of people milled about as they waited for the events to start. The hotel employees were busy checking in new arrivals and bringing luggage up to the rooms. It was a hotbed of activity. The largest convention of the year was almost ready to begin and the staff was already overloaded with guests. The hotel manager was running back and forth, obviously pleased that he had filled the hotel to capacity for this weekend. Off to one side, near the registration desk, two men stood talking very intently.

"It is nearly time to begin and he has yet to arrive," the first one said. He was of medium build, slightly pudgy, and completely bald.

The second man sighed. "After all this time, you have still not learned patience. He will be here." He was taller, thinner, and impeccably dressed. The suit, of course, was black.

"What will we do if he doesn't come? We have events planned. Do you know how long it took to put this all together? I haven't been able to organize one of these for nearly a hundred and ten years since the last one in England, and you remember what a problem that was when someone I refuse to mention went on a rampage. I'll be damned if I've gone to all this trouble for nothing!"

The second man smirked. "You're damned anyway."

"Well, yes, of course. But that's beside the point."

"Look, stop fidgeting. You always were a nervous one."

"But we can't have the convention without him. He's the Guest of Honor!"

"And he will be here. You can't expect one like him to be on time. He's very busy you know."

"I know, I know. But I confirmed these plans with him personally ages ago!"

"Then he'll be here. It is an important day. He will not miss it."

The pudgy man fidgeted. He was about to say something else, thought better of it, and kept silent. The second man stood quietly as the crowd surged around him. It would be difficult for the untrained eye to separate the conventioneers from the normal hotel guests, but it was not difficult for him. He knew all the guests. The oldest ones he had recruited himself, but he had taken the time to get to know them all personally. A few greeted him as they passed by and picked up their registration materials at the convention desk. They came in every shape and size, every race and color. Fat and thin, beautiful and ugly, short and tall. They were all the epitome of normal human beings. Which was exactly the way he had trained them. It didn't do for humans to see demons walking among them, unless that was what they wanted. And yet, even the second man was becoming irritated.

It *was* getting late. The guest of honor should have been there hours before, but he supposed it was only to be expected. After all, it was not every day that a demon was promoted out of Hell. Actually, it had never happened before. Which also irritated him. Cluchach (known affectionately as "C") was one of his oldest demons, procured shortly after the Fall and back when he still made special deals to fill his ranks. With so few people back then, he needed to be inventive when recruiting. He had long since given up using such things as contracts. Too binding—too limiting. But, back then, he was young and didn't know how to run his business properly. He'd learned since then. But C was never supposed to fulfill the terms of his contract. None of them were. Who'd ever thought that one demon would ever be responsible for the eternal damnation of almost one zillion human souls? C was only one soul short and it was certain that he would hit the mark this weekend. C never failed. Now he would be duty bound to honor the contract and release C from his service. It was to be the highlight of the convention, and he didn't like it one little bit.

"He's here!" the first man cried. He lunged for the door as a large white limousine pulled up in front of the hotel. The doorman quickly opened the door and a young, handsome, and vibrant man eased out of the car. C beamed happiness and confidence. He was dressed in a flawless white suit with a white shirt, white tie, and white shoes. His hair was dark and thin, of medium length but neatly trimmed. He walked as if he owned the world and, to a certain extent, he did.

"C!" the first man beamed. "You made it!"

He thrust his hand out and C took it slowly. "Ah yes," he said, a smile slowly breaking on his face, "Dathon, isn't it? Sorry I'm late. Celebrating, you know."

"Of course, of course. We're just glad you made it on time." Dathon was trying to hurry C along, but C was taking his time walking through the lobby. It had taken him centuries to reach this point. He was going to enjoy it.

"Now we've got you making the keynote address in the Hamilton Room in fifteen minutes, and then you've got a break for an hour or so before you're on the next panel."

As they walked, the second man stood quietly, sizing up C. It had been awhile, after all, since he had had a sit-down with C. Not since that unpleasantness in Greece a few decades ago when he'd tried to have C dismembered. He'd long since regretted making his employees immortal. Killing them only reduced them to the state of a normal damned soul.

C stopped in front of the second man. "Well, well, well. The man himself. Didn't think I'd see you here, A. Thought for sure you'd be sulking in a corner somewhere."

"And allow you to have all the fun? Perish the thought! How are you, C?"

C smirked. "You should know. One away and then *I'm* away."

"And do you have someone already picked out?"

"Now, A, that would be telling. As if I'd let you know ahead of time. You'll see them soon enough."

Next to them, Dathon was sweating anxiously.

"Gentlemen, gentlemen, I'm afraid I must insist. I have to get C to the Hamilton Room."

"Of course," A smiled happily. "I'll catch up with you later. Looking forward to your panel on damnation techniques."

Dathon hurried C away but, as he went, C turned around and silently mouthed the words "One more" to A.

A turned away and inspected his manicure but, beneath his feet, the carpet was burning.

" . . . and so, ever since the Kitchener accord of 1910, we've had to revise what we consider to be a mortal sin."

The panel had been going on for more than half an hour when she walked into the room. She sat in a back corner by herself. Even though she was not near them, several demons got up and quietly moved to other sections of the room. She pretended not to notice them. In the controlled atmosphere of the room, they had allowed their human façades to drop; but not her. She sat in her human guise, perfectly poised. She was thin, but not abnormally so. Her hair was a light blond and tied neatly into a French braid. Her face was warm and soft and her eyes were especially soothing. She was a vision of simple beauty, and she sat calmly and quietly as she listened to C speak.

"Yes," he said, "we've had to become more cunning, more resourceful. There's so much competition out there today that it's tough to get someone to commit a truly *damnable* sin. People commit minor sins every day. They lie, cheat, steal, and manage to convince themselves that they never did it at all. Guilt is one of our most powerful weapons. Only through guilt can we compel them to recognize—"

He stopped. He couldn't see her with the lights up but he knew she was there. He could smell her scent. Violets. She had always preferred that perfume. A human failing that refused to die. It was foolish. He should have known she would be here . . . everyone was.

"Uh, C? You were saying?" Dathon blathered.

"Oh, oh, yes. Where was I? Oh, guilt. Yes, guilt must not be underestimated. If properly used, it can be insidious."

"I don't think anyone would argue that, C. Any questions?"

A few minor demons asked (as a few always will) how to be as successful as C in damning souls. "Work hard," he said. "Know your victim. Everyone has weaknesses."

"Everyone?"

"Everyone. Some just aren't as blatant about it."

She raised her hand.

Dathon ignored her.

"Any more questions?"

She got tired of waiting. "What about the souls? Is there ever any hope of redemption?"

Dathon tried to bluff over it. "Well, that's all we have time for. I'd like to thank everyone—"

"There's always hope of redemption," C said, "otherwise there is no point to damnation."

He looked up where her voice had come from, but she had already left.

A stood silently in the hallway, amusing himself with the convention schedule. "Seven Deadly Sins: Should There Be More?" he chuckled to himself. "Modern Damnation Techniques: The Internet and You," "Why Can't Johnny Damn?" and "Overcrowding: New Space in Hell?" A was most entertained. If nothing else, Dathon was a capable administrator, which was probably why most of the souls he had damned had come from the business sector. "A well-placed keystroke or erasure can be as damning as the most tempting female flesh," Dathon had once said, and A was forced to agree with him.

A pretended not to notice C and the entourage of younger demons coming down the hall.

"Yes, but that bit you did with the Englishman was so inspired! How did you come up with it?"

"I just assured him that, being king, he could do anything he wanted. Abdication seemed a small thing to him after that, but it was enough to do the job."

A picked his teeth with his manicured pinky and gave the schedule his undivided attention.

"A."

He glanced up.

"Ah, C. Made any progress? My Minister of Damnation has not sent me a new Damnation Contract with your name on it yet."

"A moment, if you please."

A looked up. He appeared genuinely confused at the request, but A could appear to be genuine about anything including the most ungenuine things.

"Of course." He waved his hand and they were in the ether with mist swirling about them.

"What is she doing here?"

"*She?* And who might *she* be?"

"You know who. Charazadon."

"Oh. Well, I expect that she is doing the same thing they all are. She's here to pay homage to you and pick up some damnation tips. She certainly needs them."

"Tell her to go away."

"I can't do that."

"Of course you can. You're the devil. You can do whatever you want."

A grinned. "I suppose I can. But I won't."

"Why not?"

"I suppose because I would prefer that you do it. Actually, I prefer to make you as uncomfortable as possible."

C glared at him.

"So you will not command her to leave?"

"I will not command her to do anything, except to damn a soul. She hasn't done one in quite a long time, as you know."

C looked at him a long time. "I will win, you know. I will have my freedom."

"Of course you will, old sod, I'm counting on it."

With a wave, C was back at the hotel and A was gone.

"Cheeky bastard," C said, and turned back to his entourage.

C avoided her the rest of the day, which was not very hard. Charazadon did not try to contact him, nor did anyone try to contact her. They walked around in their demon garb, wings flapping, mouths salivating, tongues undulating, penises flapping about, letting themselves all hang out. Except her. She walked about the convention always in her human face. The others walked around her. A few threw excrement at her, but the stains always faded away on her tan sun dress. She wandered through the dealers' room, looking at the self-help books (*A Better Way to Hell; I'm Okay, You're Damned,* etc.), passing by the tables with the new torture devices, avoiding the tables with videotapes of successful damnations and the underground tapes of exorcisms. The art show wasn't much better as demons attempted to show what passed for art, but all they had were pictures of souls being damned. Charazadon walked around for a while until she thought it was safe enough to go upstairs.

After dinner, C went to see about his final soul. He had planned it for some time now and it was meant to be a big one. It was true that it had gotten harder and harder to truly damn anyone. Everyone was always committing little sins, so it was difficult to get them to recognize truly major sins. But this one was almost in the bag. He'd been working on this soul for a while, and he had arranged it so that everything would come together tonight. It was too easy to corrupt the souls of the rich and famous; they practically begged to be damned. Harder to get, and more rewarding, were the souls of everyday people—those who had spent their entire lives being devoted to their religion, their families, or their work. They were harder to tempt but, once you got them, they were delicious.

Susan's husband, Ronnie, had been lured out of town because of work; but only for a certain amount of time. If C timed this right, he would get three souls for the price of one. It had taken some patience (that was the problem with the young demons: they wanted damnations immediately, they weren't willing to work for it) and a lot of work to tempt Ronnie's younger brother Jerry with visions of Susan's nubile young body. C had had to drop the visions into otherwise harmless dreams, but, once Jerry had taken hold of it, C had been able to drop the visions in at any time during the day. In addition, he had planted similar pictures of Jerry into Susan's mind. While this was going on, C had increased Ronnie's desire for fattening foods, alcohol, and violence. Planning—it was all planning. As they had said so many times, "the devil is in the details." C smiled at that. Now, tonight, C had arranged for Ronnie to leave on an emergency business trip and for Jerry to stop by suddenly while Susan was alone. At that point, C had to step back. That was the rule. He could plant, he could tempt, he could persuade, but at the point where the final decision was to be made, he had to withdraw. The choice had to be theirs. So many had lost the souls at that point, but that was because they hadn't done the work well enough. C was certain that, once again, he would win.

When Jerry stopped by, he had interrupted Susan during a particularly heated masturbation session (filled with visions of Jerry, of course, provided by C) and she was primed and ready. C sat back and watched as the passions overwhelmed them and the clothes came off. Within minutes, they were in bed and two mortal sins were being committed. (Deep in Hell, the Minister of Damnation signed Jerry and Susan's names to a Contract of Damnation with C as the signing agent and sent it off to A.) But C wasn't done. On his way to the emergency business meeting, Ronnie received a call on his cell letting him know that the emergency was over and the meeting was canceled. As he turned his car around, Ronnie tried to call home but, for some reason, his cell chose that moment to lose power.

Pulling his car into the driveway, he saw his brother's car and wondered what it might be doing there. Opening his front door, he was confronted with certain sounds that could not be denied. Sounds of mutual pleasure, of orgasmic bliss, that he had not heard himself for some time. He slowly walked to his den and opened his closet. He took out his pistol and checked it. It was fully loaded. He walked quietly up the stairs to his bedroom, opened the door, and fired.

When A received the three Contracts of Damnation, he was alone in his penthouse hotel suite. He looked them over, but they were complete, as he knew they would be. He was not happy. Silently, he ordered the Overlords of Hell to increase the sufferings of the damned threefold. If nothing else, he would enjoy some music this night.

"I know you're here," C said to his hotel room. There was a most undemonly odor of violets in the room.

"I could never hide from you," Charazadon said. She moved away from the darkened corner where she had been waiting.

"You could. If you really wanted to. I recall that you hid from me for a few centuries once."

"Only because you didn't want to look." She paused. "How have you been?"

C laughed. It was a good laugh, full of mirth and joy. It was especially unpleasant coming from a Lord of Hell.

"How have I been? Oh, I've been doing very well. You know, of course."

"Yes, you're the talk of the legions."

"As I should be. No one else has ever accomplished this."

Charazadon lowered her head. "Do you think he will honor his part?"

A little too quickly, C answered, "Of course. He is honor bound by our contract. He has to."

"Still, it is not like him not to try some tricks."

"Why are you here, Charazadon?"

"I've been waiting here for you."

"That's not what I meant, and you know it. Why are you here *now?*"

"Is it so hard to believe that I've come to wish you well in your triumph?"

"Yes."

Something played across her face. It was difficult to tell if it was a smile or a grimace.

"I've come to ask you a favor."

"Yes?"

Charazadon paused. With an effort, C could tell that she was crying. It was a terrible thing to see a demon cry. He wanted to hold her but didn't. He stood waiting for her to speak again.

"I want you to kill me."

Downstairs, in the lobby, A was questioning Dathon. "Is all ready for the special event tomorrow?"

"Of course, my lord. All has been prepared. But, if I may, I have a small question . . ."

A stood and glared at Dathon, who began sweating. Dathon was one of those demons who could sweat while standing in the heart of a glacier.

"Um," Dathon began, "you aren't actually going to go through with this, are you?"

A smiled. Such naive faith and fear. It was positively delicious!

"Yes, of course I am! I am a man of my word."

"But you're not exactly a man, are you?"

"I suppose you might have a point there, Dathon, I suppose you might." With that, A turned and walked away, singing a particularly odious song popular among the Roman legions under Tiberius.

Dathon scurried away to the banquet hall, his steps echoing in the large room as he passed beneath the huge panoramic windows. There were times he really hated his job.

"Charazadon, don't be insane. You know I can't do that."

"Only a demon can kill another demon. Either that or A, and he'd never do it."

"No? I'd heard he'd threatened that."

"Threatened is not doing. He knows that keeping me the way I am is more painful than killing me."

"No doubt. Killing you would only make you one of the normal damned. You'd have none of the privileges of the demon class, but none of the problems either. I imagine that's why you're asking."

"You know it is. I haven't damned anyone in decades and I don't want to."

"No wonder your record is so poor lately and no one wishes to associate with you. But why? Don't tell me that whole Gein thing is bothering you again."

"It's not just that. It's what it all started. First there was Ed. Then Charles, then Ted, then David. It just kept going on and on and on and on."

"Yes! That was the beauty of it! We did great work with Ed. Not only did we damn him, but entire scores of other people who had never met him. It was magnificent!"

"No, no, it wasn't. It was just wrong. We shouldn't have done that. Look at the innocent people who died horribly in great pain because of it."

"So? That's what they are born for. To die in great pain!"

Charazadon looked at him. "I didn't realize."

"You didn't realize what?"

"That you had learned so little. How long have you dwelt among them? You are one of the oldest of us and yet you don't understand them. Have you ever tried to talk to them?"

"Talk to them? Why should I do that?"

"You once told me that you had to learn everything about your subject for a successful damnation. Have you ever listened to them? Listened to their poetry? Their music? Read their literature? Have you never gone and talked to one of them? Felt their hopes and dreams? Their joys and sorrows? Tasted what it was to be human again?"

C didn't reply.

"Once," he said after some time, "I could remember what it was like. But it's been so long that I can't remember any more. After tomorrow, I won't have to remember. A will give me my soul back and I'll be human again."

"I know. That's why I'm here. Once you're human, you can't kill me. And you're the only one who would. I can't do it anymore. I can't go on damning them knowing what they'll face, and I'll never get enough souls to win my freedom. I need you to do this for me."

"I can't. You know I can't. That's breaking the rules. You'd be free, or as free as a damned soul in Hell can be, but I'd pay the price. You know that. If I kill you, I accept your contract. I'd be responsible for gathering your souls."

"I know. I just hoped that—"

"No. I've come too far."

Charazadon hung her head lower and looked out of the hotel window. "Sometimes I just like to watch the lights. The way they dance around in the sky and on the ground. The humans attach so much importance to lights. Have you ever noticed that? Everything good is light and everything bad is dark."

"Charazadon, why are you telling me this?"

"Because I can't remember what it is to be light and I want to."

She walked by him and out the door. This surprised him because demons normally don't use doors. Those were for the common hordes of meat. C sat down on the bed (the first bed he had taken the time to rest on for a millennium) and thought.

The time had come. The players were arranged and the banquet hall was full. C's three-way triumph had already spread through the convention and all the guests were anxiously waiting the final act. Would A come through? The betting demons were given odds that A would pull something out at the last minute and save the day. No one beat him, after all, that was what his reputation was built on. But there were still other issues as well. More than a few demons were hoping against hope that C would pull it off—that he would succeed where no other demon had before and win his freedom. Otherwise, what were they all bothering with this for?

The roast was still underway. Other lesser demons were making fun of C, bringing up times when things didn't work out the way they were planned or other things intervened. C didn't care for it but put up with it, laughing goodnaturedly but always looking for Charazadon. She was nowhere to be seen. A, however, was watching C intently.

"And now," Dathon said, "we come to the main event. A!"

A stood up amidst much applause and motioned everyone down.

"Tonight," he began, "is a very special night. This is an event that has never happened before in our shared history and may never happen again! Cluchach has done the impossible. He has secured One Zillion and Two souls!"

More applause. Still no Charazadon. C sniffed the air. Something wasn't quite right.

"And so, we gather here tonight to honor him and to wish him well, for he is now leaving us for good."

A smattering of applause.

C smelled violets. That stupid human perfume of Charazadon. But from where?

"So it is with great regret that we come to the end, Cluchach and I. For centuries we have worked side by side. I'll miss him, but mostly I'll miss all the souls he brought me!"

Much laughter. C looked around but still couldn't see Charazadon. But he knew she was there. Then he looked up at the large panoramic windows through which one could see the lights of the city below. Except for one very large dark patch.

"But I am a man of my word and I am here tonight to keep my word. So without further ado . . ."

A pulled an ancient parchment out of his jacket. The dark shape on the window shifted. C tensed.

"This"—A held the parchment up high, letting everyone see—"is something most of you newer demons have never seen. It's a *written* contract!"

A smattering of laughter. There was the sound of small cracks.

"With the burning of this," A's finger burned with flame, "Cluchach is released and his soul is his again! May God have mercy on his soul!"

More laughter. A's finger moved closer to the paper as the large window collapsed and a black angry shape burst down into the room.

Demons scattered left and right as they fled like cowards. The dark shape fell upon the floor and drew itself up. It was Charazadon.

"*No!*" she screamed. There was no pretense at humanity, there was no false form. She was truly a demon in every sense of the word. And yet, C still smelled violets.

"He is mine!" she yelled. "He owes me a debt and I demand to be paid!"

"*Demand?*" A bellowed. "You demand of *me?* Who are you to demand anything from any of us?"

"I am Charazadon, daughter of the Seventh Circle. And I have come to claim what is owed me."

"And that is?"

"Cluchach's soul. It belongs to me. He promised it to me aeons ago and I will have it!"

C jumped to his feet. "I never promised you anything!"

Charazadon turned and glared at C. "Yes, you did—a long time past, but you did."

"Enough of this," A said. "Begone!"

"NO!" Charazadon screamed. Her very being seemed to come apart with the intensity of her shout. She leaped at A.

"Charazadon! What are you doing?" C yelled.

A stepped back. "She is completing her doom."

White fire burst from A's hand and engulfed Charazadon. C

shrieked and jumped over the table to her.

"Let her go!"

C tried to pull her out of the bright flame, but she was held fast. Her very being was melting from the inside out. A gestured with his other hand and C went flying across the room. "This is none of your affair, Cluchach."

Stumbling weakly to his feet, C looked quickly at Charazadon. She did not have much time left. Gathering his strength, he flung his arms together and sent a blazing white-hot sheet of pain toward A.

It hit him full in the face and caught him totally unprepared. A shrieked and fell backward, breaking his hold on Charazadon. C ran over to her.

Charazadon's body was charred on one side, yet oozing and liquid on the other. A, on the other hand, was completely motionless.

Climbing out from under a table, Dathon stared at the scene before him. His brain could not take it all in. Cluchach had killed A. He had killed the Fallen One. He had killed the First. Dathon screamed. It was not unlike the sound of a cat's claws being raked over a blackboard.

Dathon ran over to A's corpse. Smoke was rising from it. Dathon was sobbing. This was the worst event he had ever organized. "He's dead," was all Dathon said.

Beneath him, lying in C's arms, Charazadon began to laugh.

"Why are you laughing?" C asked.

"Because," Charazadon said, "because you never could appreciate a good joke."

Charazadon began to shimmer, her body acquiring a glow. C put her down and stepped back. Quietly, he called for Dathon.

The pudgy little demon rushed over. Charazadon's body continued to pulse and undulate until finally there was a completely different being lying in her place. It was A and he was laughing.

C walked back to the podium. On the floor behind it lay Charazadon. She was completely and utterly dead.

A stood up, still laughing. Dathon, not believing what he was seeing, sat heavily down in a nearby chair.

"Well, well, it appears that we have a change of plans here. Cluchach, you've killed one of my demons. You know what the penalty is, don't you?"

"Yes." C said flatly. "What was her contract for?"

"Oh, well, you know, she was one of the earlier additions, back when there were a lot more people and inventory quotas were higher."

"How much?"

"Not much more than your old one. Only two zillion."

C straightened up and slicked his hair back. He dusted off his suit and tightened his tie. "I'll make it," he said.

A walked up and looked him straight in the eye. "I have no doubt that you will, Cluchach, I'm counting on it."

In a small, remote corner of Hell, a young woman was writhing in torment, burning under volcanic fires. Every breath she took was an effort as her lungs filled with black smoke. Her flesh blistered and cracked, but she was smiling.

A man moved up near her. He was youthful and handsome and, though he no longer beamed happiness, he was still confident.

"Hello, Charazadon," he said.

She spun about. "Cluchach! What are you doing here?"

"Shh. I'm not supposed to be here. A's too busy with some earthquake and plague in northern Turkey, but it won't be long until he notices I'm here."

She wouldn't look at him and dropped her head into the lava. When she pulled up, her burned flesh regenerated itself. "I didn't want to, you know; he made me."

"'The Devil Made You Do It'? No, I don't think so."

She paused. "No, he didn't. I suggested it actually. After you refused me."

"That's what I thought."

They lay there in silence for a moment, their flesh sizzling in the molten earth.

"I am sorry, though."

"I know."

"I . . . I just wanted you to know that."

"I know that too. He would have broken the bargain one way or another. Listen, I can't change any of this, but I can leave you with something. Close your eyes."

Charazadon closed her eyes and C waved his hand over her. A scent of violets filled the air.

"Cluchach! What are you doing?"

"Just a little gift. Thought you might need it. I don't expect there's much perfume down here. It won't wear off. It's a permanent scent for as long as you want it. I've got to go. Got something going down in Florida. Social Security scam with Dathon. Might be big. I'll stop by again when I can."

He moved away and became more indistinct.

"Oh, and Charazadon?"

"Yes?"

"You forgot that we can't wear scents when in demon form. We can only wear them when we're in human form and A never cared for violets."

As his voice drifted away and the screams of the damned rose again in her ears, Charazadon silently cried to herself and said, "Thank you," even though she couldn't be sure if anyone else was listening.

Rising above the stench of burning flesh floated the fragile smell of violets.

Static

Dr. Sybaris looked at his instruments and frowned. This was not the result he had expected at all. Quickly, he double-checked the apparatus and made sure that everything was attached the way it should be. The omniscope had plenty of power, but the screen was still dark. What's more, the signal he was picking up was completely wrong. He should have been tuning into the afternoon broadcast from New York, but this was something else entirely.

An angry frown carved itself into Dr. Sybaris's forehead. His dark curly hair covered his head like a confused beaver, going in all directions at once. His beard and moustache, normally well-trimmed to the point of obsession, were wild and uneven. Even his clothes were unkempt. His shirt was wrinkled and, though his collar was attached, it was not closed and he was not wearing a tie. The full height of his lean, six-foot-two-inch frame was bent over and clenched. His very demeanor was a testament to the many days he had spent working on his latest invention. Dr. Sybaris's eyes burned angrily. He had never accepted failure before and wouldn't begin now.

Out of the speakers came a weird buzzing sound. It was almost like speech but not quite. Dr. Sybaris adjusted the receptors' strength, trying to boost the signal. The frequency was higher than the standard atmospheric band so, technically, he should not have been receiving it at all.

His frustration was unbounded. The experiment should have been a success. Everything was perfect theoretically, and Dr. Sybaris had spent months on the calculations and construction of his device. He had even modified it to include Tesla's newest designs of the electrical coil. It gave far more power than mere steam ever had but was also far more dangerous. Dr. Sybaris cursed at the fumbling of his fingers in the thick, insulated gloves. He needed more delicate, refined work but couldn't risk using his bare hands. "Why isn't it working?" he cursed.

He adjusted the omniscope again. The screen should have been showing something. It was designed to convert radio waves to images, but all it showed was lines of static. Perhaps it was the signal itself that was the problem. Dr. Sybaris moved to the instrument panel and glared at the settings. The dials reflected in his protective goggles. According to the oscilloscope, he was receiving several radio waves at once. "It's some sort of electronic interference," he muttered. "Have to try and isolate the correct wavelength." He moved dials and adjusted levels on the console. Slowly, the other waves dropped off the scope until only two remained. One was definitely stronger than the other and had to be the one he wanted, but he couldn't isolate it. Determined, Dr. Sybaris poured more power into the console. The connectors sizzled and crackled as the electricity leaped through the air. The system was quickly becoming overloaded and dangerously close to exploding. Dr. Sybaris was reaching for the emergency shut off when something started to come through the omniscope.

It was blurry at first, with no real definition. Straining, Dr. Sybaris was barely able to make out a vague shape, but it didn't look anything close to humanoid. The head looked all wrong—and the hands! He could have sworn that they weren't hands at all but some sort of claws. Suddenly, the speakers roared into life: " . . . go out among men and find the ways thereof, that He in the Gulf may know. To Nyarlathotep, Mighty Messenger, must all things be told. And He shall put on the semblance of men, the waxen mask and the robe that hides, and come down from the world of Seven Suns to mock. . . ."

Then the power grid exploded.

Several days later, Dr. Sybaris discussed the incident with his good friend and colleague, Morgan Rice. They were enjoying drinks at the Autonomic Explorers Club on High Street after a particularly heated lecture called "Artificial Intelligence and Morality" given by Cormac 217. Years ago, the mere appearance of Cormac, a free-floating brain encased in a robotic body, would have inspired fear or at least interest. But after the Biogenic Revolution of 1901, such sights were becoming more commonplace. It had become the standard method of prolonging life after the human body failed. But, of course, only for the wealthy. The poor still died as humans.

"That's extraordinarily interesting," Morgan Rice remarked as he brushed the ash from his cigar off his waistcoat. Although they had been friends for many years, Rice and Dr. Sybaris were polar opposites. Rice was plump where Dr. Sybaris was lean. Rice was slow moving and calm where Dr. Sybaris was manic and animated. Rice was grounded and content with the world where Dr. Sybaris was a malcontent and gadfly. Despite their differences, Rice had always had a soft spot for his often overly animated friend and sometimes could not resist the urge to tease him just a little bit. "Do you mean to say that you picked up something beyond the standard radio waves?"

"Completely," Dr. Sybaris responded. "Analyzing my data after the explosion, I found that the corresponding wavelength has similarities to that of radio waves but has altogether different qualities."

Morgan rubbed his walrus whiskers thoughtfully. "Are you sure you didn't simply latch on to some new video transmission? I've heard recently that Gatworth is experimenting on giving video three-dimensional depth. I believe he's calling it 'holography' or some such thing."

Dr. Sybaris was insulted. "Do you believe I can be fooled with something so simple? Really, Morgan, you insult me!"

Morgan laughed. "Oh, Anton, do be calm! I was simply pulling your leg! Stop taking yourself so seriously!"

"This *is* serious! My experiment creates video from a purely audio source. Think of it! Sound creating images! The implications are phenomenal—everything from a new art form to new methods of teaching or even military applications. But none of it will matter if I can't get it to work properly!"

Dr. Sybaris fumed as he finished his drink.

"Look here," Morgan said, "let us assume, then, that this is some new sort of wavelength. Perhaps it's something that's never been used before. Or, just possibly, something we've never known was there. What about that message you said you intercepted?"

"Yes," Dr. Sybaris agreed, "that does concern me. It simply doesn't make any sense. It's not logical. It was almost like some sort of religious ritual. The voice wasn't right either. The way it buzzed!—it was almost as if it were mechanical. It's just not right. It's out of place . . . as if it didn't belong . . . just like everything else."

Morgan's eyes rolled. He had no wish to be subjected yet again to Dr. Sybaris's pet theory that something was fundamentally wrong with their world, out of place. Morgan was about to try to divert the conversation off this well-beaten track when the telescreen behind the bar flashed a news bulletin. A calm, decidedly British announcer was seated behind a desk, his rigidly starched collars seeming out of place with the mechanical eye and microphone mounted on the side of his head. "Attention, attention! This is a bulletin from the Ministry of Air Defence. We have just received video of today's attack by the Royal Airships on the vastly inferior German fleet at Rheinsbach."

The screen changed to show a division of British airships steaming through the sky as they opened fire on a formation of German airships that were still standing on the ground outside their hangers. The guns of the massive zeppelins fired mercilessly on ship and German soldier alike. "Our forces, led by General Kitchener, conducted the early-morning raid. The German airfleet suffered significant losses from which they are not expected to recover."

At the sight of the bombing, loud cheers rang through the barroom as the British victory was celebrated. "God Save the Queen!" was chanted loudly to everyone's satisfaction except Dr. Sybaris, who merely glared at the screen. He knew, unlike most of the men there, that Queen Victoria had died several decades ago and that what passed for the Queen today was nothing more than an intricately designed robot with fake skin. He knew because he had designed the robot's power system, but he could never speak about it—not if he wished to stay alive.

"I need some air," Dr. Sybaris growled as he pushed through the cheering crowd followed by Morgan. Outside, the air was hardly better. The choking fog of the various steam-powered cars hung in the air. The steam-horsed carriages chugged down the street while, above, the richer denizens of London rode their electric bicycles through the air. "No matter what," Dr. Sybaris grumbled, "status prevails."

Morgan looked at his friend. It was a song he had heard many times before. "This is 1902 England, Anton. Would you prefer Germany?"

"What I would prefer," Dr. Sybaris retorted, "is to be able to breathe without coughing."

Pained, he looked at his friend and patted him on the shoulder. "My apologies, old fellow, I am assailed by a foul mood today. Pay me no mind. Better we speak later, hmm?"

Without waiting for an answer, Dr. Sybaris turned and walked down the street, leaving Morgan to stare after him. "It's wrong," Dr. Sybaris muttered, "everything's all wrong."

For the next week, Morgan's attention was consumed with the war against Germany. The attack by the British Air Fleet had essentially decimated the German Fleet, but the Kaiser was not one to sit idly and allow his empire to fall. He had quickly ordered his force of automata to march into Poland in a lightning strike that threatened the whole of Europe. The combination of mechanical soldiers (half man, half robot) with the electric cannons and shock tanks had virtually leveled the city of Warsaw; and the Kaiser, many felt, would win the war on land if not in the air. The Queen had sent diplomatic communiqués to the American president, Thomas Edison, via his new electric videophone. While Edison had pledged to send food and supplies, he refused to commit any troops or airships. Morgan had heard rumors that Einstein's electronic brain was hard at work developing a new kind of weapon that would render all others useless. Debate raged over not only whether the rumor was true but also what it could mean and what the country that wielded it would do.

So when Morgan entered the Dog and Duck on Tottenham Lane, he was not thinking about Dr. Sybaris. But once he saw his old friend slumped against the bar, he remembered everything. And yet, Dr. Sybaris had never looked worse.

His eyes were sunken and his skin had a hollow, yellow hue. Even across the room, Morgan could see that Dr. Sybaris's hands were trembling. He had developed the appearance of a man about to shake himself apart.

Most of the people were congregated near the telescreen that was reporting the latest war news. Dr. Sybaris sat at the end of the bar, drinking alone.

"Anton!" Morgan cried as he playfully slapped his friend on his shoulder. "What are you doing here?"

Dr. Sybaris nearly jumped over the bar in shock. Morgan quickly grabbed his friend and gently placed him back on his stool. "My God, Anton! What's the matter? Are you all right?"

Now that he had gotten closer, Morgan could see that his friend was in worse shape than he thought. The man's eyes were glazed and bloodshot with the air of a crazed madman. If Morgan hadn't known better, he'd swear that the man before him had escaped from Bedlam Asylum.

"Morgan!" Dr. Sybaris sobbed. "Is it really you? Or are you a phantom? Come here, let me test you." He started grabbing and pulling at Morgan, checking his substance.

"Anton, of course it's me. What on earth has happened to you?"

Dr. Sybaris looked around them. "Not here. Over in one of the booths. Grab the bottle."

Morgan followed his friend over to the darkened corner booth and placed the bottle of whiskey between them with two glasses. As he filled them, Dr. Sybaris placed a metallic cylinder on the table and pressed the button. It emitted a low-level hum that varied in pitch and intensity. Morgan stared at the cylinder.

"It blocks the signal, but it only works for a little while so we'll have to speak quickly."

Dr. Sybaris took a long, hard swig of the whiskey and coughed. His eyes glazed over until Morgan gently nudged his hand.

"Anton, talk to me. What's happened to you?"

"It's the signal," Dr. Sybaris muttered, "the signal. You remember, don't you, Morgan? How my Visualizer latched onto that signal I couldn't explain. Remember?"

Morgan nodded his head sympathetically.

"Well, I kept working on it until I discovered what was wrong. It wasn't an audio signal at all, Morgan—it was something more!"

Dr. Sybaris leaned forward and whispered conspiratorially.

It was something's thoughts!

Morgan sat stunned. His friend had obviously lost his mind. "Overworked, poor chap!" he thought.

"Don't look at me like that, Morgan. I know it sounds mad, but it's true. That's why I couldn't convert it to a video or picture; it wasn't an audio signal at all. I had managed to find the frequency of thought. And there's more . . . *it was the thoughts of something that wasn't human!*"

Glancing about the room, Morgan could see that no one was paying any attention to them, nor were there any policemen in the room. For the first time, Morgan was afraid for and of his friend.

"I couldn't tell where the signal was coming from, but it was somewhere in England. Most of the time, the thoughts weren't even words. They were buzzes and noises but of different tones and pitches. That was how they communicated between themselves. They only thought in English when they were speaking with a human."

"Wait," Morgan said. "You're saying that you've tapped into the thoughts of aliens who are *speaking* to humans?"

"Not so much speaking as giving them orders. I've been listening to them all week, Morgan, and I don't think I've slept at all in five days. They're here, Morgan, they're everywhere! They're on every continent, in every nation. They've been here for millennia; watching, plotting, planning, manipulating."

"Are they here now?"

Dr. Sybaris grimaced and took another gulp of whiskey. "They . . . and their cults."

"What do you mean?"

Dr. Sybaris looked around the room. "There are those who service them—their acolytes. They work for them and keep them safe and protected. These *humans*," he said with a sneer, "have pledged their lives to the cause of these creatures and made their alien goals their own."

"And where are these aliens from?"

"I know you're humoring me, Morgan. I know that tone. But it's true!"

Dr. Sybaris slammed his fist on the table, causing others to look in their direction.

"They came here from beyond space, following the trail of the Old

Ones. It's *them* that they serve and all their minds are pledged toward that goal. They shall be free again and the earth shall be wiped clean and remade in their image! Iä! Shub-Niggurath!"

Morgan slapped his friend across his face and the light of reason slowly returned to his eyes.

"I'm sorry, Morgan, I'm raving. I've already said too much. Their slaves are everywhere. I have to be careful. I think they're onto me. I don't know how, but I think that they detected my Visualizer and tracked it back to me. That was probably why I was finally able to get a clear picture of them. Oh, God, Morgan! They're horrible! I can't even describe them. They look like brains with tentacles stuck on the bodies of huge, misshapen wasps! Their wings allow them to fly through space, but they look like nothing on this planet. Myths have known them in the past and called them demons—Beelzebub, Ashtoreth, Belial. The human mind can only comprehend part of them because they are so full of the *outside*.

"And that's not the worst. I've listened to their thoughts and commands. I know what they've done and what they're going to do. I know why everything is so *wrong*. Here, take this."

Dr. Sybaris pressed a recording disc into Morgan's hand.

"I recorded what I could. Listen to it and then tell me that I'm insane. I've tried to send copies to others, but I know my mail is intercepted. They're trying to isolate me. It won't be long now. Watch yourself. Trust no one . . ." Dr. Sybaris got up to leave and pocketed the metal cylinder from the table. "Not even me."

Faster than Morgan had ever seen him move, Dr. Sybaris was out of the pub and into the street, nearly knocking down several people on the sidewalk. Then he was gone and Morgan was left sitting alone with an empty bottle of whiskey in front of him.

Although shaken by the encounter, Morgan tried to dismiss it as stress from overwork. Dr. Sybaris always had a tendency to take his emotions and theories to the extreme, so perhaps this was just another incident. Still, his eyes showed that he believed what he said, no matter how insane. The story was nonsense, of course, but Morgan worried that his friend had lost his mind. He put the disc in his pocket just as the crowd began to cheer and shout.

The telescreen showed the British line of cyborgs pushing the Germans back over the Polish border. In their hands were weapons that emitted sonic bursts that blew apart the German troops. The flesh melted off while their metal parts sparked and exploded. It was a complete rout, and the Germans had no defense.

As everyone cheered, the announcer went on to claim that the victory was due to the Americans secretly sending over the Tesla Sonic Disrupter. Hidden among the shipments of food and medical supplies, the Americans had smuggled in the latest weapon designed by Nikola Tesla. Using low-frequency sound, the Disrupter did exactly that: disrupted machines and flesh. British forces, the announcer went on to proclaim, were determined to push the Germans back to Berlin and destroy the German Empire once and for all.

The pub exploded with cheers and yells as everyone celebrated. The war would be over within a matter of weeks! The beer and drinks flowed freely, and men slapped each other on the back and boldly kissed the women. Celebrations continued into the night and for days after.

Morgan quickly forgot about his friend's wild tale as he drowned himself in beer, wine, and women for the next week. The disc sat forgotten in his coat pocket.

For three weeks, no one had seen Dr. Sybaris. He was not found at the Diogenes Club, where he had been a regular fixture for years and where the old men cheered the victory and simultaneously maintained how soldiers had it harder in their day. Nor did Dr. Sybaris appear at the Autonomic Explorers Club when Dr. Elias Payton presented his paper on "Cosmic Radio Signals," in which the diminutive academic had seriously questioned several of Dr. Sybaris's own theories and published papers. In the midst of Germany's surrender and resultant celebrations, Dr. Sybaris was almost totally forgotten.

Morgan had attempted to call on his friend several times during those weeks, only to be left standing outside Sybaris's door unanswered. He couldn't even clearly recall their last meeting. There was a drunken memory of talking about Dr. Sybaris's Visualizer, but Morgan was damned if he could remember anything more. In truth, he could barely recall anything of that crazy week. Still, when reason returned,

Morgan had sent letters and telegrams that all went unanswered.

Finally, feeling vaguely uneasy but not really knowing why, Morgan determined that he would go to Dr. Sybaris's house and, if he was not admitted, would return with a policeman. This time he would not be so easily rebuffed.

Outside Dr. Sybaris's door, the house appeared calm and quiet.

In the street, the steam-powered horses carried their carts back and forth. A newsboy on the corner offered the latest data-sheet that claimed: "Germany's surrender a hoax! New threat coming! New bomb in German hands!" Morgan ignored the people in the street and pounded heavily on Sybaris's door with his walking stick.

Morgan could hear the sound reverberate oddly in the building. Almost as if it were hollow. He knocked hard a second time.

He was about to turn away and summon a constable when the door suddenly flew open and Dr. Anton Sybaris was standing in the doorway.

"Morgan!" Dr. Sybaris exclaimed happily. "How wonderful to see you! Come in, come in. It's been much too long."

Stunned, Morgan could do nothing but shake the outstretched hand and stumble through the door.

Inside, the building had changed. The entire first floor was now a huge room. All the walls had been taken down, and the space had been converted into some sort of massive factory-type area. Clearly, something had been produced here, but now all that seemed to remain was the space where vast machines had been. To the left was a small sitting area with a few chairs and a work-table. A few papers were still on the table, but it was mostly clean.

Dr. Sybaris motioned Morgan over to the chairs where a dapper young man sat. "Morgan," Dr. Sybaris exclaimed, "allow me to present Mr. Noyes. He's a recent colleague of mine, a physicist, actually."

"Pleased to meet you, Mr. Rice," Noyes said. His voice was kind enough, but it made Morgan uneasy all the same. It was like listening to a polished politician speak—the kind of talk that said one thing but meant something entirely different.

Noyes was a youngish looking fellow but, truth be told, it would be difficult to ascribe any age to him. He was urban and fashionably dressed with a small, thin mustache. His black hair was slicked back over his skull and gleamed icily in the electric light.

"My pleasure, Mr. Noyes. Anton, I hope I'm not intruding, but I was worried about you."

Dr. Sybaris gave Morgan a puzzled look. "Worried? Whatever for?"

"Well," Morgan laughed, "I have to admit that I'm not entirely sure why. I just have a vague memory of your being very upset at our last meeting, but I can't recall any details."

Noyes smiled. "A bit too much celebrating, Mr. Rice?"

Sheepishly, Morgan nodded. "A tad. We've every reason to celebrate, don't you agree, Mr. Noyes?"

"Oh, yes, yes, indeed. Still, one can never rest, you know. 'The price of freedom is eternal vigilance.'"

"Thomas Jefferson. True, very true. Anton, I seem to recall it had something to do with your 'Visualizer'?"

Dr. Sybaris laughed. "That foolish thing? Oh, Morgan, I gave up on that weeks ago. Never could make the blasted thing work. Stupid idea anyway. Fancy trying to turn sound into pictures. Can't imagine what I was thinking."

Morgan looked at Dr. Sybaris, confused. "But . . . I thought you said you *had* gotten it working."

Noyes looked at Dr. Sybaris, who simply smiled at Morgan. "No, you're mistaken, old boy. Nothing of the sort. Look around you! All my efforts these past weeks have been on helping manufacture and refine Tesla's Sonic Disruptors for our troops. We've just finished actually. The last shipment went out this morning."

"So I see. You've been very busy."

Morgan pulled Dr. Sybaris aside. "Anton, are you *quite* sure you're all right?"

Dr. Sybaris's gaze darted over to Noyes and back again. "Quite sure, old chap. In fact, I hate to be rude, but Mr. Noyes and I have some pressing business to discuss. What if I meet you later tonight for drinks, eh? At the Diogenes Club?"

Morgan allowed himself to be led back to the door. "Yes, of course, Anton. That'll be fine. I'm just glad to see you are well."

Noyes nodded genially to Morgan. "Good day to you, Mr. Rice.

Hope to see you again."

Not knowing what else to do, Morgan nodded back to Noyes, whom he had no desire ever to see again. "Good day, Mr. Noyes."

As the door slowly closed behind him, Morgan turned back to see Dr. Sybaris's face disappearing back into the dark. It almost seemed that the skin on his face was loose, but before Morgan could be sure the door was closed. Morgan was back on the street again with the steam horses and newsies.

While he walked back home, Morgan tried desperately to remember his previous meeting with Dr. Sybaris in the Dog and Duck pub. He remembered walking into the pub, seeing his friend in the back, and sitting down at the booth. But what happened then? There was some talk about the Visualizer. No matter what Dr. Sybaris said now, they had talked about the invention—Morgan *knew* that. Then, he also knew that Dr. Sybaris had gotten it to work. But why would that be unsettling? It would prove several of Dr. Sybaris's theories, but Morgan remembered that first time—the strange signal and the explosion—and then it all came back to him. The signal being thoughts, not audio, and the aliens and the cults—and then Morgan finally remembered the disc.

Morgan could not run home fast enough.

In a blaze of activity, Morgan went through every pocket of his coats until he found it. The disc gleamed in the light. Frantic, Morgan ran to his disc player and quickly put it in. Suddenly, the speakers erupted with sound. At first it was nothing more than buzzes; then there was the sound of English speech.

"We have not worked so long to be stopped now." The voice had an odd, unnatural tone to it, not unlike someone speaking in an unfamiliar tongue.

"For years we have subverted their history, changed science and manufacturing." Another voice said.

"Agreed. By assimilating their greatest minds we have accelerated their natural evolution. We have introduced technology they were incapable of understanding or controlling. They are now at least sixty sun cycles before where they would have been without our interference."

"I understand." This was a different voice. It had a thick German accent but spoke with no hesitation. "I have completed the necessary computations. The bomb can now be mass-produced. The atomic age will begin in four weeks."

"That is acceptable," said the first voice. "Our forces are preparing the necessary manufacturing areas in the designated countries."

"And soon the earth shall be wiped clean and remade in their image," replied the second voice. "Then the Old Ones will rise and we will fly once again through space and bring the others here. Azathoth shall open the gate and Nyarlathotep, the Crawling Chaos, will reward his servants."

"Iä! Iä! Iä!" shouted all the voices.

"Wait!" shouted the first voice. "I sense an intruder here—one who is not of our thoughts. Noyes, do you feel it?"

"I do," said a voice that Morgan had only just recently met. "I shall find him, and he will either join us or Nyarlathotep shall walk in his guise."

Suddenly the disc cut off. There was no more left to hear, but Morgan had heard enough. After all those years, Dr. Sybaris was correct. The world *wasn't* right. It had been pushed, shoved into technology it was neither prepared for nor able to handle . . . and it was all around them now.

But there was still time! Morgan grabbed the disc and put it in his pocket. He had friends at the Ministry of Defence and he'd make them listen to the disc. Maybe they weren't prepared for this technology, but they had it now and could use it against these aliens just as well as they did against the Germans.

Morgan rushed from his room, the call of "cab!" already forming on his lips, when he opened the door to find Noyes standing there.

"Good afternoon, Mr. Rice," the smooth voice dripped. "I told you that I'd hoped I'd see you again soon."

Noyes pushed himself inside and closed the door behind him. No screams were emitted from the house. No blood was ever found. Still, at that moment, Morgan Rice was erased from this earth.

In the air, the sound of German airships laden with atomic bombs came ever closer and closer.

Sunspots

They come at night, mostly. Blinding, bright lights that smash their way into my mind. No matter where I am, they find me. I've tried to hide, but they always find me. I've hidden in stables, under bridges, even in the sewers—and the lights always appear.

They've been attacking me for years. Even as a child in Whitechapel, I wasn't safe. I would be asleep in the back room with my brothers and sisters, and the lights would come. There would be loud noises like a train engine wheezing as it goes up a hill. I'd clamp my hands over my ears and shut my eyes tight, but they'd find their way through. Their thoughts worming their way into my brain, becoming my thoughts, my desires, my actions. No one else ever heard or saw them. The lights would be so bright that everything else would become blurs and stretched out like sweets on a taffy pull. Heads would look squished and thin while their fingers became long sticks.

When I woke up with my mother's bloody and bruised body below me, I ran off into the streets and tried to hide from everything. I wandered through the workhouses and asylums, growing up among the poor and the mad. One night, in Bethlehem Hospital, the lights came for me while I was in the open room. Later, when I awoke in the straitjacket, they told me that there had been no lights and I had been stopped from attacking a female patient. They said that I was shouting about lights and that the patient had been hiding something inside her body.

I was in Bedlam for a while.

That's when I learned not to talk about the lights. I worked on my control, on being aware when I had my 'spells.' I couldn't stop them but, when I felt them coming, I would find a dark, tight place to hide away. That's how I learned what they were doing and what they wanted.

I begged the doctors to kill me. They would not. Men and women around me were subjected to the most horrifying treatments ever devised in the name of healing, but we were never allowed to die. So I escaped and ran back to the streets of Whitechapel, the only home I'd ever known.

On the nights when the lights did not come for me, I would dream odd, terrifying dreams. My thoughts were not my own and were nothing known to me. In the dreams, I'd see strange places with unnatural landscapes. The buildings were tall and thin and sat at odd angles to one another and there were things that flew in the air and creatures that swam through liquid that wasn't quite water. I'd see vehicles that spun and split through the skies and vast expanses of stars and dark spaces that would zip by at unbelievable speeds. I'd feel sadness at leaving those horrifying landscapes with their unholy creatures, but a sense of purpose, of need, would drive me forward. When I would awaken from these dreams, I'd be shivering and covered in a sickly, cold sweat. Several times I would look at my hands and scream, horrified at their short fingers and pink skin.

I tried to kill myself several times.

My coat pockets loaded with heavy rocks, I threw myself into the Thames, only to be pulled out by a passing bobby. I jumped in front of hansoms, but they always managed to stop short no matter how close I timed my leap. I picked fights with dangerous men in bars and let them beat me unconscious, but I never died. Each time, something kept me from death. Eventually the lights revealed that this was because I had to fulfill a great purpose, a mighty task that was the sole purpose of my life.

But I would not do it.

So the lights came more often and were more and more insistent. They pressed down upon my mind, crushing my thoughts until I couldn't tell the difference between their thoughts and my thoughts. I could see through my eyes, but so could they. I lay in the middle of Commercial Street, screaming. People ignored me, thinking that I was drunk, while children mocked me by screaming along with me. When I stood up, the lights in my mind moved my body and I watched as I walked down the street.

I found her in Buck's Row.

She looked young but said that she was older. Her name was Polly. I'd seen her around before, when I would be trying to drink the lights away at the Ten Bells Pub. She'd been nice to me and could see that I was not right. She was drunk and led me down the street when my hand suddenly shot out and slit her throat with a knife I hadn't known I had.

After that, I went away and hid in my mind. I did not want to see the things my hands were doing.

I awoke the next morning, lying in the park behind a bush. My hands ached from the activity of the night before, but there was no blood on me or my clothes. I was sure that it was all a dream until I heard the newsboys shouting about a horrible murder. Mindlessly, I plodded along.

The lights came again a few days later, but I bashed my head against a stone wall until I was unconscious. After that, they came every night and I could no longer fight.

Annie died in the back of a run-down house on Hanbury Street. This time the lights made me scoop out her intestines and throw them over her shoulder. There was something inside her that they made me look for, but it wasn't there. I could feel them making notes as my hands cut her open as if they were charting a road map.

If I couldn't kill myself, I'd give myself up. The East End was exploding in a riot of outrage. I'd confess and the police would execute me. But when I went up to a PC, my mouth would not work. The lights would not allow me to speak. The PC snorted at me in disgust and punched me in the gut with his nightstick. I lay in the gutter, sobbing soundlessly.

The next weeks were spent in an alcoholic blur. The lights pushed me out into the streets but, thankfully, the women were so terrified that none would approach me. We were searching, ever searching. Eventually, even terror subsides and a tall woman fell beneath my knife. Many times I'd thrown the knife away and just as many times it found its way back to my pocket.

But another had spotted us as the tall woman bled onto the sidewalk and my fear overcame the lights to allow me to flee, but they pressed ever harder on my mind. The world became nothing but a bright white space, and people were blurs. As I stumbled mindlessly through the white light, they would direct me with arms raised and fingers pointed. Their hideously long fingers and weird, misshapen heads with large, doll-like eyes were always before me.

I found myself in Mitre Square. My hands were digging inside some woman I'd never seen before. They had me looking inside her for something. I cut and pushed squishy things aside until I saw it—a tiny little light, no larger than a pollywog. It was what they'd been looking for for so long and which had been denied them. It was the mother/brother/sister/father/lover/killer that hid beneath the flesh. The lights inside my head rejoiced and my hands lunged for it, but it slipped through my fingers like quicksilver and was gone into the night.

The lights screamed and ripped through my brain. I pounded my head relentlessly, but they would not stop. Dazed, I fumbled along, trying to follow the prize.

"I would know it now," the lights told me. I had seen it and would be able to spot it wherever it hid or whomever it hid in. When I captured it, it would mean the end. That's what the lights promised me. I didn't know if that meant I would finally be allowed to die or taken into the stars or ripped apart by an angry mob—and I didn't care. It meant that I would no longer be here and I would no longer be me and the lights would no longer need me and that's all I cared about. What did it matter if it was the peace of oblivion or the hell of the afterlife? I would no longer be me.

It took nearly a month. Several times I thought I had found it, but it jumped before I could lay my hands on the woman. It was watching for me now, so I had to be careful. When I saw it, fluttering behind Mary Kelly's eyes, I kept my distance. I put laudanum in a dark green bottle of gin and gave it to a girl to share with Mary. As they walked out of the Ten Bells, I followed closely behind. Barely standing, they made it to Mary's room and I waited outside. When the other girl came out later, Mary was drunkenly signing a song about a violet on her mother's grave.

She was passed out when I walked into the room. I built the flame into an inferno to keep the lights at bay. Then I started my work.

An hour later, with pieces of Mary about the room, I found it.

I cupped my hands softly around it and slipped it out from the dead body. The lights jumped and leaped about as I raised it before me. I heard the sounds of the wheezing engines whirling about my head as their hideously thin fingers stroked and caressed the little, errant dot of thinking light.

I smiled as they gorged themselves on the small, tiny soul and took me away and ripped me apart among the stars. I still smiled because I knew, sweet Mary, that because I took you and the others with me, we walk among the cosmos and dance among the eons. We are immortal and, in the space between the stars, there are, finally, no lights.

My Brother's Keeper

Grandfather used to let me out some nights so I could walk in the grass and stare at the stars. "Yew too big for that naow," he says, and there are no windows in the attic. Sometimes I think he's afraid of me.

He doesn't say it out loud, but I can hear it in his mind. When he reads to me from the old books and teaches me what to say, he gets a look in his eyes that makes me think he hates me. It'll pass quick-like, but I see it. I can't help being what I am.

There was a time when I lived in the shed. It was small and I would spread out all over it. Grandfather would come and tell me to stop making so much noise, especially if the man with the cows was around. I couldn't help making noise. I needed to spread out and let all my limbs uncurl; but the shed was so, so tight.

The first time I was out in the air and could feel the grass on my skin and mouths and reach toward the sky, I cried out for my father. Noises from under the hill answered me, but that only seemed to make Grandfather angrier. "Damn ye! Don't be going on like thet! Ye'll only rile 'em up moaning thet way. Ye're here to sarve Willy, don't forgit!"

I don't like Willy. He's mean to me when Grandfather and Mother aren't watching. Just because they can't see me, he thinks he can get away with cutting and hitting. I don't know why they can't see me. I see myself just fine and can even count all my legs and mouths and eyes. Grandfather says it's because there's more of the 'outside' in me, but I don't know what that means. I guess I get that from Father because Mother isn't at all like me.

I make Mother nervous. She doesn't like me to be around. When Willy is away, she has to feed me and I can tell she hates it. I try to talk to her, but my words aren't right. It's hard to manage all my mouths to talk or be silent. She is always pale and her face is dull as if she's somewhere else. She makes me sad.

Some nights I slip through the corners and my mind goes to the 'other place.' That's where my friends are, and they teach me things that even Grandfather doesn't know. Willy thinks he's so smart because he can speak the Aklo language, but any child can do that. Father talks to me sometimes. He tells me things about how the world will look when he comes to visit, but all I know of the world is wooden floors and walls. I want to burst free and stretch myself out, but I can't. The attic is too small now.

Once Grandfather and Willy had brought me my food and there was a sound at the door they use to come up into the attic. The cow was stronger than I was used to and I had to get my arms and mouths around it in order to feed right, so it was making noise. Grandfather looked frightened, but Willy wasn't. "Let 'em come up," he said. "He needs to feed anyway." I could hear Mother through the floor telling someone not to open the door.

When the noise stopped and the voices went away, Grandfather slapped Willy. "Ye fool! Ye ain't ready and nor is it! Ye're too weak right naow. All it takes is one damn fool to see somethin' he oughtn't. Then it'll be a mob and fire!"

"Yew said that fire cain't harm him," Willy said. His voice always sounded as if he had too much spit in his mouth.

"Hurt *yew* well enough," Grandfather said. "Remember that ye be more of this place than it!"

They won't bring me along when they go and make the services anymore. "Ye be too big naow," Grandfather said, "we cain't risk it."

I didn't mind. While they are out, I have my own services and they are better than theirs. I did all the ceremonies the way the 'others' taught me, even though my mouths wouldn't work right and my limbs wouldn't always go in the right direction. The Scarlet Ceremonies are the best. They let me see further outside. They tell me things. I know more than Grandfather and Willy now. My learning did not come from books but at the feet of the 'others' who are depending on me. I have a great role to fulfill. I just don't know what that is yet.

Why are there no windows in this attic?? I must see!

Birds are flying around outside the attic in large numbers. I hear them but cannot see them. There are voices downstairs that I do not know. They are loud and concerned. Something about Grandfather. He is 'dying,' but I do not know what that means.

The birds chatter in a rhythm. I can hear Grandfather wheezing in the same pattern. It must be some sort of a game, so I move back and forth over the floor in the same rhythm. I hear Grandfather talking to Willy downstairs and then, suddenly, he stops talking and the birds go silent. I'm the last to stop, so I've lost the game.

Later, Willy comes upstairs and tells me that Grandfather is dead. I don't understand. Willy tells me that it's like the cows when I feed too much. I go looking for Grandfather in the spaces in-between, but he is not there. I'm beginning to think that Willy and Grandfather and Mother are less than me. This makes me happy.

Willy keeps trying to explain 'Time' to me, but I don't understand. There is no 'time' outside. He gets angry and tells me to call him "Wilbur," but I begin to see how small he truly is. Father does not talk to Willy. Sometimes he asks about my brother, but I do not answer. Willy cannot open the way without me. I am more important than him.

I asked Willy why he wears clothes sometimes. He answered that it is to protect him when he goes out among what he calls 'people.' He explains that there are others like Grandfather and Mother, but I have never known anyone but them. I hear voices downstairs sometimes and hear minds that are different. Are these 'people'? What are they?

I like when the light comes through the seams between the planks in the wall. It feels warm on my skin and it makes me lazy. I have never felt the rain or what Willy calls 'snow.' It sounds cool and fresh. Willy refuses to let me out to feel it. He makes me say the rituals over and over again even though I know them better than he does. I correct him on his speech now, and he does not like that.

I hate my brother.

I hear yelling. Mother is yelling at Willy. She is calling him words that I do not know, but they sound dark and ugly. I hear her mind and it is angry and sick and full of hate. She wants to go somewhere, a place Willy will not let her go anymore. Why are the birds here again?

What are you doing, Willy?

The noises in the hill are louder, louder than I've ever heard them before. They growl as the birds gather about and shriek. I have never heard so many birds. Downstairs, Willy is doing something to Mother. I cannot see clearly. His mind is nothing but red.

I pound on the floor.

Stop it, Willy! Leave Mother alone!

The birds shriek louder and louder in a rhythm that gets faster and faster. Someone is gasping for breath. I catch an image of fingers clutching a throat and the birds burst into a mad song.

There are no sounds from downstairs. I pound on the floor. Willy comes upstairs slowly.

"Ain't no use moaning like thet," he says. "Mother's daid. Like Grandfather, 'member?"

I made some noises which made Willy madder.

"Jes' be quite naow," he said. "Daid naow or later, makes no difference."

He left and I could hear him pulling something across the floor downstairs and then the front door slam shut. Later, I got a flash of a fire up on a hill and Mother on some kind of stone table. I remembered that table. Grandfather had taken me there before when I was smaller and told me that "one day, ye'll be a-callin' yer father's name up here."

There was a fire and Willy placed Mother in it.

Now I had no one but Willy here in this place. My friends 'outside' could not come here yet, so I was alone. My eyes felt warm and moist.

I got larger again. Both Willy and I did, but I was bigger and always would be. I was learning faster than Willy and it made him nervous. He moved out to the shed I used to stay in and tore up the attic floor.

At last I can stretch!

I can go to my full height now. No longer cramped and I feel stronger. Willy knows it too and eyes me strangely when he feeds me. I instruct *him* now on what is to be done. He tries to hide his thoughts from me, but I can still see them. He is worried that he will fail.

So am I.

There are certain things that only he can do. I can't say some of the words or move properly while on this sphere. I can open the way but only a thin crack; nothing large enough to go through. We need each other for now. But later, when Father is here and the world is wiped clean, Willy will know what it is to fear me.

He came and admitted his failure to me. Grandfather had told him what was needed, that a page out of a book had to be found and he waited too long. He claims that he tried to get the book from others, but his words made no sense to me. I know nothing of 'mail' or 'libraries.' I only know that he should have resolved this before. Willy claims that he was afraid to leave me alone and go and get what we needed. I chastised him greatly for this. If my welfare was of such a concern, he could have gone away while Mother was still here to feed me. I've ordered him to go and return quickly. After so long, my will reigns.

I fed greatly before he left. Alone, my mind traveled beyond the spheres and echoed through the stars. I conversed with mad Azathoth and debated with creatures who had left earth aeons before and others who were yet to come. Father praised my efforts and search for knowledge but warned me that the convergence was imminent.

My consciousness expanded and I could feel Willy far away from our home. He was tense, irritated because he was foiled in his attempt to retrieve the page. An image of another shimmered in my mind. It was a strange creature that appeared somewhat similar to Willy but smaller and older like Grandfather. "Wal, all right," Willy said to the animal, "ef ye feel that way abaout it. Maybe Harvard wun't be so fussy as yew be."

I ebbed away from the scene and fled into my center. Willy's desperation came through to me as I felt him appeal to another creature, similar as the first, and receive the same response. I impressed the need upon him. Forces were moving together. He must take whatever action was needed. A vision of some four-legged animal with a long snout appeared suddenly before me, and I jumped away as it lunged toward me; but it was Willy, not me, that it attacked. It growled and bit and tore and I could feel Willy's panic as he tried to throw it off. With a groan, Willy left this sphere the way Grandfather and Mother had, and I howled with him.

Now only I was left.

Because I do not understand 'time,' I do not understand its pass-ing. Many scenes appeared to me of Grandfather and Mother and Wil-ly, but they were without form or weight. Grandfather demanded that I rise, that I was the only hope left. The hill. I had to make it to the top of the hill.

Groaning, I pressed against the walls of my prison. Outside, I could hear the hill noises growing louder, as if they were encouraging me to break free. I expanded, contracted, and expanded again. The wood in the walls and the ceiling grew weaker. Pushing, straining, *grow-ing.* With a last heave, the building exploded and I was free!

The air smelled sweet and warm. I looked around me with all my eyes. There was a slight wind. I remember the times Grandfather took me to the hill. The trees. *The trees were so tall.* But now, as I reared up, some trees were shorter than I was. And I was so *hungry.*

Not far away I found cows. More cows than I had ever seen! I leaped upon them and fed. Some screamed, but most did not have that chance. Half I ate completely, not even leaving bones, while I sucked the others nearly dry. The more I ate, the hungrier I got.

But where was the hill? I could not remember the way. Everything was wrong, out of proportion. What should have been large was now small, and trees blocked every way I looked. Tired, I moved down into an area that seemed familiar. There were more of the birds here. Now I could see them, flying back and forth. Bugs lit up for a second, then out and then up again. I pushed the trees aside and fled. When the light came up over the trees, I nearly screamed. It was so *bright!* Bright-er than any light I had ever seen. I huddled close and pulled all my limbs to me and cried.

Grandfather! Help me!

The dark was cooler and I could move about again. I found a large wooden box like my home. I shook it, wondering if one like me was imprisoned inside, but only sounds of animals came out. I smashed it and ate what was inside. Another box was nearby, but this had win-dows. I could see things inside but walked away.

The way was not clear. I moved about, looking at the curious marks I left as I walked, and hid again in the maze of trees. Grandfa-ther and Willy could not see me. Maybe these others could not either. I might be safe then. The light came and went. I reached out but could not feel anyone. I had to look inside myself.

"Thar, up that hill," Grandfather said, *"here's ware ye'll open the way."*

Willy clumped up the hill ahead of me. His furry legs kicking and stomping in irritation. I came behind. My legs were too clumsy to move fast. Why didn't I look more like Willy?

"What's 'pecial abaout here?" Willy asked.

Grandfather slapped him, which made me smile.

"Watch yer mouth, boy," Grandfather said. *He walked toward a stone table on the center of the hill. "This is a holy place," he said; "years of rituals were done here. The lines between the spheres is weak here."*

I climbed onto the table and looked around. If I stretched, I could see our house. Other buildings were away in the distance. There were lights in them and I wanted so badly to go see them and look into their windows.

"Remember," he said, *"remember."*

I followed the dream but got lost. In the dark, I came upon a cliff face that towered even taller than me and I climbed it to the top. There was the stone table! I climbed upon it and reached into the stars, calling the words and moving in the required way—but nothing happened. I could not make it work. In anger I thrashed about and upended trees and bushes. Exhausted, I went back the way I came and slept and thought.

The anger had grown by the time night came again. I pushed through the woods, mad with hate. I hated Grandfather and Willy. I hated this world. I hated the things that walked here and, when I found another box, I crushed it as easily as a stick. Some puny thing screamed, "Help, oh, my Gawd!" but I grabbed her and the others and consumed them. I could feel them dissolving in me, but it was not enough. I needed more. I crashed through the trees while the birds screeched furiously and ate anything I could find that walked or crawled.

Deep in the woods, I brooded and thought. My mind slipped sideways through the gap to the other places, and I sought counsel. There were ways, I was told, to compensate for my loss. Changes to be made. Different words to be spoken. I would not be able to open the break enough for Father, but others could come through and they would begin the work. In the end, the result would be the same.

During the day, I felt something. It was a mind I had known before but could not place. It wasn't Grandfather or Willy. But it was close and I felt its anger and fear. Perhaps I could use it. I know anger.

The rain began to fall.

I looked up and felt it splash upon me. Moaning, I reached as high as I could. I'd never felt the rain, never known how it could make me feel clean and new. I laughed and cheered. *This is an omen,* I thought. I had to move now. Forces were aligning both for and against me.

The way was now known to me. I followed the path I had made. The rain fell hard and then soft. The light was dimmed so I could move easily. The hill came closer and closer. I leaned on a wooden box that stood over a river. It creaked but did not fall. Ahead was another box with lights and voices coming from inside. It made me angry. It should not be here. *They* should not be here. This world is not theirs, but they infest it and scurry over its corpse. I launched myself against the front of the box, but it held. Something inside screamed hideously, so I hit it again and again until it fell in pieces before me. I ate the few inside, but something else screamed from a small box. A voice came out of it screeching, *"Sally! Sally! Oh, Gawd, SALLY!"*

I picked it up and sniffed it. There was nothing inside but wires. Where was the voice coming from? I stepped on it, and the sound ceased. The rain had stopped and the light was back out when I got to the bottom of the hill. I slowly crawled to the top.

Calmly, I reviewed in my mind what I needed to do. I said the words to myself and repeated the motions in their correct order. I had nearly reached the stone table when I became aware of something on a higher rise nearby. The mind was familiar and the same as I had felt earlier. I looked about, searching for something to hit, when I saw them.

There were three of them. Creatures similar to Willy but smaller, and one of them I knew. I looked and remembered the flash I had gotten from Willy of the man who denied him the pages from the book. It was the same creature that faced me now. He had some sort of thing in his hands and, although I knew he could not see me, he stared at me. I roared and moved to strike him down when he sprayed something at me which pushed me backward.

It was some sort of powder, such as Grandfather used in certain ceremonies, but different, stronger. I felt it covering me, suffocating me. I thrashed about, but it only made it worse. *Why couldn't it rain now?*

The creature raised its arms and began chanting rhythmically. Its face was white and intense. Suddenly the birds were about again and shrilling evilly and in ever-increasing volume. I struggled and felt that the binding was losing force.

"*Morgan! Rice! It's fighting me! You have to join the chant now before it's too late!*"

From beneath the hills came loud growls and I could sense something trying to help me, but now the three of them were together and singing against me. I looked around. *Why is no one here to help me?* Grandfather and Willy were gone. I tried to conjure them up from my mind, but they would not come forth. I began to feel sick with dread.

Maybe it wasn't that Willy thought he would fail. Maybe he was afraid that *I* would.

Terrified, I began to scream.

"*Ygnaiih . . . ygnaiih . . . thflthkh'ngha . . . Yog-Sothoth . . . Y'bthnk . . . h'ehye—n'grkdl'lh. . . .*"

I tried to say the words, but they got mixed together. I yelled as loudly as I could, but nothing was happening. I could not feel *them* helping me.

The will of the creatures pressed down upon me, smothering my mind. I felt myself falling apart into pieces. I cried and sobbed, but they would not release me. Instead, they pressed on and on and I dwindled more and more.

Softly I sensed something reaching for me. Through the gates, between the spheres, *he* reached for me, but he was still so far away.

The birds screeched louder and, terrified, I heard their shrill call match the rhythm of my breathing.

I was losing myself . . .

Finally, in a last burst of strength, I reached out and screamed, "*Eh-ya-ya-ya-yahaah—e'yayayayaaaa . . . ngh'aaaaa . . . ngh'aaaa . . .* h'yuh . . . h'yuh . . . HELP! HELP! . . . *ff—ff—ff*—FATHER! FATHER! YOG-SOTHOTH! . . ."

Then everything exploded.

Now I dwell in the spaces beyond. I soar through the cosmos and spread terror. I ride with hideous beings on the night-wind and roam through nameless catacombs and unknown valleys. Father does not blame me. He says that there will always be more chances and that time has no meaning here. Hundreds might fail, but all it needs is for one to succeed. Together we scheme and plan. Father loves me.

"How Does That Make You Feel?"

The door smashed easily beneath my fist. I dived quickly into the room, only to find it empty. Doctor Primordial had already fled. The warehouse was still full of strange equipment, so I was not too far behind. I could see weird incubator-like machines posted in lines throughout the room. There were at least a hundred of them. I thought that they had been empty but, as I turned to leave, I could see something moving inside one of the glass coffins. I walked up to it slowly, afraid of what I might find. I holstered my .45 and reached out a gloved hand to the glass. It was cold to the touch and covered with condensation. I rubbed until a small window appeared and I looked inside. There was a corpse lying within. It was wearing a Nazi uniform, and I could clearly see the "SS" insignia on the collar. The flesh was gray and sunken with death. Whoever he had been, he had been dead for some time, preserved in this ghoulish freezer. As I stared blankly at the poor creature, he opened his eyes and turned to look at me. I burned the warehouse to the ground.

"And what happened then?" Dr. Gull asked.

"I woke up," Ed replied. "Just as I always do."

Dr. Gull made some notes on his pad. They were sitting in Dr. Gull's office at Rhode Island Hospital. It was a room like any other psychiatrist's office. Simple but neutral furniture. Just a couch for the patient and an easy chair for the doctor. A desk sat nearby with a closed laptop on it. Diplomas hung on the wall along with various pictures of family, including one photo that looked very old. It was a black-and-white picture of two men smiling happily at the camera.

"So let me make sure that I understand what you're saying. You've been having a recurring dream that you're some sort of 'pulp hero' named 'The Crimson Scorpion' in New York City in the 1940s?"

Ed shifted nervously in his seat. For a fairly small man, he was uneasy in his body. The addition of extra weight had made him clumsy and unable to be comfortable. 'Middle-aged spread,' Ed assumed; although it bothered him, he never considered joining a gym or going on a diet.

"Well, yes and no. You see, I'm always the Scorpion but it's not a recurring dream so much as it's an extended one."

"You mean that it's like a movie?"

"Yes. Every time I go to sleep, it picks up where it left off. I keep seeing new chapters. Like one of those old serials, you know?"

Dr. Gull nodded.

"That's very interesting. And how long has this been happening?"

Ed shrugged. "I don't know. Past couple of months, I suppose."

"And you are always this character? The hero?"

"Yes. It's weird, because it's not me and yet it actually *is*."

Dr. Gull looked over at Ed. He was an unassuming man—the type that people would pass every day on the street and never remember. To many, Ed was invisible. Small wonder then that he had become an accountant in a nondescript dividends department for a large Rhode Island bank. The profession fit Ed like a glove.

"Mr. Conners," Dr. Gull intoned, "I don't think that you realize the importance of this session. You were found sleeping at your desk and, when awoken, attempted to shoot people with a non-existent gun while shouting . . ."—Dr. Gull flipped back the pages of his notes—"I have it here. You said, 'Beware the wrath of the Crimson Scorpion!'"

"I have no memory of that."

"Of course not. That's why we're here." Dr. Gull sighed. "I am being paid by Fleet Bank to counsel you and determine if you are fit to return to work without being a hazard to yourself or your co-workers."

Ed shrugged. "I don't feel like a threat."

Dr. Gull agreed. Ed looked about as threatening as a cartoon mouse. But still, there was something odd here.

"Mr. Conners . . . Ed, I'd like you to keep a sleep log for me if you would. Just write down whatever you dream about."

"If you think that'll help?"

Dr. Gull stood up and shook Ed's hand as he walked him out the door.

"I do. Let's see if we can figure out what your dreams are trying to tell us. Maybe then we can understand why you're having them."

After Ed had left, Dr. Gull went to his laptop and searched several websites. Unsatisfied, he turned to his many volumes of psychiatric references but could find little to help him. Anguish patterns in dreams he had known about; those were easily definable. But what to do with a man who dreams he is a 1940s pulp hero in an ongoing dream?

Before the warehouse had hit the ground, I was in my Ford Coupe with the engine racing as I sped back downtown through the streets of Manhattan. No one knew the back streets of the city better than I, and I knew my time was running out. Somewhere out there was Dr. Primordial, and he had to be stopped! Even I could barely believe that the Secret Nazi Program was the reanimation of the dead. With an army like that, Hitler could march across the world and no one would be able to stop him. And they had chosen to start in America! In the city I had sworn to protect and save from evil!

I punched the button on the dashboard, and the video screen rose up out of the console. Russell's face immediately came on-screen. "What's the deal, boss?" he said.

"The warehouse was a bust, Russell. Dr. Primordial had already skipped out. But I found out what his secret project actually is . . . he's making Nazi zombies!"

Russell didn't answer. His brain was trying to process the information. Even though he was the smartest person I'd ever known, he was sometimes annoyingly unimaginative.

"I don't understand. Why would he do that? What would he gain?"

"Don't be stupid, Russell. An army made up of zombies would be practically unstoppable. No matter how many times you'd shoot them, they'd just get back up again. Not to mention the rate of infection. Every enemy they kill and eat becomes one of their own."

I sped past Broadway and the late-night theatergoers. So smug in their ignorance.

"Gotcha, boss. But how is he doing it? Resurrecting them, I mean?"

"I don't have time to go into it, Russell, but he's using some sort of incubation tubes. There were hundreds in the warehouse, all hooked up to machines and Dr. Frankenstein junk."

"OK, I'll run over and examine them right now. I can tell you what he's using—"

"Don't bother. I burned the warehouse down."

Russell was silent.

"All of it?" he asked. "But, but . . . I could've learned so much from that equipment! I—"

"Stow it, Russell! We're not competing with Dr. Primordial. We're shutting him down, remember?"

"Right. Gotcha. OK. If he's using tubes, he must be using electricity. Let me check the utilities files for high usage. Something like that is going to use a lot of power, and we can track him that way."

I swerved to miss a pedestrian who cursed as I drove by. You're welcome, citizen!

"But, boss, we've got another problem."

"What's that?"

"No one's heard from Miss Sarah in five hours. She's not answering her phone and our mole at the New York Herald *says she hasn't been in all day."*

"Understood." I shut off the video screen and screeched into a high speed U-turn. If Dr. Primordial had guessed the connection between me and Sarah Kent, ace reporter, her life would be in incredible danger.

Dr. Gull flipped back through the pages.

"And then what happened?"

Ed shrugged. "That's all I have so far."

"Ed, the amount of detail you have here is amazing. Tell me, when you're having these dreams, how do you feel?"

Ed appeared to sink within himself. His chin lowered onto his chest and his voice was low and deep.

"When I first started having these dreams, it felt weird, you know? I'd wake up all panicked. But, as they continued, I got used to them. Now I look forward to them." Ed looked up and, for a moment, Dr. Gull felt that it was not Ed who was behind those eyes. "Because when I'm having them, I *am* the Crimson Scorpion! I feel everything he does. When he shoots his gun, I can feel it up through my arm. When he punches some goon with his right hand, using his scorpion ring to leave a mark on the guy's ugly mug, I feel it.

"The smells. The *sounds!* They're all real to me—as real as my sitting here, talking to you. Sometimes the dreams feel more real than this world."

Dr. Gull made a note on his pad: "Becoming disconnected with reality."

"You realize," he said to Ed, "how that makes you sound?"

"Yeah, I know, like I'm a few bricks short of a load. But hear me out for a moment."

For the first time since they had begun these sessions, Ed was animated. His voice was excited and, even though he had lost no weight, he moved strongly and decisively as he gestured.

"When I was young and in college, I studied a lot of different things. I settled on accounting because it was a way to make money and I was naturally good at it without having to work very hard, even though I hate it with every fiber of my being. Anyway, before that, I studied a lot of philosophy and physics. Have you heard of the 'alternate universe' theory?"

Dr. Gull pretended that he had not so he could hear Ed's explanation.

"It's a theory in physics that there are an infinite number of other dimensions that exist and are alternates of our own universe. That's where a lot of science fiction novels come from. It's the concept that because you turned left instead of right at a certain intersection at a certain time, your life changed. But somewhere, the universe that was created when you turned *right* exists! It's an amazing theory and one I've wondered about all my life. What if those dimensions were out there and you could just *shift* over to one of them as easily as you walk through a door?"

"So what you're saying is that you believe that this 'Crimson Scorpion' universe is *real?* And you've somehow tapped into it?"

"Why not? I mean, when I'm having those dreams, I feel *alive!* More than I've ever felt before. Do you know what my life is like, Dr. Gull? I'm not married. I have no kids. My parents both died over ten years ago. I have two brothers whom I never talk to anymore. I haven't even had a girlfriend since I left college. I don't even remember what sex is like anymore. Here, *right here,* in *this reality,* I am dead.

"But when I'm the Crimson Scorpion, I'm *strong!* I knock bad guys out with one punch. I'm confident and I'm effective. *I get the job done!*

And that's why, every time I wake up from one of these dreams, I cry."

Dr. Gull was quiet . . . and worried.

"Ed," he finally said, "the next time you come back, I want to try a little experiment."

"What kind of experiment, doc?"

"I want to hypnotize you, Ed. I want to talk to the 'Crimson Scorpion.'"

I had left Big Ben guarding Miss Sarah but, when I reached her apartment building on the West Side, he was nowhere in sight. It was close to midnight and there were no lights on in her place. Carefully, I went inside and walked up to the second floor. I could hear mumbled voices but couldn't make out what they were saying. One of them was male and his accent was certainly German!

Not waiting for an invitation, I broke down the door and was greeted with a horrific scene. Big Ben, one-time heavyweight contender, was on the floor in pieces and there were several zombies chewing on his flesh. They wore tattered, torn military uniforms of the Third Reich but were lowly soldiers, not commanders.

Miss Sarah was tied to a chair and gagged. Her eyes pleaded with me to rescue her, but all I could see was the SS officer standing near her with a gun in one hand and a detonator in the other.

"At last," he hissed, "we've been waiting for you."

My eyes followed the detonator wire to a pile of dynamite on the floor nearby.

Without hesitating, I leaped forward. The Nazi fired and the bullet tore through my left shoulder. I couldn't allow it to slow me down. I kicked him out of the way as the others finally realized that there was new meat available. In one move, I grabbed the detonator and Miss Sarah. As one, I hurled us through the window as I pressed the detonator and the apartment exploded behind us.

We landed on the street-level awning and bounced down to the street. Miss Sarah's chair burst from the impact and she landed with a broken arm. I fell hard on my left shoulder and pain ripped through my mind.

I quickly got Miss Sarah to her feet and we ran for my car. "They were waiting for me when I got home! They . . . they killed poor Ben. Ripped him apart right in front of me and started eating him. What are these things?"

"Zombies," I said, "Nazi zombies. Dr. Primordial created them and he's going to use them to help Hitler take over America."

Miss Sarah cried, "You've got to stop them, Rex! You can't let this happen!"

"I'm working on it," I replied, and the dashboard monitor lit up again.

"Boss," Russell said, "I've got a lead. There's a warehouse down by the docks. It's chewing up electricity like it's bubble gum. Doc P's gotta be there!"

"On my way!"

I looked over at Miss Sarah. She was crying and nursing her broken arm but determined.

"I'll drop you at St. Mary's on the way. They can set your arm."

She looked at me with such anger and resolution in her eyes.

"The hell you will. I'm going with you."

"You've got a busted wing. You'll be no good in a fight."

She lifted her right arm. "All I need to shoot a gun is one good arm."

I smiled. There was a reason I loved this woman.

"How are you feeling today, Ed?" Dr. Gull asked.

Ed looked nervous; more on edge than ever. "I dunno, doc. I just don't feel right."

"Can you be more specific?"

Ed shrugged.

"I can't explain it. I just feel anxious, as if something is about to happen. I haven't even been able to sleep for the last couple of days. Every time I try, I jump awake. The last dream I remember is being on the way to the warehouse for the final confrontation with Dr. Primordial."

"So I see. Why do you think that is?"

"I'm not sure. I think . . . I think it's getting near the end. As if the story is almost over. *But I don't want it to be!*"

"Every story has an ending, Ed. Maybe it's a sign of a new story beginning."

"I suppose. But what if it doesn't? What if this is all I'm left with?"

"Would that be so bad, Ed? It's a great life—"

""—if you don't weaken'"

Dr. Gull looked at Ed, puzzled.

"That sounds familiar. What's that from?"

"An old song from the Thirties. Never mind. Let's get on with it."

Ed lay down on the couch. Despite his girth, he tried to get as comfortable as possible.

Dr. Gull took out a pocket watch and sat down next to Ed.

"Isn't that a bit 'old-fashioned,' doc?"

Dr. Gull smiled—a rare and frightening thing.

"It just seemed appropriate, somehow. Now I want you to just relax, focus on the watch, and listen to my voice."

Dr. Gull quietly counted down as Ed slowly closed his eyes.

"Can you hear me, Ed?"

"Yes."

"Where are you?"

"I'm in my car with Miss Sarah. We're heading to the warehouse to stop Dr. Primordial."

"Tell me what happens."

It was easy to find the warehouse. It was lit up like Macy's Department Store on Christmas with bolts of electric light streaming out the windows. I gave Miss Sarah my .45 and extra clips. She winced from pain as she put them in her pocket. I opened up the trunk and took out some things. When Miss Sarah came to look, I was holding my trusty tommy gun and was stuffing my pockets with grenades.

"Criminy!" she said. "Do you drive around with all this in the trunk all the time?"

I smiled. "You never know what you're gonna need, doll."

I knew that we were likely not to come out of the warehouse alive. I'd briefed Russell before we'd arrived on what to do if we failed. There were a few similar guardians he could contact as well as the special emergency channel for the president and the Army. I set the car's engine running, pointed directly at the heavy front door, wedged the gas pedal down, and put it in gear.

The car took off like a bullet with us behind it.

We ran through the open door and were greeted by a mob of zombies. Most were wearing soldier's clothes, but it disturbed me to see that some were dressed normally like civilians. I flung a grenade into the middle of the crowd and watched as it blew them apart. In the back, I could see an office of some kind and people moving out.

I pointed it out to Miss Sarah. "If he's here at all, he's up there! Make for the stairs!"

I laid down a covering fire of bullets from the machine gun as Miss Sarah ran for the back of the room. She fired as she went, hitting a few of the zombies, but they kept on coming. "Aim for the head!" I cried. "Or their legs! If they can't move, they can't fight."

I was horribly wrong about that, of course.

I threw another grenade into the crowd but, to my horror, I saw more zombies piling into the room through the side doors. Beyond them, I could see hundreds more along with lines of incubators. This must have been Dr. Primordial's main lab.

I'd taken too long in throwing grenades and had fallen behind Miss Sarah as she ran up the stairs firing.

At the top of the stairs, she turned to the right to go through the door.

"Rex!" she called to me. "He's in . . ."

I screamed to her to get back, but it was too late. Bullets ripped through her and she fell over the railing into the sea of zombies below. The ones whose legs she had shot off got to her first. She was screaming as they ripped into her flesh and tore her arms off. Crying, I did the only thing I could do and shot her through the head, killing her instantly.

"PRIMORDIAL!" I yelled.

I ran into the room, ready to shoot anything I saw, but I wasn't prepared for what greeted me. Primordial was standing between two giant pieces of machinery that took up nearly the whole wall. Sparks and electricity jumped through the air. The smell of burning ozone was overpowering.

"Schwein!" Primordial spit. "Did you think that you could defeat me? I, who have conquered death itself? My armies are all over the globe, ready to rise and bring on the Thousand Year Reich. And I, not that paper-hanger, shall rule over all!"

Suddenly the air around Primordial shimmered and . . . broke. I fired the machine gun at him, but it had no effect. The bullets passed through him and shattered the wall behind as he laughed.

"Where I go, you can never follow!" His body grew thin, like a ghost. I shot at the machines next to him, but the process could not be stopped.

There was only one thing to do as Dr. Primordial began to disappear. Gritting my teeth, I threw my gun on the floor and leaped.

"*Ed!* Ed, you've got to wake up. Wake up now!" Dr. Gull screamed.

Ed's eyes shot open wide in fear and terror. His hands gripped Dr. Gull's arms and squeezed.

"I've got you now!" Ed yelled triumphantly. "You thought you could get away, but I followed you."

"Ed, you've got to calm down. Nurse! Nurse!"

The middle-aged nurse from outside ran into the room. The sounds of the hospital echoed in from outside.

"Nurse!" Dr. Gull shouted. "Quickly! I need a tranquilizer for this patient!"

She left the room. Dr. Gull looked down at Ed but could not believe what he saw. Instead of the thirtyish, pudgy accountant, a thin man clad in a black leather aviator jacket with a red mask was gripping his arms with a strength that suddenly became titanic.

"Through oceans of time I've chased you, you bastard! And now you'll pay for what you did to Miss Sarah!"

The Crimson Scorpion threw Dr. Gull against the wall, knocking all his old photographs off the wall. "I don't know what you're talking about! I'm not who you're looking for!"

"Oh, yes, you are, Billy Boy. Think back to when you were a little snot-nosed brat. Remember how everyone played superheroes? But not everyone could be the hero, could they? Someone had to be the bad guy, and you loved it. You were never Superman or Spider-Man. You were always Lex Luthor or Dr. Doom. Because you knew how they thought. You knew how to *be* the bad guy."

Dr. Gull backed up against the wall as far as he could as the Crimson Scorpion came closer and closer. "No, no, I'm not listening!"

"Think about it, *doc!* Why else do you think you became a 'doctor'? He's there, inside of you, and I'm gonna make him come out if I have to rip you apart!"

The Crimson Scorpion pulled Dr. Gull to his feet and punched him hard in the face. Dr. Gull flew across the room and landed behind his desk. Slowly he climbed back up, but what stood there was no longer Dr. Gull. His face was long and pointed with stringy, crazy hair that hung down in front of his eyes, which shone with a special kind of madness.

"*Schwein!*" Dr. Primordial scowled. He touched the mark on his chin gingerly where the Crimson Scorpion's ring had left its mark. In red, the skin already bruising, was a tiny scorpion. "I will *never* surrender! *Never!*"

The Crimson Scorpion quickly slammed the door shut and lunged for his enemy. From outside, the nurse pounded and called for the doctor.

"Get security!" she cried as the sounds of fighting and screaming came through the closed door. The sounds of running feet came up behind her as the security officers tried to open the door.

"Dr. Gull!" they yelled, but no response came. Suddenly, there was the loud sound of something heavy hitting the floor and then something swirling, like a sound effect from a science fiction movie.

"There's no time to get the keys. Just stand back!" the security guards warned as they used their shoulders to smash open the door.

Inside, they simply stood and stared.

There was no one there.

The room was in a complete mess and looked as if a football team had been using it for practice. The desk was overturned. The couch was ripped and crushed. Bookcases were smashed and there was a burn pattern on the far wall that looked suspiciously like a concentric circle. But no bodies, no people, and no sign of where they could have gone. One of the guards checked the windows and found they were all shut tight and unbroken.

"I'm calling the police," a guard said as he ran out the door.

On top of a pile of debris was a smashed photo. It was in black and white and very old. Previously it had held a place of honor and respect on Dr. Gull's wall, but now it had been ripped apart as if in a psychopathic fury.

"What's that?" asked another guard as the nurse bent to pick up the picture.

"It's a picture of the doctor's grandfather. This is dreadful. Dr. Gull loved this picture."

The guard held out his hand and looked at the picture. It had been taken in the '30s or '40s and showed two men standing side by side, their arms on each other's shoulders. The taller man was on the right and was wearing a scientist's lab coat. The man next to him was smaller and more compact and was wearing a black leather aviator's jacket with goggles on the top of his head. They were both smiling and laughing at the camera while, in the background, a military airport hummed busily along.

"Who's the guy on the left?"

"Dr. Gull used to tell me the story. That was his grandfather's best friend. He was the man who smuggled the doctor's grandfather out of Nazi Germany and into America. His grandfather went on to do some top-secret science work for the government or some such thing. The doctor would probably never have been born if it hadn't been for that man!"

On the photo, in a tight script, was written simply, "To my best pal, Rex."

What Was That?

It all began, as most things generally do, rather slowly. It's like gaining weight. You never notice the pounds you put on until, one day, you walk by the mirror. Then it all starts to come together: the late-night snacks, the extra helpings at dinner, that scoop of ice cream you just couldn't resist. The result is always so much easier to see than the hundreds of little causes along the way. That's the way it was with Tim Ghee. He'd never really thought too much about it until the day he stopped and realized that Cthulhu was everywhere.

Tim had always been aware of him, of course, operating somewhere on the periphery of his sight. One couldn't be a fan of fantastic literature without knowing who Cthulhu was: the creation of writer H. P. Lovecraft. The big "C" was a member of the Old Ones who existed before man and would rule the world again in the future. He, like all the other gods Lovecraft created, was a way for Lovecraft to symbolize man's insignificance in the cosmos. Cthulhu was a symbol of terror and horror, of the universe's indifference to man. It was a frightening concept when Lovecraft wrote it back in 1926—but now? Now it was just a commodity.

Without anyone realizing it, Cthulhu had become commercialized. Suddenly, Cthulhu had become plush dolls in a variety of costumes (including Santa Claus!), T-shirt logos, toys and even, perhaps the most frightening of all, slippers! His influence had spread through media and movies to the point where even the most uninterested of people knew who he was. Perhaps they did not understand exactly *what* Cthulhu was or what he stood for (other than some lumbering giant monster with a squid face), but he had ceased to have any power as an image.

It was right about when Tim came to that realization that he finally realized something else as well: he'd gotten stupider.

When he was younger, his mind was on fire. Filled with concepts and ideas, it burned like a creative inferno. Tim understood things so much better then. Now it seemed that he could barely understand anything anymore. His brain couldn't hold concepts in his head, and he found himself having to relearn things he had known instinctively years ago. Not basic things, of course. He could still walk, eat, and drive his car. But his thoughts were jumbled, unfocused, and his memory was shifty. Tim could no longer remember large portions of his childhood. He could remember where he was, such as "in 1970, I lived in New Milford, Connecticut," but he could not recall any details of it. He could only remember what he could see in old pictures. The graying black-and-white figures stared back at Tim, who knew that "this was me and my mom on the beach . . . somewhere . . . the lake maybe?" But he had no connection to those people in the pictures. He might as well as been looking at pictures of World War II GIs marching into Europe for all these family snapshots meant to him.

The doctors all examined Tim and concluded that there was absolutely nothing wrong. "It's perfectly normal," they said, "to experience some loss of memory as you get older." It's not Alzheimer's, they said, just age. "The brain is a muscle; you need to exercise it more."

But it was more than that.

The more Tim worked, the harder he pushed, the worse it became. That's when Tim noticed that he wasn't the only one. He even found that there was a name for it, a title: "The Dumbing-Down of America." It wasn't just Tim Ghee; it was everywhere. Once he realized that, he started seeing it all around him. It was just like when you buy a new car and you suddenly notice all the other cars like yours on the road. So Tim went out and talked to people and, the more he talked, the more frightened he became.

Now, it wasn't that big of a surprise. Tim fully expected to find that people didn't know a lot about history or literature or even how the government works. He expected that. For years, the average person's attention span was getting smaller and smaller. Some blamed television and some blamed video games, but the explanation could never be all that easy. There was something else at work here.

Even as he talked, Tim was prepared to find that most people couldn't answer the simplest questions. But what was disturbing was how often Tim also forgot the answers and had to check his sheet. It soon became clear that most people only had the vaguest idea of what was going on around them. Tim would ask: "What happened in Salem in 1692?" Most people would give him a blank stare. A few might answer, "Something to do with witches, I think?" Worst were the ones who were certain that was when the Pilgrims landed. It was true that most people had short-term attention spans, but even when they were asked something like which politician lost the presidential election because of problems with vote counting in Florida, all Tim would be greeted with was more blank stares.

The worst offenders were the young people. Most of the older people who were questioned would be embarrassed or even ashamed when they couldn't remember things (even things Tim had no way of validating, like "Who was your fourth-grade teacher?"). But the younger the people got, the worse it seemed to be. Not only could they not answer the questions, but they became angry that someone was even asking them these questions. Tim soon came to the conclusion that, among the young people, it was 'not cool' to be smart and, actually, the dumber you were the cooler you were.

Like Cthulhu, being dumb had become accepted.

It was when Tim got home from one of his survey sessions (a particularly depressing one that found most people unable to do any math higher than simple addition) that he found the card in his coat pocket. It was a plain business card with just a name on it: "Edward P. Gorga." There was no telephone number listed or profession. On the back of the card, in a light pencil was written, "You have just begun. Meet me at Prospect Terrace at 6 p.m."

Tim had no idea how the card had gotten in his pocket. He had a vague recollection of being jostled in a crowd on Westminster Street, but couldn't recall any particular person. The thought of being in Prospect Terrace at that time wasn't thrilling either, but Tim was curious enough to be there early. There was no one in the park, so he sat down on one of the benches and looked out over the city that Lovecraft once called home and tried to remember how it must have looked in his day. Oddly, Tim could not even remember the way it had looked when he first saw it in 1982. Were those buildings there back then? Surely the great bridge hadn't been torn up yet, had it?

After a few minutes, a man walked up and stood beside the bench. He was standing just far enough behind that Tim could not see him clearly. "You're not mistaken," he said. His voice had a slow, measured tone, as if he were not entirely confident in speaking English. "There is something going on."

Tim turned to look at him, but he moved further behind and stayed just out of sight. "Please," he said, "do not look at me."

Smiling, Tim said, "What? Are you going to tell me there's some big conspiracy? And you're going to be the . . . the . . . the whaddaya call it? In that movie?"

"'Deep Throat.' In the *All the President's Men* movie."

"Yeah, yeah, that one. So it's all a conspiracy, right? The government's trying to keep us all dumb and stupid?"

"Not the government, no. But they have been reaping the benefits of it. And it's not a conspiracy: it's a plan. It was hatched here, actually, even though he didn't know it."

"Who didn't?"

"Lovecraft, of course."

Tim sighed. Already he felt as if he'd had enough. Tim had had enough run-ins with kooks before: the nuts who thought that everything Lovecraft wrote was real, not just stories. Most of them were just sad people, looking for something to believe in. But this guy didn't sound like them. He didn't sound as if he was about to run around chanting "Iä, Shub-Niggurath!" He sounded almost sad, defeated.

"It's not just the overall decrease in intelligence, either," he continued. "Lots of things have changed. It's the whole sense of apathy, of giving up, that makes it worse. People have just lost hope. They expect bad things now and, more often than not, that's exactly what they get."

"I don't understand what you're talking about." Tim turned to look at the man and, this time, he did not turn away. He was wearing a gray overcoat that was tightly buttoned. A dark gray hat was on his head, and he had a full beard and moustache, both gray. Even his skin, what little Tim could see, looked ashen.

The man stared at Tim for a few minutes, sizing him up. "No one does," he finally said. "Some people tumble onto bits and pieces of it but never see the whole picture. Studies are done measuring our society's intelligence as it falls. Sociologists track trends and cycles of morality talking about changes in families and increases in violent crimes. And all the while we become more and more complacent. The easiest way to make people comfortable with a concept is to make them pay money for it."

The man handed Tim a large envelope. His hand was, of course, inside a gray glove. "Here, take this. Read it through. Then, if it makes sense to you, pass it on. Information begets information and so on. Often the best defense is to mirror your opponent's offense."

Tim took the envelope, and the man moved as if to walk away but thought better of it. "I should warn you," he said, "you've been marked. It won't be much longer now."

"Longer for what?"

"Oh, nothing very dramatic. No 'men in black' are going to visit you. But 'they' know you are aware now. If I could spot you, so can 'they.' These days you're easy to spot. You all stand out like sore thumbs."

With that, the gray man turned and walked away rather stiffly. Tim took the envelope and went home, anxious to avoid nightfall in the park. When he got home, Tim simply threw the envelope on a pile of recent mail, already forgetting about the encounter.

It was not until several days later that Tim found the envelope again. He didn't even remember what it was at first. There was nothing written on the envelope to identify it, and Tim had no idea what was inside. As he opened it, a bunch of clipped newspaper articles and several pages of handwritten notes dropped onto the table. Most of the articles had to do with studies showing different things happening over the last two or three decades. Following them, Tim could spot an alarming trend. The earliest articles were well-written, in-depth examinations of their subject, while the newest ones read like to-do lists—nothing more than bullet points and sound bytes. The decrease in attention spans was obvious. So too was the subject of the articles. Many had to do with declining test scores of students, while others were about the increase in Alzheimer's disease. Confused, Tim turned to the handwritten pages. The script was tight and hard to read. Almost every inch of the paper was covered and, at times, it was hard to follow, but he struggled through it.

"It seems unbelievable and I know that you will probably discount anything I write, but I have spent years tracking down the evidence. If you follow my lead, you will find your own proof and that, more than anything, will convince you that this is the truth.

"We are being invaded.

"It began more than eighty years ago. A writer, unknown to any but a few, began to have some singular ideas. They were unlike any that anyone had ever had before and, after a short time, he began to express these ideas in stories. To the writer, the stories were nothing more than disappointments, as he could never convey in words what he had seen in dreams and imagined. In time, the writer died, convinced that his work was worthless; but, despite all odds, the stories survived.

"Not only did they survive, but they thrived! Many other writers could have faded away amidst the changing tide of fickle reading trends, but this one writer's work flourished and gained more and more readers every year. Even when his work was not easily available, it was sought out and devoured. Eventually, the ideas that made up his work moved outside of his stories. They gained a life of their own and slowly reached out to other writers and new media. They began to show up on television shows and in movies and, especially, in comic books. It was as if comics were particularly suited for them: the minds of the young readers soaked the ideas up, carrying them along as they grew older.

"New writers took those ideas and expanded them, brought them into new and different areas. Even more amazing, they leaked into games and toys. They became so well known that they were now familiar to almost everyone . . . which was what they wanted all along.

"The beings that this writer once depicted never existed. Their images were manufactured so that They would be comprehensible to man. Their actual existence was as far beyond those pulpish images as man was once beyond the simple ant. They were so much more than sea-creatures and walking octopi. But that was all that the human brain could understand, and it was barely the tip of the iceberg breaking the water.

"And the earth was never going to be 'wiped clean.' There was no need for that when humans were so eager to just give it away. With the increase of their influence, They became more and more powerful. They had become an idea, a concept, something that could not be wiped out with a gun, a pitchfork, or a torch. They jumped from mind to mind to mind, increasing their influence every time someone new read their books or saw their movies or played their games and toys.

"And, as Their influence grew, we lessened. Our minds grew weak and unfocused. Without anyone noticing, our society began to lose its intelligence. Their thoughts were never meant for humans brains, and we are suffering the consequences. Eventually, we will all deteriorate to the level of mindless amoebas, helplessly flopping about on the ground. At that point, They will simultaneously leap from our minds, thought becoming flesh, and spread over the earth that we so willingly gave them. Their escape from our brains will leave man as a bloody, wet mess on the carpet of Their 'new' world.

"So complete is Their victory, so insidious Their plan that I cannot even mention that first writer's name or his creations without you, the reader, laughing and throwing these pages into the trash. They have become as dangerous to us as a wide-eyed kitten, romping through a field. How could there possibly be any danger in images that are sold in toy and book stores? In characters that adorn T-shirts and coffee mugs? Concepts that are packaged and marketed like hot dogs?

"The damage is already done. Nothing can change the inevitable result. Decades of preparation have set the pattern for the future—a path that They are zealously guarding. Even now, Their attention is being turned toward you as you read this. You will feel yourself starting to forget what you have just read. In time, your mind will disintegrate and you will not even be able to remember who you are or were. It will be called Alzheimer's, but that is such a poor term for it. Such is the fate of all and just because once, *at one time,* They reached out to a writer and gave him an idea."

Tim put the papers back into the envelope carefully. So much of it made sense to him, but almost as much was just too ridiculous to believe. It couldn't be true. Even now, he was having difficulty holding onto the entire concept of it. Scoffing, Tim put the envelope on a pile of junk and sat down to watch TV. One of the channels was having a marathon of old Vincent Price movies including *The Haunted Palace*. Tim smiled as the movie began. He knew he'd seen it before, back when he was a kid watching Creature Features shows; but for some reason he could barely recall any of the plot. In a way, it was if Tim had never seen it at all.

For the next several days, Tim would walk by the envelope. Sometimes he would stop and look at it, trying to remember what it was and why it was important. He felt an intense urge to give it away, sensing that he was supposed to give it to someone but couldn't remember who. Inevitably, another thought would come into Tim's mind and he'd put the envelope back down. Eventually, it would become lost in the clutter that his home had become.

Slowly, as all things happen, Tim began to be almost a prisoner in his own house. Trash piled up around him. Unread books, magazines, and newspapers grew into towers that dipped and swayed drunkenly. At times, Tim would go into a frenzy, tearing through the piles and looking for something that he couldn't put his finger on. A pressure grew behind his mind, pushing, forever pushing and growing in strength and weight. His thoughts became like mushy oatmeal, unable to take any real shape or form. Tim was sure that there was something, something very important that he'd forgotten. If he could just remember what it was . . .

"The Dreamer in Fire": Notes on Robert Winslow's "Sutter's Corners"

> It was a room like any other room in a town like any other town. Four blank walls with faded paint. Nothing much to look at and nothing much to see. I'd been in Sutter's Corners for three days and still had no clue why I was there. A cryptic note, sent by a woman I'd loved years ago, had brought me here. Now I was at a loss for what to do next. I stared out of my room at the Addams Hotel (the only one in town) and watched the traffic in the street. There was very little to see. A lone automobile passed every so often among pedestrians who all looked the same. Where was Lauren? What was I doing here? Following the trail of a woman I'd thought I'd left far behind. For that matter, why was anyone here in this desolate, forsaken town? Why did the sight of them, shambling aimlessly over the streets, frighten me so?
>
> —Robert Winslow, "The Dreamer in Fire" (*The Dreamer in Fire and Other Stories*, Sargasso Press, 1952, p. 135)

When Robert Winslow first wrote those words in 1947, he could not have imagined the impact they would have on his writing and his life. In a letter to longtime friend Dexter Wilson, Winslow stated, "I've just started a new story called 'The Dreamer in Fire,' which looks to be substantially longer than any of my other stuff. Which means that no one'll be interested in this one either. But I still feel an urge to write it. It's yet another story featuring my doppelgänger, Richard Clay, and I'm trying to examine what lies underneath the surface of a forgotten

American town. I have no idea where I'm going with this . . ." (*The Winslow Letters*, Vol. 3, p. 89).

By the time he finished the first draft in August 1947, the story stretched to more than 20,000 words and developed into an examination of Winslow's personal fears and doubts. It was the most intensely personal story he had written to date. While this abrupt change in focus from his original conception was unplanned, it can be seen as the most significant step Winslow had taken in his development as a writer.

In the story, Richard Clay travels to the town, Sutter's Corners, after receiving a plea for help from his long-lost love, Lauren Price. Clay still harbors great passion for Lauren, and the summons impels him to rush to what he believes will be her rescue. Upon arriving in the town, Clay cannot find any evidence of Lauren ever having been there.

Perplexed, he begins to research what he considers to be her disappearance. The townspeople, openly polite and helpful, insist that she was never in Sutter's Corners. Clay begins to believe that he is going insane and has been imaging the entire incident. He begins to question if he is really in the town at all.

Clay then starts to receive more messages from Lauren warning him away. The notes begin to appear from out of nowhere in places Clay knows no one has been but himself. Eventually, Clay discovers the truth behind Lauren's disappearance, but no longer cares. He has become one with the town and joins their collective mentality. In the end, it is Clay who is writing to others, bringing more people to Sutter's Corners.

After careful editing and revising, Winslow sent the completed manuscript to *Weird Tales,* and it was eventually published in the February 1949 issue. Inheriting Lovecraft's curse, Winslow never managed to achieve cover story status. It has only recently been discovered just how much difficulty Winslow had in selling the piece. *Weird Tales* requested extensive rewrites that Winslow, to his credit, ignored. The piece was eventually run exactly as it was written.

The story was largely ignored by *Weird Tales* readers. The letters section for later issues showed no particular response. The story did, however, attract the attention of Lucius Boyd, who immediately wrote to Winslow asking for more stories. Boyd had recently started his soon-to-be-legendary Sargasso Press, named after William Hope Hodgson's infamous haunted sea, and was interested in publishing the story in book form. Winslow was hesitant at first, questioning where Boyd had obtained his address and suspicious of his intentions. Eventually Winslow, warming to the idea and to Boyd as well, agreed to write two new stories for the collection. These stories, "An Afterthought in Haägen's Field" and "Dancing on Memories," reflect the influence of "The Dreamer in Fire" on Winslow's writings. Clearly, something had happened between Winslow's last story, "The Face Behind Mine," and "The Dreamer in Fire" to enable him to write these amazing weird tales. The other stories were clearly from Winslow's earlier period, and recent evidence reflects their composition to somewhere between 1935 and 1942. They are, for the most part, competent but forgettable. It was the three new stories that cemented Winslow's reputation and established him as a growing master of weird literature. This career was, of course, cut tragically short by Winslow's death in a car crash in 1955.

With the recent discovery of previously unknown letters and notes, found by Winslow's only surviving heir, William Carson, we are afforded an unexpected glimpse into Winslow's life and work. The cataloguing and indexing of this material is still in progress, but even at this early date many new facts are being discovered.

For years, scholars of weird literature have speculated on whether Sutter's Corners had a real-life counterpart. Considering the huge contribution "The Dreamer in Fire" made to Winslow's work, it is a valid question that has remained unanswered.

Previous speculation has ranged from viewpoints of "total fabrication" (Barlow 23) to "based on a combination of actual locations" (Jackson 10). The actual truth, as detailed in the letters and memos of the Carson collection, presents an amazing and unbelievable story. Not only was the town of Sutter's Corners based on reality, but it came completely from the inspiration of one town: Northport, New York.

In December 1945, Winslow received a letter from a fan named Arthur Daily. In it, Daily expresses admiration for Winslow's work (it is still unknown how Daily got Winslow's address, as Winslow was notoriously private about such matters) and a desire to meet someday. Daily enclosed a snapshot of himself standing in front of his house at

53 Orms Drive in Northport. The picture shows a somewhat sad-faced individual wearing dull, worn clothes standing in front of a small converted farmhouse. The house itself had obviously seen better days and appeared barely able to stand upright. There is a faint shadow of mountains in the distance. The letter apparently intrigued Winslow for some reason, and he sent a response. This is consistent with Winslow's frequent insecurity over his work and almost slavish devotion to anyone who praised his efforts. A return letter from Daily arrived almost immediately.

> Dear Mr. Winslow:
>
> I was delighted to receive your letter of 12/17 as I had never really expected to hear back from you. I know that you must be terribly busy with your writing, but I deeply appreciated the time you took to respond. In answer to your question, that was indeed a section of the Adirondack Mountain range behind me in the photo sent you. Northport is in a very secluded area of New York State and we're pretty much in the wild up here. The mountains are Mt. Marcy and Mt. Pharoah and are an excellent place to hunt and fish. If you should ever be traveling through this area, I would be pleased to offer you a tour of the local scenery.
>
> (Letter from Arthur Daily to Robert Winslow, 12/22/45, from the Carson Collection, University of Rhode Island Special Collections.)

Found in the Carson collection is a series of random jottings and notes that form a disjointed diary for Winslow from 1940 to 1948. In an entry dated 12/20/45, Winslow writes: "The picture haunts me still. The sad-faced youth standing alone before those mighty mountains which seem to be trying to overwhelm him. There is a quality there that continues to intrigue me. I must learn more about this fellow and his surroundings." The next letter from Daily is dated 1/4/46 and contains more information designed to increase Winslow's curiosity:

> I have tried to decipher some of the remaining records regarding the early history of Northport but have had little luck so far. The few pages are disjointed and often make no sense. There is a record of the town charter, signed in 1709, and witnessed by some of the founding citizens like Jeremiah Bradley, Eziah Small, and John Stanley (all families that still survive in Northport), but there is little else.

I have begun to think that Northport was never really settled, simply discovered in a state of perpetual being.

(Letter from Arthur Daily to Robert Winslow, Carson Collection.)

Equally interesting is Winslow's diary entry for this period. Dated 1/7/46, he writes: "My fascination with this mystery increases! A town without a history! I simply must get Daily to take some photographs of the town and send them to me. I feel revitalized for the first time since writing 'The Face Behind Mine.' This may be just what I need to get myself writing again."

This last comment ties in with the recent allegation by T. S. Craig that Winslow periodically suffered from bouts of depression and writer's block (*The Masters of Modern Horror,* University of Texas Press, 1989, p. 382). What was unknown until now was the depth and length of the depression Winslow was experiencing at this time. He wrote the final draft of "The Face Behind Mine" in 1943, and notes in the Carson Collection point to the fact that he had written nothing since. The reason for this particular writer's block is still unknown, but it is possible that Winslow may have been affected by the difficulty he encountered in getting "The Face Behind Mine" published and its poor reception afterwards. It is also possible that Winslow was suffering from one of his many bouts over his fear of being nothing more than an unsuccessful hack writer. This self-doubt had plagued him ever since he first began writing professionally in 1925 and would continue for the rest of his life. Another possibility is hinted in his note of 5/24/44: "Still nothing. Originality completely escapes me." Winslow obviously felt burnt out in his writing and was looking for something to recharge his creative juices.

On January 16, 1946, Daily sent Winslow photographs of Northport. They appear to have been everything Winslow had been expecting. The Carson Collection contains fifteen black-and-white photographs that accompanied Daily's letter. "Here are some of the photographs you asked me for. As I have said, Northport is a very quiet, forgotten town and the residents seem to appreciate that. My picture-taking was met with polite but hidden resentment. Of these seventeen pictures, the ones of the town square seem to be the best and appear to capture, in my opinion, the general feel of the town."

The mention of *seventeen* photographs having been sent is definitive proof that the Carson Collection is missing two of them. Their current whereabouts are unknown. The remaining pictures show an extremely small town of the type that can only exist in very rural communities. There are few automobiles on the street, and the general outlook of the town is poor and worn. The town square is a small grassy area circled by an off-white church, several unidentifiable buildings, a hotel, a general store, and a town hall. In layout, they follow the buildings described in Winslow's story exactly. The town hall appears to be the only center of local government in the town and probably, as in the story, contained all public offices as well as the sheriff's office, jail, and library. In every picture, there is the vague shadow of mountains in the distance.

All the photos are worn and bear evidence of having been consulted many times.

If these pictures do indeed "capture the general feel of the town," as Daily suggests, than it is a somber mood indeed. None of the people in the photographs appear to be smiling or laughing, and their actual figures (as opposed to the buildings) appear indistinct and undefined. Most unusual of all would seem to be the lack of children in the pictures. Farm machinery and rural living is evident in many cases, but nowhere is there one child to be seen.

Winslow marked the occasion of the photographs arrival with this note dated 1/19/46: "They are finally here and are everything that I'd hoped they would be! The town is exactly as I had pictured it from Daily's letters, and I cannot wait to see it for myself. Already I feel myself brimming with the possibility of new ideas and plots. Who knows what this place could inspire in me? What new thoughts may occur, isolated from all reality in this comfortable cushion of forgotten society? Hideous versions of human cruelty? Bizarre rites of forgotten alien races? Or something far, far worse? I shall have to wait and see, but not for long. I will write Daily that I am coming."

Daily's response was immediate.

"To say that I am ecstatic over your coming visit would be to seriously understate my enthusiasm. I look forward to your arrival and hope that you will find Northport the peaceful haven that you have been searching for."

Winslow's notes detail his optimism over the coming trip. "I am all nervous with anticipation. What shall I find there? What is waiting there *for* me to find?" (1/25/46). "Confirmation came from Daily today. He will pick me up at the bus station in Lake George on January 31 in his aged auto, and I shall stay with him in his house for two weeks. At that time, I will judge whether a longer stay is necessary" (1/26/46). "Daily is certainly a strange chap. He apparently has plenty of time on his hands and speaks of no particular occupation. I do not believe him to be a farmer, and the remote town of Northport seems a strange place to find a wealthy man. Then there is the matter of his age. He is only in his twenties (he will not admit his exact age), but that first picture still haunts me. His face is so sullen and deflated that I can only wonder what he was thinking of when that picture was taken. For that matter, who was holding the camera? . . . I have straightened my affairs in town and impressed the need upon my uncle to keep an eye on the house and pick up my mail. He is used to my strange ways and habits of taking off at a moment's notice. I feel sure that he will gather my mail for me, after what happened last time! I only hope that this trip accomplishes its purpose. Otherwise, I may give up writing for good and turn my hands to more mundane and practical tasks" (1/27/46). "Strange dreams last night which I can only attribute to nervousness over my pending trip. I seemed to be drifting through an immense area of trees with mouths that sang my name over and over again. I could feel a strange pull upon me from the ground below, and I saw a small settlement of buildings in a clearing nearby. For some strange reason, the sight of these places filled me with an overpowering dread, although I cannot remember why. They were not modern buildings, nor did they belong to any historical period of architecture that I could place. They seemed to be a strange mixture of brick, stone, and wood that pulled me toward them. As I got closer, I became more and more afraid as I felt some force beginning to push in upon my brain. Someone (or something) else was trying to force their thoughts into my mind. As I fell closer, I began to feel myself thinning, growing more and more indistinct. I began to fight the urge to go lower but was losing the battle. Then I seemed to move toward something in the center of the buildings, and it filled me with such repulsion and horror that I awoke suddenly. It has been a very long time since I've had any dreams this vivid, and I don't know what to make of this. As always, I've written it down here for future use, but I don't know what I can do with such a vague, undefined concept. I have no time for such things anyway. I have to try and start working on some new writing. But I find myself still blocked. I cannot produce one single word of note. So I shall placate myself with jotting down plot ideas in the hope that Northport will inspire me with the ability to do them justice" (1/28/46). A short list of possible story ideas follows which Winslow, apparently, never used.

There is no entry for January 29, but his entry for January 30 is significant.

> More unsettling dreams last night, but I shall not let them bother me! I am off on the great journey tomorrow and nothing shall stand in my way. As I look around my small apartment, checking that I have packed everything that I could possibly need, I feel at once both elated and depressed. But I am unsure why. Even if my stay is slightly longer than two weeks. I know I will return home eventually, so why this strange feeling of finality? Perhaps it is just my sense of this damned writer's block finally coming to an end.

On January 31, Winslow caught the bus out of Boston and began his long trip. A hastily scribbled note (on a diner napkin) was the only notation he made of the event. "On the way at last! It will take over ten hours to reach Lake George, but I have just purchased ample reading material and am ready for the long ordeal ahead. My fellow passengers appear to be the worst that I could possibly have feared, ranging from mere ugliness to horribly ignorant. I shall keep to my own seat at all times and will NOT use the common bathroom."

The trip was apparently accomplished without any mishaps. Winslow arrived safely in Lake George and Daily was there to meet him. Although the bus arrived several hours late, Daily had waited for his guest. Winslow did not make any more entries for that day except the one line: "I am here!"

The following days were apparently very busy as Daily showed Winslow around the town and surrounding areas. Although we have no entries for 2/1 or 2/2, they did exist at one point. Winslow's entry for 2/3 clearly makes reference to them, and this is especially disappointing as they obviously contain Winslow's account of his first meeting with Daily. While, at first, they appear to have been quite amicable, Winslow begins to show some doubts about his host.

> Daily is still a mystery to me and I fear that I shall never understand him. Today, I asked him point blank how he came to be here and what his particular story was. He had been annoyingly vague and noncommittal the last few days, dropping subtle hints about a recently deceased relative and having been injured in a factory accident, but nothing definite. He was taken a bit aback by the directness of my question but answered politely enough, yet I still feel that there was a slight hint of resentment behind his manners. He stated that his grandfather, who had lived in Northport all his life (was born in the house, so it seems), died recently after a long illness of an undisclosed nature. The grandfather had no other surviving heirs and had left the house and a sizeable amount of money to Daily. This all seems very improbable to me, but I suppose it must happen to some people sometime. Of his accident, he spoke very little. It happened in a garment factory in New York when a belt on one of the large machines broke and slashed his face quite severely. He has a long, whitish scar running along his face and down his neck (it supposedly goes even lower, but I declined his offer for a full viewing), which perhaps accounts for his taciturn manner. He claims to have come here to live out the rest of his life in quiet contemplation, but is one of the most dull-witted men I have ever met. Then again, there is one disturbing fact: since I have been here, I have yet to see the man smile.

Winslow spent the next few pages talking about the effect Northport had on him. Surprisingly, it was not what he expected.

> Northport is, in itself, an enigma but one that seemed more interesting from a distance. The actual town is a dirty, scrungy affair with people who seem to have completely lost their sense of humor or good nature. I suppose part of that may have to do with the fact that they are barely living in the twentieth century and have a bare minimum of life's luxuries. And a life of constant toil may have something to do with it. Their entire demeanor reminds me of the pictures I used to see in the papers of striking coal miners who had been rousted by the owner's gang. Their life is leaking out of them. Even

Daily, a relatively recent immigrant to the locale, cannot escape this affliction. The town is small and consists of but a few buildings. There are some farms a short distance away, but there do not appear to be very many people around here. The buildings are surprisingly new, perhaps no more than twenty years old, but look far older. Their paint is peeling and they appear to be little more than ceremonial shells. Instead of being inspired, I am becoming even more depressed. I have begun to wonder if my face is growing as grim as theirs.

The cure that Winslow was hoping for was still eluding him. Instead of feeling his energy revitalized, he was beginning to feel more and more drained. Winslow had brought his beloved portable Smith-Corona with him but found himself unable to write anything worthwhile. He was still missing that essential ingredient which would enable him to escape his depression and make that final leap into creativity. He found his first clue when Daily took him to the local library.

The most amazing thing about the place is the fact that it is in the same building as the jail. I suppose this helps if prisoners get a sudden craving for Shakespeare in the middle of the night. The library is woefully inadequate. Northport has no local paper and very little local activity of any kind, and the library only carries a small group of outside newspapers and magazines. I notice that *Weird Tales* is not one of them, not surprisingly, but the general store does not carry it either. This makes me wonder again if Daily did in fact see my story, "The Face Behind Mine," in that issue. I don't see how he could have found it in this place. Which, of course, leads me back to wondering how he found me. Anyway, the library serves as a sort of combination library/historical society, with the exception that the historical papers are few and far between. Daily was correct when he said that the early records were indecipherable. The only things I can make out on several of them are the names. Small and Bradley appear quite frequently. The librarian, Mrs. Sarah Bradley, is a direct descendent of both lines but can add little to the official records. The actual incorporation of the town is also interesting. The articles of incorporation are not the same as they usually are for other colonial towns. Rather, they give the impression that the town was already here when Bradley and Small showed up, but there is no indication of who or what was living here. It was most probably one of the many Indian tribes that inhabited the Adirondacks, but I cannot tell which one. I am not familiar with Indian languages, so cannot tell if this writing is foreign or simply worn. I also cannot recall if these local tribes even had a written language. I never did pay much attention to such things, unfortunately. I will probably have to check with the Adirondack Historical Society and see if they have any information on the local tribes that might help. Due to the lack of a local paper, there is absolutely no way to tell what has happened in the town for the last two hundred years or even last week! History seems to be handed down verbally within the families, but I have been unable to get them to tell me anything. Daily says that they still consider him an outsider despite the fact that his grandfather was a lifelong resident. Otherwise I would have to accept the notion that nothing has ever happened to anyone in Northport ever! I cannot even find any records of local boys sent to fight in either the Revolutionary War or the Civil War. As for the World Wars, the townsfolk appear incredibly indifferent and uninterested. Wilson's isolationist policies would have done well here! There is a box with some old papers and diaries in the basement of the library which I shall try to decipher. They appear to be quite old and may shed some light on this curious matter. I am still incensed, however, at the terribly slipshod and lazy manner in which this library is run. Documents this old should be cared for, not shoved away into a corner somewhere.

Later that night, Winslow made another note.

I managed to convince the old librarian to allow me to take some of the old papers away with me to study. Actually, looking back on it, she didn't give me much of a fight at all. She actually seemed completely uninterested in the whole matter! This worries me, as I wonder if there may have been more papers at some time that have wandered off or been 'borrowed.' Anyway, I brought them back to Daily's hovel for further study this evening.

I had planned on doing some writing but did not get very far. Daily has been most cooperative in that he has freely (I say freely instead of happily, as it does not seem that this man does anything happily!) given me plenty of space and time to work. I've set the machine on the battered old writing desk in his living room and sat staring at it for over two hours. I was unable to think of a single thing.

What I did think of were bits and pieces that weren't worth putting down on paper. Nothing coherent or complete. I am beginning to wonder if I will ever write again, or even if I should. Daily has been most interested in my work but not the 'avid fan' he appeared to be in his letters. His interest seems almost clinical in a way, focusing more on where my ideas come from and what their 'hidden meaning' is. I've told him that the most distinct hidden meaning in my work is money, but he doesn't believe that. He has been a most charitable host, however, going out of the house for hours in the evening to give me the time to contemplate and work. (Contemplating work is more like it!) I've told him that there is no need and that all I require is to be left alone, but he insists on leaving the house. I'm beginning to wonder where he goes during those times. Where could he go? There is nothing in the town open or vaguely interesting, and it's at least an hour's drive to the next town. Perhaps he goes and worships trees while I torture and misuse their remains in these futile efforts. Maybe I should eye my pile of papers before they come alive and seek retribution for the many of their kin I've wasted.

The next morning Winslow made several notes which are written in a hasty, scrawled hand. He appears to have been in great excitement over something he found in the library papers.

No sleep at all last night! Have been going through the library papers all night and have made an incredible discovery! The majority of the papers are written in the same strange language as the incorporation papers and are virtually indecipherable. They appear to be some sort of business papers or contracts of some kind, but I have no idea what. The big thing is that mixed in with these pages are leaves from someone's diary, possibly one of the founder's or their families, and I would estimate that they were written in the early eighteenth century and are extremely brittle with age. But they are written in English! I have to check the library and see if they have any more of the papers or possibly the book itself. Will write more later!

This entry was written (as near as I can tell, for it is undated) about the morning of February 6, 1946. There are no further entries for that day or the next. All that remains of the entry for 2/8/46 is the enigmatic line, "Have rented a room in the town's only hotel and pray to be out

of here by tomorrow." There is no indication what has occurred in the
past two days that has led to Winslow leaving Daily's house and staying in town. The mention of 'pray' is especially disturbing given Winslow's violently atheistic philosophy.

The next memos in the collection are dated February 10 and February 13, 1946, and are annoyingly vague and noncommittal. "Have
finally reached home after several sleepless nights. My room is a com-
fort to me, but I have had to stuff my ears with cotton. The town's
constant murmuring is too much for me."

Winslow never directly discusses Northport again in his notes and
there are no further letters from Daily in the collection. There is, however, a brief comment that Winslow makes in an entry dated 4/20/46:
"I've given it all to my uncle for safekeeping. I cannot bear to have the
things near me, nor can I destroy them. I kid my uncle by saying that
he should hold on to them for the future 'Winslow Collection' at some
university. Unfortunately, he does not understand the joke or the *hidden meaning"* (my italics).

Sometime later, it is not clear exactly when, Winslow would begin
writing the rough draft of "The Dreamer in Fire." Even though he was
writing again, he appeared neither enthusiastic nor relieved about it.
There has been speculation that this may have been because he des-
paired of ever selling the piece, but a sense of oppression and resignation runs through the entire story. Clearly, Winslow was purging
himself of whatever happened to him in that lonely hillside farmhouse.

For the next nine years, Winslow would never talk about where his
inspiration for the story came from. This is interesting considering his
overwhelming response to any praise. When he was having so much
trouble with *Weird Tales* over its acceptance, Winslow lamented to
Dexter Wilson: "Better that it never see print. Damn the impulse that
made me write it or ever become a writer in the first place! I should
have been a ditch digger instead. I only sent it to *Weird Tales* because
it's too bad for any other magazine and this way it will hopefully lie
buried and forgotten. I never want to see it again" (*The Winslow Letters,*
Vol. 3, p. 213).

The coming years would see an increase in attention to Winslow's
writing and a mysterious decrease in his ambition. He no longer de-

sired to write, and friends and editors were forced to drag stories out of him. While he would continue to produce fine stories (like "The Alabaster Dimension" and "The Lime Network"), he would never hit that same level of intensity that drives "The Dreamer in Fire." I have written in length elsewhere of the enormous similarities that exist in Winslow's later work, so much so that one could consider each story a variation of the same theme: loss of identity and self.

When he died in 1955, a victim of a hideous car crash while driving in the outskirts of New York State, he was recognized as a growing master of the macabre. Yet, strangely, he never wrote about Northport again in any of his notes, memos, or many letters. In an effort to further understand the thinking behind this seminal Winslow story, I made a special trip to Northport.

The Adirondack region of upstate New York is, in many ways, the same as when Winslow saw it in 1946. Although there are more residences built into this wooded region, there are still vast pockets that are quiet and unspoiled. As one travels along I-93, it is impossible to ignore the spectacle of the mountains rising above the horizon. They dwarf everything in sight and leave one feeling alone and insignificant. These mountains were here hundreds of years ago and will, hopefully, be here hundreds of years from now. Except for the small pockets of commerce, like Lake George and Lake Placid, one can travel on the roads for hours without meeting another car. Northport, a two-and-a-half-hour drive from Lake George, remains much the same as when Winslow saw it almost fifty years ago. In its own way, it is as timeless as the mountains that surround it.

The town is a short distance from I-93 now and is entered by Rural Route 33. The highway, of course, did not exist when Winslow visited the region in 1946, so it was likely that Daily followed Route 6 out of Lake George and connected with Route 33 where they intersect outside of the small township of North Hudson. The road is a long, twisting affair that wanders slowly past farms and towns but most often plunges through some of the thickest forestry in the Adirondack region. There are no streetlights in this area, and travelers are forced to use their high beams when driving on moonless nights.

There are no road signs for Northport, and the people at the travel stations are hard pressed to find it on the local maps. But, unlike most Lovecraftian towns, if you look hard enough, you will find it printed in small letters between Mt. Marcy and Mt. Pharaoh. While there are many hiking trails marked along the way, there appears to be few people who hike in this section. I was told that it was due to the often steep inclines and poor drainage of the area.

Traveling along Routes 6 and 33, I was struck by the feeling that this was exactly the way Winslow saw it in 1946. While there are no existing notes for his bus ride from Boston to Lake George, his meeting Daily, or his traveling along this road, he cannot have helped being impressed by the sheer weight of the nature surrounding him. Perhaps this explains the passage in "The Dream in Fire" that runs: "I have begun to loathe the sight of the trees with their gigantic stature and lofty stares. They crowd around me like an army that cannot be bothered to take notice of an insignificant colony of ants . . ."

There is no warning when entering Northport. Suddenly the sign "Now Entering Northport, Founded 1709" appears out of nowhere and you are there. The road circles around a few small farms and houses, mostly set back from the road and in varying states of care and decay. Some almost appear new with their bright red roofs and silos, while others are silent and forlorn. Crossing the bridge over the small river brings one directly into the town center.

It is, in fact, a center in name only. The townsfolk do not cluster around the various buildings, and its solemn appearance looks more appropriate for a graveyard than a town square. Actually, Northport is somewhat unusual for even having a town center. Most towns this size in upstate New York survive without a town center at all, with post offices set in the basements of private homes and firehouses and schools appearing suddenly along the road.

As I stood in the center of the commons and stared around, I could not escape the feeling that this town should have died years ago and was only pitifully holding onto a sort of cancerous life. The white church had long ago faded to a dull gray (what did this indicate of a flock that would allow its temple to wilt so?), the general store stocked everything one could possibly need assuming one's needs were small and not picky, a town hall that was built to accommodate a town that never grew larger, and a hotel where there would be no customers. Who put this place here? In the middle of nowhere, what purpose could it serve? Or did any of that make a difference?

The town commons of Northport is roughly the equivalent of a football field; and while it does not appear to be regularly tended, it is not overgrown or unkempt. The general store is the first building one passes when entering the center and is the only place of activity in the square. A few trucks were parked outside, and there was a haphazard display of farming supplies on the porch. Looking at the building, I would assume that it had been built somewhere in the late nineteenth century and barely touched since. Parking among the unwashed trucks, I went inside.

The interior of the building mirrored its exterior: functional and simple. There were several men holding a discussion near the counter. I wish I could say that all activity ceased the second that I, the unwelcome intruder, entered the store, but it did not. I was completely ignored. The store was only half stocked, many of the shelves being empty and dusty. I grabbed a soda from the cooler (definitely a 1940s model and a collector's dream) and a bag of chips. Stepping to the counter, I paid for my purchase and left. Not once did anyone speak to me, acknowledge my existence, or tell me a cautionary tale about the dangers in following the trails of dead men. Neither, I noticed, did anyone ever smile.

The hotel is across the commons from the general store and I made my next stop there. The hotel, which is actually named The Addams Hotel just as in Winslow's story, is a short two-story building that could have been built around colonial times. Entering the reception area, I saw a plaque stating that this is exactly so and that the hotel got its name from the fact that John Quincy Adams had once stayed there. Before that it was known as The Stanley Tavern, possibly indicating what one of the original town founders did for a living.

Upon registering I asked the owner, a young woman named Elizabeth Bradshaw, if they kept records of their guests going back to 1946. I explained my research on Winslow to her, and she appeared quite interested and promised to check if they had kept their records for that long. She appears to be only around thirty or so, so obviously she was not the owner when Winslow stayed here in February 1946. She explained that the hotel was a family-run business, with the recent addition of a small restaurant on the side of the building, and that she inherited it when her mother, Mrs. Anne Bradshaw, died in 1980. Since then she had run the hotel by herself with a small staff of local girls who helped clean and cook.

I noticed, while signing the hotel register, that not many people stayed at the hotel and no one else was staying there now. Miss Bradshaw explained that they occasionally got skiers or hikers or salesmen traveling through the region but that their business was usually very small. When questioned as to why she even kept the place open, she appeared very confused, as if such a thought had never occurred to her. "Because it's supposed to be open," she replied, and I left the matter at that.

I was given Room 203, overlooking the town square.

I had, of course, requested this particular room as it was the one that Winslow describes in his story, and I believed it to be the same room in which he had stayed himself so long ago. The hotel is tastefully but plainly decorated, and the room even more so. In fact, it follows Winslow's descriptions exactly.

> There are no paintings on the wall or decorations of any kind. The only thing here is a bland wallpaper that begins to insult your eyes if you stare at it too long. The furniture is sparse and dangerous. I felt glad that I was not too heavy and likely to strain the limited resources of the thin guest chair. The bed is a small thing tucked into the corner almost as an afterthought. Clearly, little consideration has been given to taste or pleasure. It is a functional room and that is all. No excesses, no frills. Just a bed, a roof, four walls, and two windows. The windows look out upon the street from the second floor, but there is very little to see. Even after so long sitting here waiting, I have seen practically all that Sutter's Corners has to offer me. It is not a particularly large offering.

I set my things into the plain dresser and looked out of the window. The angle appeared to be the same, as Winslow describes. The general store across the commons, the town hall a little further down, and nothing else but trees. I hoped to be able to find some of the people who might have been around when Winslow visited, but was not sure of how much success I was likely to have. It had been over forty years, after all. I actually hoped to find Daily's farmhouse, if it was still standing, and maybe even Daily himself. I believed that Winslow based the deserted farmhouse of his story, where the unspeakable revelation occurs, on Daily's home but was unsure if Daily appeared as a character in the story himself.

One of the first things I wanted to do was to visit the local library. I felt as if I did not need anyone to guide me or point it out. After reading the story and Winslow's own notes, I felt that I knew the town well enough to practically pass for a native. I walked out of the hotel and started down the commons toward the town hall.

There was no one on the street and I noticed, not for the first time, the strange sense of motion in the air. It felt as if someone or something were whispering or talking softly close by. I attributed it to the closeness of the hotel restaurant and filtering noises from the general store, and entered the town hall.

The small, red brick building housed all the governmental offices of the town, such as they are. When I walked inside, I noticed that the general reception area was closed. I thought that this was unusual given that it was a weekday, but figured that reduced needs had forced the town officials to cut down on staff. Below me, I knew, would be both the jail and the library. Walking down the stairs, I noticed that there was no sound of conversation anywhere in the building. It was utterly silent.

The library, luckily enough, was open, and I walked over to the reception area. An old librarian—not the Mrs. Bradley whom Winslow speaks of in his notes—came to the counter. I explained that I was an historian of sorts and was looking for local information. I was politely told that there was very little and that I should try the larger library over in Lake George. Briefly, I outlined the story as I had gleaned it from Winslow's notes about his finding the papers tucked into a corner of the library.

The librarian, a Mrs. Martin, was aghast. Never, she told me, had she ever heard of such a thing. She had apparently taken over from Mrs. Bradley in 1958, when the latter retired. At that time, she said, the library was a horrendous mess and nothing was in any kind of order. It took her months to put the library into shape, a feat she seemed sincerely proud of, and never during that time had she found any such papers. She hoped that, if they had existed, whoever found them (implying Winslow) had donated them to the Adirondack Historical Society instead of leaving them out to rot. After that was done, she escorted me on a grand tour of the library. I was able to discern, however, that Mrs. Bradley was still alive and living in the area. Consulting a regional phone book, I could find no listing for her. On an off chance, I asked Mrs. Martin if she knew where her predecessor was living.

Mrs. Martin replied, in the easily offended tone of the elderly, that she certainly did know where Mrs. Bradley was living and gave me exact directions to the house. I would not be likely to learn much from her, Mrs. Martin warned, as she was well into her eighties and not entirely comprehensible. On a whim, I casually asked if Mr. Arthur Daily had been in lately. Mrs. Martin said, somewhat confusedly, that Daily had been in only the day before. Extremely pleased, I consulted one of the local maps and was able to get a general idea of where Daily's house had stood in 1946. It was certainly off in the woods, and I had a suspicion that it was as remote now as it had been forty years ago.

Before I left the library, I asked Mrs. Martin if she was a native of Northport and was not surprised to learn that she was a recent arrival. Apparently, even people who had lived in the town for more than thirty years were still considered 'newcomers.' She was imported, she explained, to clean up the mess left by Mrs. Bradley and get the library into working order. I thought that it must have been so, as she had been the first person I had seen in Northport who cared about anything.

Her directions were, of course, exact and I soon found myself outside a small, tan house with the name 'Bradley' on the mailbox. Going to the door, I knocked timidly and wondered what I could possibly say to this woman that would make any sort of sense.

A large shape moved behind the door and slowly opened it. A rather brutish-looking man stuck his head around the corner and asked what I wanted. When I replied that I had come to see Mrs. Bradley, he seemed unimpressed and acted as if she received visitors every day. He opened the door for me and started down the hall. Mrs. Bradley was in the sitting room, and he left me to make my own introductions.

As I walked into the room, the first thing I noticed was an over-whelming smell of mustiness. The room was decorated in a grand-motherly style and the shades were wide open to let in the afternoon sun. Mrs. Bradley was sitting in a chair in the corner, looking out at the window at nothing in particular. She looked to have been a large wom-an in her youth, but old age had shrunken her body so much that she appeared to be a midget wearing a giant's clothes. I wondered how clear her mind might be. I introduced myself, and she seemed to be extremely uninterested in both me and whatever I had come to talk about.

Luckily, I had brought along a portable pocket tape recorder and started it before the conversation began. Although her speech rambled at times, she seemed remarkably clear-headed for her eighty-plus years. Amazingly, she remembered Winslow exactly.

"Oh, yes," she began in a weak voice, "you're interested in that writer feller, eh? Haven't thought about him for years and years now. I wonder how long it's been?"

"He visited your library during a trip here in 1946," I prompted. "Do you remember anything about him?"

"Remember? Hell! I remember everything about that man. What a strange one he was! Comes into *my* library with that mousy little Arthur Daily and starts poking around. 'Why don't I have more papers?' he says. 'Where're all your magazines? Don't you have any information on this?' Stupid little whiner was all he was. Complaining about the way I ran *my* library and after I had the kindness to sit and help him person-ally with his research. Some gratitude. Then! You should have heard him when I mentioned the box of town records in the back. Nearly threw a fit!"

"Why was that?"

"Oh, he was screaming about how they should be in the historical society or a museum somewhere. As if anyone'd be interested in them. That's all I needed. Some nosy little busybody coming about complain-ing about the way I do things. Most racket I ever heard out of anyone. And then you should have heard him the next day!"

"The next day? What happened then?"

"Well, he come running in bright and early that morning. I knew he hadn't slept all night, 'cause he had on the same clothes he'd worn the day before. Thought I wouldn't notice. Anyway, he's all hot and bothered about something he found in the papers. All that fuss after I was nice enough to let him borrow them. I figured Daily would make sure that nothing happened to them, if they was worth anything anyway. So he's waving these sheets of paper in front of my face screaming as how they're pages out of the diary of someone and did I know where the rest of the pages were. I told him politely that I didn't have the faintest idea what he was talking about and let him look around in all the restricted areas to see if he could find his precious book. Some thanks I get. After a couple of hours he starts whooping and hollering as he'd found the foolish thing. Didn't look like much to me, just some old diary of someone who died a long time ago. He went and sat down and started reading it."

"Mrs. Bradley, do you remember whose diary it was?"

"Nope, not a clue. He didn't show it to me and I didn't ask. About an hour or so later, I notice he's just sitting there. Not moving, not turning the pages, nothing. It was as if he was listening to something. So I went over to him and touched him on the shoulder, and he jumped a mile! I swear! Almost gave me a heart attack! Damn fool. He's just standing there looking at me. Then he rushes by me out the door and that's the last I ever seen of him."

"What happened to the book?"

"He took it with him. Never saw it again. That's how I remember him so well. Only had one book thief while I was librarian and it was him."

"What about the other papers he borrowed?"

"He stole them too! Along with the book. I really let Daily have it over that. I loaned this Winslow feller the papers because Daily vouched for him. Said he was a famous, well-respected writer who was doing historical research on the town. Just a plain little thief, if you ask me!"

"And that's all you remember?"

"You're lucky I remember that much. You see, it was the look on his face that did it. It was so strange that I've never forgotten it. I seen it once or twice before in my life. Once, back when I was a young girl, we all went to see a Lon Chaney film at the movie theater in Lake George. Some of the looks on my friend's faces were like his. You know . . . frightened, scared almost to death . . . but mesmerized, as if they couldn't look away. That's what he looked like."

I thanked Mrs. Bradley for the information and she seemed almost instantly to forget that I was there. It was as if a switch had been thrown in her mind. I saw myself out into the street and could hear the son puttering about somewhere in the house as I left. She appeared to have shut down the instant she finished what she had to say. Just as if someone were giving dictation to me through her.

By the time I got to town, it was approaching nightfall. I decided to have a quick dinner in the restaurant and retire to my room. With luck, I would track down Arthur Daily the next day and hopefully solve the remaining riddles. Why *did* Winslow leave Daily's house so suddenly, and why was he so anxious to leave but take so long doing so? Strange things indeed.

The meal was enjoyable if somewhat bland. The fare consisted of meat and potatoes but of such a plain variety that I was forced to cover mine in salt and ketchup in order to give it some taste. Miss Bradshaw, the hotel owner, stopped by and asked how my research was going. I related the strange story that Mrs. Bradley had told me along with my reservations over finding out that Winslow had stolen important historical documents. I still felt, however, that there had to be a rational explanation somewhere.

I was comforted by the fact that she had managed to find the hotel records for 1946 and was happy to lend them to me for the night. Ecstatic, I followed her back into the hotel lobby and took the large register up to my room. It was a thick, clumsy book and actually held the records for 1940–1960. Even in the earlier years, there did not appear to be a lot of business in the hotel.

Opening the door to my room, I noticed a faint odor but brushed it aside as mustiness in my eagerness to examine the register. I placed it on the small desk and leafed through the pages. I knew the exact date I was looking for: February 8, 1946. I recognized Winslow's handwriting immediately, but it was not his name. The same spidery script that I had seen in letters and memos had, almost painfully exactly, signed the name 'Richard Clay.' That was the name that Winslow sometimes signed on his lesser work. The records indicated that he had signed in early on that day, about ten o'clock. Flipping through the pages, I found that he checked out on February 10, also early in the day. Evidently, Winslow traveled all day in order to return home the same day. It still did not answer the question about why he had left Daily's and why he stayed those extra days in the hotel.

On a whim, I flipped through the later pages in the book. There were very few entries, but on the page for February 8, 1948, I found the name 'Richard Clay' written again! Exactly two years to the day. Winslow had returned to the hotel and to Northport. Stunned, I flipped ahead to 1950, and found another entry. It was the same for 1952, 1954, and 1956. A year *after* his death, the name appeared again. Amazed, I continued to scan the pages. He appeared again in 1958 and 1960, at which point the register ended.

I went back and checked the signatures more closely. They were definitely in Winslow's handwriting. Mentally, I reviewed the facts surrounding his death in 1955. He had been driving on some on the mountainous roads in upstate New York when the vehicle spun out of control and plummeted off a cliff. The car was positively identified as being Winslow's, but the body was so badly injured and ravaged by the forest animals that visual recognition was impossible. Checking some of my research material, I found that the decree of death was given by the coroner in Gloversville, New York, who identified the body by dental records. Something did not make sense.

Why would someone impersonate Winslow to the extent of using his literary pseudonym? And yet, if (by some extreme stretch of the imagination) Winslow was still alive, who was that in the car? With a sense of events spiraling out of control, I made some notes and went to bed. My impending visit to Daily was slowly becoming more important.

That night, I had what became, in retrospect, a significant dream. I remember that I had been floating above a stretch of trees that, as in Winslow's dream, cried out to me. Suddenly my aspect changed and I found myself underground. Not in a coffin or a cave, but encased in the earth through which I was able to move effortlessly. I swam through the dirt, following some need to move forward, and came to a spot that I could only call 'blighted earth,' into which I dove. The dream became more confused after that, and I was left only with the memory of being engulfed by something that both filled and devoured me, leaving an empty shell behind.

I was not entirely oblivious of the significance of having such a dream in the same room that Winslow himself had occupied not once, but apparently many times. Quickly washing and dressing, I carried the register book down to the lobby. Miss Bradshaw was not in sight and, loath to leave the book just lying there, I brought it along with me. I was still troubled with the information I had learned, but hoped that Daily might be able to shed some light on it. After all, if Winslow had been making continuous visits to Northport, surely Daily would have known about it.

I followed the route I had planned out the day before, but was less comfortable on these roads. The trees along this trip seemed uncomfortably close and tight to the road, as if they were slowly seeking to encircle me. The condition of the road left much to be desired, and it wasn't until I had gotten halfway there that I remembered I hadn't eaten breakfast. Doubtless, these events conspired to put me on edge as I inched closer to Daily.

Rounding one of the curves, I nearly missed the small mailbox by the side of the road with 'Daily' printed in small, precise letters. The driveway was dirt and my car tires groaned as I pulled off the highway back into the horse age. I could not see any buildings through the trees but moved slowly down the road. Coming through a particularly thick group of trees, I finally saw what I had previously only known in fiction.

> The farmhouse stood alone and away from the road. It was clearly the oldest thing I had seen yet in Sutter's Corners and I wondered at the fact that it still stood at all. The walls were made of some dark wood that looked horribly absorbent and warped. There were only a few cracked and broken windows in the thing, and it was one of the most disgusting hovels I had ever seen. I was not frightened so much as entranced by it. That such a center of ugliness could exist amidst such natural beauty! I had no wish to do so, but my obligation to Lauren demanded that I enter the building. Only there, all my fears

told me, would I find the answer to her disappearance and my pain. Not for the first time, I wondered if I really wished to know the truth. Trembling, I opened the door and stepped inside.

The door opened slowly and I stood face to face with Arthur Daily. The sunken-faced youth had become a sunken-faced old man whose scar had not lost its power to fascinate. Once again, I explained who I was and my desire to learn more about Winslow. Daily seemed to take it all in stride and invited me into his house, where he insisted that I sit and drink some iced tea with him. In between sips of the horrid liquid, he unfolded a tale that was amazing in its lack of interest.

"Don't really know what I can tell you about Winslow," Daily began. "He only stayed with me for a few days and then went home. Never heard from him again."

"Why was that?"

"No particular reason, I guess. We just had different interests and nothing really in common. Not a heck of a lot for us to talk about. Him being the city fellow and everything and me just being a country boy."

"But you spent some time in New York City, didn't you? Isn't that where you got that scar?"

"How'd you know about that?"

I explained about the existence of the letters and their importance to my work.

Daily, miracle of miracles, actually smiled.

"He always thought that there'd be a 'Winslow Collection' someday. 'Something to leave everyone who'd come after me,' he said. Guess he was right about that."

"When did he tell you that?"

"Oh, during one of our talks. He liked to talk about his work and how he felt it'd be important one day. Didn't have much else in his life, you know."

"What else did he talk about?"

"Just the usual type of stuff, I guess. Things that I'd been wondering for a while, like where he got his ideas from and how he wrote his stories. I just liked his stuff and wanted to know how he came about it. Haven't you ever wondered about that? That quality of imagination that inspires literature and creativity? Haven't you ever wondered where that stuff comes from? And why people are the only ones who do it? You don't see monkeys or animals drawing pictures or writing stories. What about you? Where do you get your ideas for articles and stuff like that from?"

"I . . . I don't know. I never really thought about it before. I just respond to something that interests me. I notice something in a writer's work that speaks to me and I try to explain it to other people."

"Uh-huh. I was kind of the same with Winslow. I've always wondered where stuff like that comes from. Dreams, thoughts, that kind of stuff. Like there's a place that only certain people can reach where these things live. A kind of world that keeps making itself up every time someone reaches it. That sort of thing."

I had a feeling that the pragmatist Winslow wouldn't have appreciated this viewpoint any more than I did.

"I spoke to Mrs. Bradley in town and she mentioned to me that Winslow had found some sort of diary in the library. Do you know anything about that?"

"Only what she told me a long time ago. Winslow had been up late reading those old papers, and he had me take him down to town early the next morning. She told me he found some sort of diary, but he never showed it to me. When we got back that day, he just took his stuff and left. Went back home."

"And you never saw him again?"

"Nope. Heard about his accident but never saw him again."

"What about the hotel?"

"What about it?"

"You didn't know that he stayed at the hotel in town on the anniversary of his visit here every two years?"

Daily hesitated. I couldn't read what he was feeling. He looked to be both confused and triumphant. For an old man with wrinkled skin, his face was amazingly flexible.

"No," he said at last, "I didn't know that."

I didn't need to be Sherlock Holmes to know that he was hiding something, and yet his voice sounded sincere.

"Why would someone sign Winslow's name in the register if he never came here?"

"Well, people do all kinds of strange things. Sometimes they just can't help themselves. Could be another fan like yourself."

Registering under a pseudonym on a date that no one knew was important before I found the papers? Doubtful.

The remainder of the interview was pointless. Daily didn't know why Winslow left, why he stayed in the hotel the extra days, why someone would sign his name in the register, or where the diary was. I was astonished at the amount of information that Daily didn't know. In fact, he seemed more interested in learning what had happened with Winslow's work since his death. Hoping to draw him out more, I explained (in great detail) how the original Sargasso Press editions were collectors' items now and that many current writers cited Winslow as an influence. Daily listened intently, with an uncharacteristic interest when I explained about the publication of *The Collected Works of Robert Winslow* as well as the volumes of letters and criticism that had appeared in the previous two decades. I was talking about how the bulk of criticism focused on "The Dreamer in Fire" when his face went blank.

"I didn't like that one," Daily said. "Didn't like it at all."

"But it was his greatest work!"

"No, 'The Face Behind Mine' was his best work. Nothing after that felt like his voice."

"Of course not! That's because this place had made such an impact on him."

"Didn't seem to make that much of an impact on him when he was here."

I tried to make Daily understand the importance of "The Dreamer in Fire" to Winslow's canon, but he refused to listen. Only the early stories, Daily said, were important. Everything that came after was as if it had been written by someone else.

By the time the interview was over, I had (perhaps) one or two significant anecdotes but little else. The sun was beginning to set as I walked back out to my car. Daily stood at the doorway, waving good-bye, and, for some strange reason, I took out my instant camera and snapped a picture of him. I dropped the undeveloped photo into my coat pocket and drove away. Daily had been a pleasant host but hadn't answered any of my questions. He had encouraged me to come back and talk anytime I liked, but I had no doubt there would be nothing more to learn from him. He was deliberately hiding something from me and I couldn't picture Winslow, chronically underconfident, bragging about a future "Winslow Collection." Nor was he even in the habit of talking about writing, preferring not to discuss something that he didn't even feel he was particularly good at.

When I arrived back at the hotel, Miss Bradshaw was working at the front desk and I returned the register to her. She replied that she hadn't had the time to find some of the past records from 1960 onward but felt that she would turn them up sometime soon. I didn't think that the register would tell me much more, but it might confirm if the mystery guest had been at the hotel recently. To my surprise, she invited me to dinner in the practically deserted restaurant. During the meal, as tasteless as it was the day before, I detailed my findings for the day and she listened attentively. I told her it was unlikely that I would be able to find much more information and would probably be leaving in the morning. She seemed genuinely sad to hear this, and I began to contemplate prolonging my stay a little longer. I had noticed that she was a particularly attractive woman and was feeling some decidedly unscholarly feelings for her.

After dinner, she excused herself to finish some paperwork and I walked upstairs to find myself suddenly alone. Entering my room, I discovered that the musty smell had become overwhelming, so I opened one of the windows. Taking off my coat, I remembered the photo of Daily and took it out of my pocket. The picture was startlingly similar to the one Daily had sent Winslow so many years ago. There he stood in front of his house with the mountains oppressively in the background. The house looked even older and more worn than it had in person, and Daily himself seemed vague and blurry. Perhaps he had moved when I snapped the picture, but the house and mountains were in sharp detail.

I threw the photo on the desk and piled my other materials next to it. For the next few hours, I was engrossed in the kind of satisfaction that only a scholar can know as I updated my records and made additions based on my new information. I had now conclusively proved that the town of Sutter's Corners did exist and, more importantly, that the townhouse that was the setting for the horrific climax was a real building. I regretted, however, not taking the opportunity to view the basement that Winslow had portrayed so hideously. Perhaps I would swing by on my way home tomorrow and ask Daily for permission to take a few pictures of the infamous basement for my article.

I cleaned up and packed my few clothes and belongings away so I would be ready to leave in the morning. There really seemed little left to be done. Perhaps if I had been a professional detective, I might have found more clues to pursue; but, as an amateur critic, I had little experience in such matters. Satisfied, I drifted off to sleep, thinking about Miss Bradshaw.

Sometime during the night, I was awoken from a deep sleep. At first, I dreamed that Miss Bradshaw had come to me, naked and pale in the moonlight; but such things do not happen to a dull, overweight English teacher. I switched on the light and, when my eyes adjusted, found that there was nothing wrong. Everything was where it should be, and the door was securely locked. The musty odor, however, had returned with a vengeance.

Throwing my robe on, I walked around the room, trying to discover the reason for the smell. It was strongest near the desk, but there was nothing there to cause such a stink. I looked at my files, neatly stacked and ready to be packed into the car, and noticed something I hadn't seen before. There was a slim, red book nestled between the files.

Taking it out, I examined it thoroughly. It was a small book of antique vintage. Opening the cover, I read the flyleaf and discovered that it was the diary of Eziah Small, Jr., the son of one of the town's founding fathers. Amazed, I flipped through the volume and found what I was expecting to see. There was a section where several pages had been torn out. This was the diary that Winslow had found more than forty years ago! I did not know how, or why, it had appeared here but gave it little thought. The door was locked, so presumably only Miss Bradshaw had access to the room. Perhaps my dream had more to it than I thought.

I sat down and began to read.

It is difficult to remember what happened after this.

The diary began in broken, old English and detailed the founding of Northport through the eyes of young Eziah, Jr., who did *not* like the place. There are a few pages missing from the beginning.

> There has been much talk lately among the men who have spent most of their time in the woods. Father and the others are intent upon staying here despite the protestations of Mother and myself. I do not like these woods and wish we had stayed in Albany with the others. At night, Father leaves the camp and goes into the forest. I have stayed awake waiting for him, but he doesn't return until early morning, well after the dawn. He has been very tired lately and has lost so much weight that his clothes are becoming loose. He says that he is bargaining with the natives for our right to stay. Some question whether we should have to bargain with such heathens, but Father silences them quickly. Despite the many mountain tribes about, I have never seen an Indian in these woods.

A few pages later . . .

> The men returned this morning with their bargain. We can start clearing land and building now. Father has locked a large parchment away in his strongbox but has told me that it is the legal document that the natives have signed granting their permission for the settlement. I have never heard of such a thing being done before, but Father assures me that this is not anything unusual. Still, I have picked the lock and looked at the paper. It is not written in any language I have ever seen before. Father's signature is plain, as are the others, but I cannot read anything else and I am reminded of the Albany maid's tales of the Devil riding through these trees. I must pray for Father.

The woods were partially cleared for the settlement but, according to the diary, there was one place that was already cleared.

> Father was proud of the spot, lording it above the rest of the settlement, but I saw Mother go white at the sight of it. There is a strange stone building here which Father says was made by the natives. I've never seen any Indian dwelling like this. Don't they all live in tents? I moved to touch the stone, but Father pulled me back. "It's sacred,"

he said; "the natives will come and move it themselves." At night, in my bedroll, I heard the sounds of work being done, but no voices. Father seldom sleeps now.

The new farmhouse was built on the site and, apparently, once contained a barn as well. There was also a basement.

I've refused to sleep in the house and Father has beaten me for it, but I will not set foot in there again. I am convinced that the stone for the foundation and chimney came from that cursed native building. It is cold and slimy to the touch. Mother does not talk much anymore but has become more and more withdrawn. But that was all nothing compared to what has happened today. Three days earlier, Father had gone into the basement and locked the door behind him. Mother would not listen, but I could hear him murmuring down there like a madman. His voice would become harsh and shrill but would suddenly drop back to his normal tone. At night, a sickly light came from beneath the door. Suddenly, this morning, Father stumbled back upstairs. He was covered with blood and there was a large gash along the side of his face which travelled the length of his body. Mother put him to bed and stitched the wound shut. Neither said a word. Father never screamed or whimpered. He just looked at me with a stern face. Once he murmured, "The Mark," but that was all. Since then, he has never stopped watching me. On one occasion he grabbed my arm and feebly tried to pull me towards the basement. I pulled away and ran to the barn. With any luck, I will be able to grab a wagon out of town or else I will walk out. I cannot stay any longer.

The boy tried to run away but was captured by the village elders. They seemed to have an unusual interest in the young boy and returned him to the less than tender graces of his father.

I cannot escape. They will not allow it. I feel their eyes upon me at all times. The door is locked and Father has bolted all the shutters. He sits in his chair, staring at me and fingering his scar. It is clear that I am abandoned to my fate. Still, they will not find me unprepared. I have hidden a large kitchen knife and will wait for the right time. There is a light coming from beneath the basement door all the time now and, on several occasions, I have heard something behind the door breathing heavily.

There was a noise behind me.

> I am cursed. Father means to take me downstairs. I am to be "marked," he preaches. It is my destiny to follow him in his service. The stones sing to me at night. There cannot be much time left! He has told me much these past few days and would destroy this diary if he ever found it. Or would he? He seems far more interested in attracting more people to the settlement. The town has been growing greatly recently, as he reaches out to others to join him. Several others have already been "marked."

Unfeeling fingers wrapped themselves around my head. Turning, I saw that Elizabeth was there, pale and naked in the moonlight as in my dream. She pulled me close to her. Her body was cold and did not respond to my touch. She kissed me harshly and I felt myself drain into her.

I felt, rather than saw, the room change around me. Suddenly it was no longer the hotel room but a strange building with stones that moved and breathed and sang. I felt Elizabeth pull me downwards, and it seemed to me that I was in a strange, alien version of Daily's home. My legs felt weak and insubstantial as I moved further and further down through the floor of the building into the basement. There was a strange light that pulsated and glared sickly. It followed a weird rhythm that, I realized, echoed the breathing of the now transparent stones around me. In the center of the room, Northport waited for me.

The mass throbbed and breathed with a life of its own—a vast, amorphous thing that, I knew, was only partly exposed. Elizabeth pulled me closer, and I began to see features of people that I had spoken to over the past few days. Arms, legs, thighs, breasts, all poked out intermittently only to be swallowed by the common whole. Taking my hand, she pulled me inside. What little remained of me could only offer weak resistance. But there was little desire to resist left in me.

We plunged inside and I lost myself within the creature that was Northport.

My mind exploded with thoughts and images. People who had lived centuries before flashed through me, and I saw the beginnings of the town unfold around me. I could see the strange, unnatural building that Eziah had taken for his own and, going further back, the unwholesome creatures who had made it and brought it to life. I saw the town grow and shrink, the perpetual replenishment of the well that was Northport, this unholy creature encased below the breastplate of earth that covered it.

Ideas and concepts passed like lighting through my mind. Hopes, dreams, fancies, daydreams, and fantasies of hundreds of years pummeled my brain. I felt the passage of people I had spoken to travel through me while some lingered longer. Winslow avoided my thoughts, ashamed at his inability to resist and keep others away. Daily passed by, triumphant with his victory and reveling in his acquiring another dreamer. Lastly, I felt Elizabeth again as she entered my mind and thoughts and consumed what remained of myself. My thoughts melted into hers, into the community, and I suddenly found myself thinking the thoughts of hundreds of people simultaneously. They pushed me further, beyond where I had existed, into an area I had never seen before. Passing through the veil, I felt their pleasure at the sense that surrounded me. The thoughts, ideas, stories, and concepts floated by and through me while they were consumed by the town. Moving forward, ever forward, beyond all caution, pushing harder and harder for more and more. I felt myself shattering, breaking into smaller pieces of myself and felt no more.

When I awoke, it was already morning. I moved stiffly through the room, packing my belongings and fingering the mark on my still tender face. I moved my things into Elizabeth's room, where she had already made a space for them. I slipped into the mainstream of the town as if I had always lived there. To visitors, we are husband and wife, running the local inn. At night, in the shelter of the woods, we are Northport, glowing and exultant. To Winslow's horror, I have brought more and more scholars here, adding to the community. I have been careful to instruct the others in the need for politeness and, above all else, smiles. We mustn't let anyone think that life in Northport is anything less than what dreams, and fancies, are made of.

He Whose Feet
Trod the Lost Aeons

For the first millennium, I sought knowledge purely for knowledge's sake. Nothing was outside my purview: literature, history, medicine, philosophy, science. I studied at the feet of the learned creatures and heard what they considered wisdom until I had heard it all. But knowledge is mutable: what is known today is forgotten tomorrow. So I moved on.

The next millennium I consumed religion—a damnable thing that remade itself into the vengeful hand of God. I walked through lands with a sword of righteousness in one hand and pious salvation in the other. I found that I was better at dispensing one than the other, so I moved on.

Sin was next. I excelled in debauchery for another millennium. I knew the touch of women and men as well as of avatars of darkness. I embraced the essence of the Asian flower and unspeakable harbingers of joy and doom. I gave pain and received it. I knew great love and fiery hate and, at last, when all was spent, I knew ennui and I did not move on.

I drank from the cup of time and know not where or whence I was. My thoughts roamed wild and unfettered through interior and exterior realms of madness. I was of this world and outside it. I was Alpha and Omega. I trod among the atoms and the galaxies and left and came back again but could not move on.

When the veil finally fell from my mind, my eyes beheld a different world. Contagion had spread to all points and cracked open the world, and I ached for an ending that would not come. But I had remembered all that I had learned, even though most of it had fallen into ar-

159

chaic mists, and I knew what had to be done and I had the patience to see it through.

I would create the end of everything.

But true anarchy takes planning.

Anyone can create chaos. All it takes is a careful word in the right place or a sword thrust where it is least expected. But if one desires to create anarchy, *true* anarchy, the kind that can topple a civilization or remake a world, it takes meticulous planning.

I learned how to plan when I walked in the dust with ancient pharaohs who both revered and feared me with good reason. Their minds were filled with superstitions but their skills were many. I turned my skin dark as the space between the stars and they bowed before me. They were efficient tools.

They erected the first of the secret temples, places where the fabric between worlds had become thin. Among the religions of animal-headed gods grew the silent sect infected with a particular madness that would, like flowers, sprout into a worldwide insanity.

The minds of men are easily manipulated, unlike those of the earlier civilizations which I was forced to eliminate. The stubbornness of lizards was particularly legendary. Of creatures that had descended from the stars or oozed through from various dreamlands, the less said the better. Those that were useful I kept and bent to my own needs. The others were eliminated. The nameless cults spread where I desired and corrupted those who were useful. The Egyptian dynasties begat the Romans who begat the Europeans who begat the Asians who begat the Americans and so on and so forth. Humans spread across the globe like a virulent disease that ran rampant through its host. And in every place, in every culture, in every forgotten realm of antiquity, I had trodden and left madness in my wake.

In the distant past, I had taught the sorcerer kings of ancient Valusia of the things that had once called the earth their home but now slept, waiting to be reborn. All that was needed for their return was for certain conditions to be achieved, for a state of anarchy to rule and for ancient obstacles to be removed. In essence, what appears to men to be untold years of planning but which would be, for me, merely a blink of my eye.

The movement grew quickly; for men, especially those with blackness in their souls, are ever ready to destroy their neighbors and their worlds. A sect near the top of the world sought to impress me with their bloodlust, but they were like children playing with toys compared to other races whose barbarity had leeched down from the stars centuries earlier. At the bottom of the world, I walked through forgotten corridors made by creatures long since extinct and talked with those that had affected that extinction. They would have a part to play in the events to come and the world that was yet to be. Their eagerness was both appealing and pitiable.

Block by block, I laid my foundation.

Blood was spilt in the right places at the right time. Men will commit more atrocities in the name of religion than of any king. In time, the spaces between the sleeping and the awakened grew less and less. Puritans discovered the practices of certain forgotten tribes in what would be called America; and many, cut off from their home nations, would embrace in secret the customs that their forbears would have deemed worthy of fiery death. I spread the word personally to many as the colonies slowly grew and indulged in their feverish delusions of my origins and designs with books containing bloody signatures and rites of nameless portents. The art of revenation was taught and essential salts given so that each time they would reverberate on the wall between the worlds. Creatures were brought forward from the depths of the sea to meld with men and women to produce constructs that would, in time, provide the ballast needed to crack open the gates.

And still men prevailed upon the land with his machines and refusal to commit. Each time the event drew near, men would retreat or allow themselves to be defeated. That was when I saw that more direct intervention was needed. A firmer hand was required.

Despite their love of war, the imaginations of men were limited. An idea dropped into the unconsciousness of several individuals resulted in the first weapon capable of cracking the seals of reality. And yet, with the power within their grasp, men grew timid and retreated from what I had shown them to create. So the idea had to be spread further and amongst those whose emotions were more easily inflamed or controlled. A campaign was initiated.

The culture of man divided. There were those who worshipped science and embraced rational thought while those who worshipped gods, both light and dark, rejected science and clung to their faith and superstitions. Once again I walked amongst men and brought them the conclusions they needed. My followers, and the followers of those who waited beyond, grew—and then, quickly, the first stroke was made.

To others, it might appear as if the end of the world was random, chaotic, and without plan. But does the watch know the hand of its maker? Does the machine, once started, see the finger that pressed the button? They simply move along in their preordained paths without knowledge or lustre or name.

The dreamers, in their sleep, glimpsed the beginning. Many refused to awaken after that sight. The mad felt the presence of the others pressing on their minds and either screamed or tore out their eyes or throats. Men at sea in boats reported leviathan shapes on their radars or beneath their ships before falling silent in their watery graves. Like blocks in a child's game, the bindings fell away rapidly once the bombs began to explode in an atomic chorus.

Each ignition pounded against the barriers, which began to crack and slowly give way. The ocean creatures, their bodies finally melting away to their true shape, congregated in the weak places in the seas and flung themselves against the wall like soldiers in an ancient war. They ran like acid into the cracks and pulled them open as they died.

Titans rose from the forgotten areas of the world.

I closed my eyes and spread myself over the globe. Voices rose up in fear and terror as dark, virulent creatures walked above ground for the first time in centuries. Cities crumbled as cracks opened in the earth. I heard my name cried by the faithful who were struck down as easily as the ignorant. I felt the wave pass through me, and the final vestiges of the barriers fell like trees before an autumn hurricane.

A vast shape the size of a mountain left his house at the bottom of the ocean to the symphonic screams of a million dreamers. The far-off sound of mad pipes grew closer and the beating of black wings flew through the air like raindrops. The pieces had all been perfectly placed and the players had given their last soliloquies. The civilization of man, built by accident or design, was nothing more than burnt embers on the wind. Those few who survived would be pets or fodder as needed. The earth shook to its core and broke apart into new and frightening continents of dark malevolence. The shapeless creatures from what had been the bottom of the world surged out like daemonic swineherds and took their place in the new hierarchy.

At last the deed had been done and I, the Dark One from Ancient Khem, walked the length and breadth of the world and surveyed what I had wrought. With those for whom I had paved the way, I charted new depths of depravity and monstrosity. My cruelty knew no bounds, and we cavorted across the tops of the new mountains that we had pulled from the interior of the earth. For a millennia I was one of them and rejoiced in what we had created.

But even for one as ageless as I, time passes and I felt the return of the inevitable ennui and listlessness. All things were transitory and, in the finality of the universe, there was no meaning. So I began planning again and, this time, I looked toward the species that had shown itself to be the most enduring and unchanging of them all. It might take another millennium or two, but eventually the cockroaches would reign supreme where the Old Ones reigned now and man had once reigned.

Or not.

"Good Morning, Innsmouth!"

"I'm Kelly Shapiro, reminding everyone that all next week we'll be visiting the lovely town of Innsmouth. One of our 'Forgotten Gems'! We'll go to their lovely shoreline, take in the shops, and talk to local celebrities about the revitalization of this once-deserted town. That's all next week on 'Massachusetts Morning!'"

At the last word, Kelly brought the microphone down from her lips, barely bothering to disguise her contempt. "How the fuck did I get this shit story?" she asked her cameraman.

Perry Langham sighed and brought the camera unit down off of his shoulder. "You know the drill, Kelly. Mandy got the co-host spot and you didn't."

"And you know how she got that chair, right?" Kelly flicked her bright red hair out of her eyes and fixed the cameraman in her gaze. Her perfectly tailored dress suit had been color-coordinated to match her hair and makeup while her freshly manicured fingernails shined in the sun. At twenty-eight, Kelly was already feeling that WCGB-Boston was too small for her. Particularly now that Mandy was sitting in the co-host seat with John Lohnes. She needed to set her sights higher.

Loading the camera back onto his shoulder, Perry languidly responded, "I don't listen to office gossip, Kelly. Let's do it again."

"Again? What the fuck for?"

"You need to be more bubbly. You shut down before you ended the segment. This is morning TV, remember? 'Upbeat! Lively! Happy! Moronic! News for idiots!'"

Kelly did the promo again and didn't drop her smile until Perry shut off the recording.

* * *

They were standing on the Federal Street Bridge with the Manuxet River below them. In the distance, the waterfall was busily churning on its way through Innsmouth and out to the sea. Perry, ever the perfectionist, had scoped out the town earlier and chose this spot especially so he could get the waterfall in the background.

The river essentially split the town into two sections. At one time, most of the buildings were decrepit except for a few old family mansions. After the gentrification of the '80s, most of the inferior buildings were simply demolished and replaced with condos or townhouses. Where there had been squalor before, now there was affluence and opulence. It cost a pretty penny to live in Innsmouth today unless you had inherited the land.

Kelly lit a cigarette and stood by the WCGB van, out of the wind. On the side of the van were large stickers of Mandy and John, smiling vapidly. The sight of them was more than Kelly could bear. "How quickly can we wrap this up?"

Shrugging, Perry loaded the equipment back into the van. "Depends how long you take. We can do a couple of promos down at the shore. I assume you don't want to go on the whale watch?"

Kelly looked at him with contempt.

"Yeah, didn't think so. Well then, we go do the interview with the Mayor at 3 P.M. After that, we talk to Richard Gilman, who's the real estate developer responsible for all this. His office is over at Marsh Landing."

She stamped the cigarette out with her heel and climbed into the van. "Let's just hurry up and get this over with."

"What's your rush?" Perry asked as he got into the driver's seat and started the van. "You usually love rich, fancy places like this."

The van drove down Federal Street and took a left onto State Street, heading for the shore. Kelly looked at the line of expensive townhouse façades, which all looked the same. They could have been from Boston's Back Bay or Portland's downtown area. Well-dressed people walked happily, calmly, in the streets as they talked and texted on their cell phones while children played cheerfully on the sidewalk. The streets were lined with BMWs and Audis and SUVs.

"I don't know," Kelly said, "it just feels fake, you know? Like it's just a covering."

Perry shrugged. "No faker than any other of WCGB's 'Forgotten Gems.'"

* * *

"Innsmouth had quite the struggle many years ago," Mayor Vincent Waite said with a smile. "Back in 1928, the town was practically destroyed due to a Federal raid on some bootleggers. And, like so many other towns and cities in New England, Innsmouth had been dependent upon a manufacturing base that eventually collapsed."

"Um . . . you are taping this, right?"

Kelly smiled her 'morning news reporter' smile. Vapid and empty. "Of course, Mr. Mayor. Don't worry, we'll get everything."

Mayor Waite smiled happily. He was a pudgy man with virtually no hair anywhere on his body. When he shook Kelly's hand, she had the definite impression of something clammy. They were standing on one of the docks in the harbor. Behind them stood the towering mammoth that was 'Marsh Landing.' It was a massive condominium complex that looked to have been built from the remnants of an old factory, part of the current 'gentrification' methodology. It was fancy and expensive and built over the Manuxet River. The view from the penthouse must have been amazing, and that was where the man who had revitalized Innsmouth lived—the legendary Richard Gilman.

"Excellent! Well, as I was saying, the town was suffering and came very close to becoming completely deserted. Many of the people had moved away and there was no industry here to speak of until we started the Innsmouth Foundation."

"When was that?"

"Back in 1984. A few of us, descendants of the original town families, formed a corporation to promote and rebuild the town. Of course, it was mostly due to Richard Gilman that we succeeded. He bought up most of the deserted properties and spent his own money developing them into the thriving town you see here today."

What that really meant, Kelly thought, was that Gilman bought up everything cheap and is now selling it off to the rich. Soon they will be the only ones who can afford to live in Innsmouth.

"What about the manufacturing?"

"Well, the only industry here now is tourism. Back in its day, of course, Innsmouth had been a major center for shipbuilding and even gold refining. But, as you know, the jewelry industry isn't what it was. What you see behind me, Marsh Landing, is where the old Marsh gold refinery used to be. Gilman used as much of the foundation as he could in the rebuilding to preserve that old New England flavor."

Suddenly, Mayor Waite got intensely serious. "One of our long-term goals, you see, is to bring people back to Innsmouth. After 1928, so many of our townsfolk left Innsmouth and spread out over this land far and wide. They're our children and we want them to come back home. Believe me, once you come here, you never want to leave. Innsmouth gets in your blood!"

"Isn't that your PR campaign?"

"Oh, my, yes. 'Innsmouth: the town of your dreams!' It's been quite successful. We've had many families come back home."

"And one can easily see why! In Innsmouth with Mayor Waite, I'm Kelly Shapiro for 'Massachusetts Mornings Forgotten Gems.'"

The camera came off Perry's shoulder. "And we're clear."

Kelly sighed. "Great. Can you send that off to the studio, Perry?"

Without waiting for a response, Kelly turned back to the mayor. "What was that you were saying about 'bootleggers,' Mr. Mayor?"

"Please, call me Vincent," he replied, slipping into politician mode. "Oh, that was just some foolishness. Supposedly back in '28, when they still had Prohibition, the Feds raided the town. Massive thing, I guess, big operation. They took away a lot of people and blew up several buildings, including the Marsh Refinery. Wasn't much left of it before Richard rebuilt it. Now it's a lovely building, isn't it?"

"Yes, yes, it is. You mean the Federal Government blew up a large portion of the town? Are they allowed to do that?"

"Back then the Feds could do anything they liked. No one with cell phones or digital cameras or YouTube watching. Anyway, there weren't many people left here after all that, and most of those left soon after. So when we started the Innsmouth Foundation, we really wanted to bring people back here, back to their roots. Of course, having such prime real estate so close to Boston didn't hurt either!"

The mayor laughed.

Waiting until he was finished, Kelly asked, "So most of the people here now are 'transplants'? From other places?"

The mayor nodded. "There's still some old families left. They're mostly in the 'old town' section." He gestured off to the north side of town. "But I'd say that a goodly part of our residents now are from somewhere else. Probably about 75%. But, after all, isn't everyone from 'someplace else'? Innsmouth is a 'melting pot'!"

* * *

"What the fuck do you mean, Gina?" Kelly snarled into her cell phone. "I can't make the footage any more exciting! This place is fucking boring! It's full of a bunch of rich old farts that probably haven't had a good bowel movement since 1979. What do you want me to do? Give the fucking mayor a blow-job on camera?"

Kelly listened and nodded her head. She clearly wasn't liking what she was hearing. Off to the side, Perry checked his watch. Their day was running late and they still had the interview with Innsmouth's 'savior' to do. Finally, Kelly swore some more into her phone and jabbed it into her pocket.

"What's the deal?" Perry asked.

"Stupid, fucking Gina is the deal. She thinks the footage we shot is too boring. She wants us to talk to some locals. Christ! I hate talking to fucking locals. Damn editors. Why the hell did they pick this place anyway?"

Perry shrugged. "Way I heard it was that someone from the town called the head of WCGB, Mr. Wayne Eliot himself. I guess some money changed hands somewhere. You know these things are nothing but PR for the towns."

"And where the fuck am I going to find locals to interview?"

Perry smiled. "I know just the place."

* * *

The van pulled to a stop outside a large building that, at one time, might have been a church. The building, like much of Innsmouth itself, had the air of something that had been decaying for decades and then hidden behind a mask of new paint and fixtures. A fancy wood carved sign was above the door. It read simply, "Esoteric Order of

Dagon." The sign was expensive and new. Next to the door were two smaller plaques. One designated the place as an historic building while the other said "Social Club" and listed hours of operation.

As they got out of the van, Kelly was already unimpressed. "'Esoteric Order of Dagon'? What the hell is this?"

Lugging out the camera, Perry replied, "I saw it when I did my scout-out last week. It's some kind of social club or something. They have a website."

Kelly looked at him, disbelieving. "Are you shitting me? I can't even get a good signal out here. How do *they* have a website?"

Perry pointed at the door. There, a small sticker proclaimed, "Wi-Fi."

"Fuck you, okay?" Kelly said as she walked up to the door.

It took a few minutes for their eyes to adjust to the dark interior. Inside was a small hallway with closed doors on each side and a stairway on the right leading upwards. Typical New England Church design. At the end of the hallway were two bay doors with the customary nine small window panes in each door. Through it, they could see a larger room with tables and chairs. Some people were milling about.

When they opened the doors, a few people turned around but not many. There was a bar on the right side of the room with a large television tuned to the Red Sox game. More were watching the ball game than paid any attention to them. Kelly walked up to the bar where an older man was rinsing glasses. He looked up and smiled. "Afternoon, folks. You do know this is 'members only' time, right?"

Kelly put on her 'news reporter' smile again. "Hi, I'm Kelly Shapiro from WCGB's 'Massachusetts Morning' show. We're doing a segment on Innsmouth for the 'Forgotten Gems' portion of the show. Mind if ask a few questions? Maybe film a few interviews with your members?"

The bartender laughed. "'Forgotten Gem'? Ain't that a laugh? Hey, Harry!" The man motioned to one of the others sitting at the bar and watching the game. "We're a 'forgotten gem,' whaddaya think about that?"

Everyone laughed. "Sorry, Miss," Harry said, "but Innsmouth is a town better left forgotten. All of us here? We're old folk. Some of us got family going back generations in this place. When everyone else up and ran, we stayed put. And what do we have to show for it? Rich bastards who bought up our homes cheap, knocked them down, and put up houses none of us could afford to live in. They been pushing us out of here for the last thirty years, so excuse us if we're not too anxious to bring more of 'em here."

"But the mayor said that they want the old families to come back."

The bartender smirked. "Sure they do. But only certain ones. Ones with the right blood and money. The rest of us? They'd rather we just die off. Make more room for their rich friends. Make no mistake, Miss, they're remaking this town into a playground for the wealthy. They're all the same, you know. Deep down."

The Red Sox scored another run against the Yankees, which brought the room to a cheer and grabbed everyone's attention. The bartender took a piece of paper out from under the bar and started writing on it. "Look," he said when no one was watching, "I probably shouldn't do this, but if you want to be a real reporter for a change, go to this address and talk to the man there. He can tell you more about what's really going on in Innsmouth. Unless you just want to report about things like 'the world's largest whoopee pie' for the rest of your life."

He passed a piece of paper across the bar to Kelly and then walked away. The rest of the men had lost all interest in anything but the ball game. As Kelly and Perry walked out the door, Perry leaned back and said one word: "Buckner."

The men yelled at him as if he had run over their dogs with a lawnmower.

"Why'd you do that?" Kelly asked as they climbed back into the van.

Perry shrugged. "I hate baseball."

* * *

The next few hours were spent getting 'local color.' They interviewed the owners of the fancy, high-priced gift stores, the shoppers at the trendy clothing shops, and fashionably dressed couples in the town square. Perry made sure to get the shops and freshly restored buildings in the background. The people were almost universally the same: "Innsmouth's such a wonderful place to live! Everyone's so friendly!

Great shopping! Beautiful shoreline! History! Everything you could ever want in a town!"

Of course, all the people interviewed were young, rich, and upbeat. That's what the producers wanted. They were everywhere: coming off the whale watch cruises, cruising around the Innsmouth Yacht Club, walking along the shoreline, and filling the expensive, gourmet restaurants on the wharf. There were some local fishermen or clammers digging in the low surf, but these were few and far between. The feeling was that such 'old-timers' were indulged but only in small doses. When encountered on the street, they were avoided and ignored. There was a clear divide between these social groups. Although the 'old town' residents weren't banned from the stores or new places, they were clearly not welcome and they knew it. There were few of them on the main streets, so the 'local color' was the young and wealthy newcomers, which was fine because that was exactly what the producers, and the viewing public, wanted to see. No one really wants to look at the man behind the curtain. They want the Wizard and they want him large and upbeat, not a hint of reality or anything depressing. That's what morning news was all about. All flash.

The sun was beginning to set as Perry set up for the Gilman interview. The penthouse office at Marsh Landing was indeed impressive, with panoramic views on three sides. On the right and left were scores of rebuilt buildings showing their new prosperous faces to all, but it was the ocean view that was the most spectacular. Marsh Landing was tall enough to look over every inch of Innsmouth's coast and beyond. There were clear views of the new wharfs and docks as well as the busy yacht club and pleasure boaters lazily drifting along. A dark line appeared on the horizon with a small monolith atop it. There were no boats near it, and it seemed as if every vessel gave it a wide berth.

"Lovely view, isn't it?" said Richard Gilman as he walked into the room. He was an older man than Kelly had expected and painfully thin. His clothes were stylish and neat, but his face and neck were wrinkled like an orange left out in the sun too long. He walked toward Kelly, smiling carefully, and held out his hand.

Kelly nodded, put on her reporter's smile (which was making her face ache by this point), and went into her well-rehearsed speech. "It certainly is, Mr. Gilman. I'm Kelly . . ."

Gilman smiled. "Oh, no need to introduce yourself, Ms. Shapiro, I'm a big fan. I watch your show all the time."

Startled because no one ever admitted to watching "Massachusetts Morning" off camera, Kelly stumbled. "Um, this is my cameraman, Perry . . ."

Gilman shifted quickly and shook Perry's hand vigorously. "Wonderful! Now I suggest we get to this quickly before we lose the light, yes?"

Without waiting for an answer, Gilman maneuvered Kelly over in front of the large window looking over the ocean and started the interview. It was the usual, typical morning news segment. Kelly asked simple questions ('softballs') and Gilman answered happily. He told stories about growing up as a child in Innsmouth during the '50s and swimming out to the reef. Later he went to college, studied engineering, and returned to revitalize his hometown. It was the quintessential 'local boy makes good' story and smelled as bad as the ocean at low tide.

Soon they had more than enough footage for the segments, and Perry busied himself with packing up the equipment. The sun had set and the lights of the town were sparkling through the windows. Kelly walked over to the ocean view, now dark and indistinct, and asked, "What's the name of that reef out there?"

Gilman came and joined her. "Ah, that's 'Howard's Reef.' There's a sharp drop into the ocean just beyond that. We renamed it some time ago."

"What did it use to be called?" Kelly asked.

"Devil's Reef," Gilman answered. "Of course we had to change that. Not good for the tourism, you know. Some of the old locals still call it that though. Old habits."

"Yes, about that," Kelly replied, "where are all the old locals? All I see are rich yuppies."

Gilman nodded. "It may look that way, but I assure you that many of those 'yuppies' are descended from old Innsmouth families. They just haven't lived here for a few generations."

"So you don't see yourself as creating a town just for the rich? Pushing out the locals?"

Gilman chuckled and nodded. "Sounds as if you've been talking to some of the old locals already? Look, no one forced them to sell and those who haven't have been welcome all the same. No one can argue that real estate like this (on the coast and close to Boston) isn't a valuable commodity. We saved this town. Others would have let if fall apart and rot. We brought it back to life and gave it purpose again."

"And what purpose is that?" Kelly asked.

"To celebrate the past and prepare for the future." Gilman smiled.

* * *

The WCGB news van was heading down Dock Street and out of Innsmouth back to Route 118. Kelly was looking at the piece of paper that the bartender had given her. There was a name and an address written in spidery script that said, "Robert Olmstead, 18 Water Street." Still looking at the paper, she asked Perry, "Do you know where 18 Water Street is?"

He thought briefly. "Yeah, I think so. That's in the old part of town. Why?"

"I think I might have one more interview to do."

"What? What for? We've got plenty of footage. I've already uploaded it to the studio and they're editing it now."

"There's just something 'off' here, Perry. This town: it's too shiny and perfect, you know? And it's not just that the rich people have taken it over. There's something else here."

"Yeah? So what? Don't get all 'reporter' on me now, Kelly. You're a morning news host. You're not Diane Sawyer."

"Fuck you, asshole! Didn't you say you used to shoot footage in Afghanistan? Kuwait? What the fuck are you doing filming this crap?"

Perry looked at her and made a U-turn in the middle of the street. "Probably just some old fuck who's pissed that he didn't cash out when he had the chance," he said as the van made for the 'old town' section.

Eyes behind expensive designer glasses watched the van drive away and passed that fact onto others.

* * *

Even by the standards of homeless people, 18 Water Street was a hovel. It was a one-level colonial of 'salt-box' design and looked as if it might fall over if someone sneezed on it hard enough. A slight rain had begun to fall, which made everything look slick and wet. There were no BMWs on this street. The few vehicles that were there were old, beaten-up Ford and Chevy trucks. No children played on Water Street, but that didn't mean that there weren't people who noticed the news truck with its garish sticker of smiling, happy, and rich newscasters come to a halt in front of the silent house.

There were heavy curtains in place behind every window. If there was a light inside the house, it wasn't possible to see it from the street. "Let me go in and scope this out first," said Kelly. "I'll see if there's anything here worth taping."

Perry shrugged, pulled out his cell phone, and started playing a game.

The front door looked as if it might break apart if she knocked too hard, and there was no bell. Tentatively, Kelly knocked on the door. She could hear the sound of something shuffling inside toward the door when it started to open slowly. The bartender peeked out and looked around nervously.

"It's late," he said. "Figured you weren't coming. Best get inside quick."

He opened the door and rushed Kelly inside.

"I don't get it. *You* gave me this note to come and talk to *you?* Are you Robert Olmstead?"

The bartender shook his head. "No, my name's Sargent, Joe Sargent. My family's been in Innsmouth for generations. My great-grandfather was friends with Olmstead. That's how I know him."

The inside of the house was dark and gloomy. A few low-level lamps were on, but their light barely extended beyond themselves. The furniture, such as it was, looked old and unused, as if it were an afterthought or attempt to provide 'normality.' The air was close and stale, but there was a sour taste to it lying just underneath the senses. They were in a living room, and a hallway led off to the left while the right had an empty doorway that opened onto an unused kitchen. For all the sense of abandonment, the place was exceptionally clean.

"You don't really know about Innsmouth," Sargent said. It was a statement, not a question. "You don't know how it used to be or what went on here. There was a reason the Feds raided the town in '28 and bombed the reef. Olmstead was that reason."

Sargent walked down the hall to the last door on the right. He knocked lightly, and some type of noise answered him. "Stay here a moment," Sargent said. "I'll see if he's up for talking to you."

He entered the room and closed the door behind him. After a moment, the door opened again and Sargent motioned Kelly inside.

It was a small bedroom, of sorts. Or, at any rate, it had a bed in it. There was a weak-looking wooden chair next to the bed and a small bureau off to the side. The bed was on the right, against the wall, and unreachable by the hall light. There was a figure moving slowly on the bed. No other lights were in the room, not even a candle. An unpleasant odor filled the room, but Kelly couldn't place it. Sargent turned to the figure. "This is the reporter I told you about."

Something on the bed wheezed as if breathing were too difficult to attempt. "This is Robert Olmstead," Sargent said, "the man who brought the Feds to Innsmouth in '28."

Kelly looked at Sargent and suddenly became very frightened for her safety. Sargent was old, she reasoned, and she'd not seen anyone else in the house. She could probably knock him out of the way and run for the door if she had to, because the man was obviously crazy. He'd as much as said that Olmstead was more than a hundred years old.

"Please . . . sit . . ." the voice said.

"Mr. Olmstead," Kelly said as she slowly sat down on the wooden chair, "my name is Kelly Shapiro and I'm from 'Massachusetts Morning.'"

"He doesn't know what that means, Miss," said Sargent behind her.

"You're . . . a reporter, yes?" the voice wheezed. Kelly peered into the black spot, trying to get more of a definition of the person before her, but it was as if the light refused to enter that corner.

"Yes, I am. Mr. Sargent says you have something to tell me? About the town?"

"It's all my . . . fault," the voice in the night said. "I was the one that brought . . . them here. When I came here, I . . . didn't understand.

How could I? At first, all I saw was the . . . terror. Then it was the joy, but that didn't . . . last long. The Feds came with their . . . soldiers and their . . . submarine and bombed the trench beyond Devil's Reef. Even the . . . Deep Ones hadn't known what lay there, sleeping in the deep beneath Y'ha-nthlei. The torpedoes . . . woke it up and it came up out of the deep rift in-between the realms."

"What came up? What are you talking about, Mr. Olmstead?"

The wheezing became faster-paced now, as if the speaker were gasping for breath because he had too much to say.

"Old . . . Obed Marsh should've known. There's *always* a bigger fish in the sea. Breeding with . . . Deep Ones was bad enough, but it wasn't that bad. Once the change came, you were almost . . . glad. The sea. It's so . . . peaceful. Then it's the time on land you dread. I came back here with my cousin, and he was one of the . . . first to die."

"From the police raids?"

The shadow shaked a furious 'no.' "From what came after."

A noise came from outside, but Kelly didn't notice. Sargent had and became nervous.

"There were . . . others, those who welcomed it and made a pact. Same way that ol' Obed did and for the . . . same reason. Nothing . . . ever . . . changes. Time is a noose around our necks. Everything that happens has happened . . . before and will again. Y'ha-nthlei fell, but *another* rose in its place—this time more terrifying and dark. And behind that will be another."

Sargent left the room and did not return.

Kelly could just barely make out Olmstead's face as her vision began to adjust to the blackness. His eyes were large and bulging, and his lips were thick and misshapen. He had no hair and his skin was rough and scaly. His head seemed unnaturally flat.

"Then they started to come . . . back. We thought that they were returning to . . . help us, save us, but we were . . . wrong. They had *another* use for us. All for gold. Always for gold. We . . . sell our past and ransom our futures for nothing more than . . . pennies."

"What are you talking about? Who's using you? For what?"

Footsteps came down the hall. Kelly ignored them, thinking that it was just Sargent returning to the room.

The shadow wheezed out one word: "Sacrifices."

"Well, Miss Shapiro, I think you've seen enough 'local color' for today, don't you?" came the voice of Richard Gilman.

Kelly jumped from her seat, but Gilman's hands clamped onto her arms and held her firmly.

"Let me go, you fucking asshole!" Kelly yelled, but Gilman just smiled.

"Not quite 'morning TV' language, is it?" He let go and quickly punched her hard in the stomach. Kelly bent over and began to vomit on the floor.

Two other men stood in the hallway, waiting for instructions. They were thick, strong men who were used to following orders.

"Throw her in the back of the van and take her over to the center below the Landing."

They picked Kelly off the floor, and she immediately bolted and attempted to run for the door. One of the men slammed her into the wall, and she slumped unconsciously into the hall.

"What about him, sir?" The other man motioned to Olmstead.

Gilman shone his light on the terrified figure on the bed. There was little left of what had once been human in Olmstead. He was mostly a Deep One, with all the signs of the sea about him. Skin had become scales, nose flattened into slits, gills working desperately in the air, and a skeletal frame that bore little resemblance to a hominid.

"Oh, Bob and I are going to have a little chat, he and I, about the price of freedom."

* * *

When Kelly woke, she could not tell where she was. There was no light, and her side pulsed with pain from where she had been shoved into the wall. She was lying on a rough wooden floor that felt old and unsanded. Her hands were tied in front of her with a thick rope that was, in turn, tied to something else. She felt her way backward and found that the rope had been tied to a cold, iron ring set in the floor. She pulled on the ring as hard as she could, but it did not move. Crying, she started to scream for help.

After about fifteen minutes of sustained yelling, her voice started to give out. Then she heard the sound of a door unlocking and opening.

Bright light poured in from outside. A figure stood framed in the doorway. Kelly was blinded by the sudden light and couldn't see it properly. The figure flicked a light switch beside the door, and the rest of the room was illuminated by lights in a ceiling that was at least fifteen feet high.

There was nothing in the room. No furniture, no trash, no bones, nothing. On the side opposite the door, there were two large openings that were framed in bricks. They could have been the openings to old sewers from colonial times. A soft sound of water drifted up from them.

Richard Gilman stood in the doorway. Silently, he came inside and closed the door behind him.

"Please," Kelly said, "you have to let me go. I won't say anything, I promise."

Gilman grinned and nodded his head.

"You were only supposed to film some 'fluff' pieces. 'Come visit beautiful Innsmouth by the sea.' That's all. No Woodward & Bernstein theatrics. But I can't really blame you, can I? Its Sargent's fault . . . and Olmstead's as well. They'll be dealt with presently." Gilman sighed. "It's always the old ones that are the hardest to convince."

Kelly cried. "Please, let me go. People will notice if I'm missing."

Gilman laughed. "You overestimate your importance, my dear. You're just a minor reporter on a regional morning news program. You won't be missed by many."

"People will know. I've got family. I . . . I have followers. On Twitter. And Facebook!"

Reaching into his pocket, Gilman pulled out her cell phone. "Oh, we've got that covered. My secretary is already posting on your behalf. See?" He held up the phone, which showed a large seafood dinner. "On Facebook: 'Having a marvelous dinner at Almeda's on the Innsmouth shore.' Lovely what technology can do, isn't it? And later you're going to be posting on Instagram all the great things you're buying at the shops on State Street."

"That won't work! People know me!"

Gilman looked disapprovingly at her phone. "It's already done. Tomorrow you'll announce how you've just been offered a co-host job out in Montana somewhere. The details will come later, but they're not that important anyway. A few posts, some videos and then you'll just fade away. We've done it before."

Kelly pulled on the rope.

"Perry! Perry knows where I am. He'll tell the police."

"There are no police around here—or haven't you noticed that? Private security firm. Owned by me. As for Perry . . . well, hard for him to talk without a head."

Kelly started shaking. "What the fuck do you mean? What did you do?"

"When Bob came to Innsmouth in '27 (and, yes, he is *that* old), do you know what he saw? Monsters! That's how he thought of the people here. He was afraid of them, so he brought the government here to wipe them out. But once he started to change, he realized that they weren't 'monsters' at all because he was one of them. What he forgot to ask was: 'What are the monsters afraid of?'"

The phone chirped.

"Hmm. Your dinner's gotten 83 'likes' already."

From far down the tunnels came the sound of something rising out of the water.

"What came out from beneath Y'ha-nthlei was as far beyond the Deep Ones and Dagon as they are above us. Below that chasm lies a nightmare made flesh which came to us, and we served it. In response it gave us all we wanted and desired, for the affairs of man are a trifle to it. All it required was the sacrifice of the Deep Ones, which we gave gladly.

"But," Gilman sighed sadly, "we were greedy. We 'overfished,' so to speak. The number of Deep Ones diminished to new lows, but the hunger and demand never left. So we had to attract more people to come here and settle. Hence the 'revitalization' of Innsmouth. Many of those with the old blood came willingly and, when they cooperated, their fortunes blossomed. And if they're sacrificing the lives of their future children and grandchildren, what of it? They get to live well, and that's all that's really important."

The sound of something wet, like flippers, slapping on bricks came out of the tunnels and grew louder.

Kelly cried, "Please . . . please . . ."

"There's always a minority to exploit, always. At first it was the degenerate townsfolk, then the Deep Ones and later it'll be something else. We have to replenish, you see? We need to 're-seed.'"

Slowly, Kelly was beginning to understand.

Watery, lidless eyes caught the light and reflected back from the darkness of the tunnel.

"What does a farmer do when the herd fails to reproduce? He brings in new cows from outside. He brings in new blood and then steps away and let's nature take its course.

"You're young and healthy. You're got a lot of productive, or reproductive, years ahead of you."

Kelly watched what was coming out of the tunnels. Some of them walked, some crawled by the use of rudimentary flippers. Skin had been replaced by scales and fins jutted out at anatomically impossible angles. Only a semblance of humanity was suggested.

Gilman walked back to the door. "And after all, anything's better than morning TV, right?"

He flicked off the lights and walked out the door while Kelly screamed.

Weltschmerz

I woke up alive again today.

Looking up at the bedroom ceiling, I silently cursed the fact that I hadn't died in my sleep. I awoke to another day in the same hell as always; facing a lifetime of days to come exactly like this one. Scratching my head, I swung my feet out of bed onto that tan carpet I hated so much. I shut off my alarm, and the sound of Ann snoring filled the room. I looked over at my wife. As usual, the covers were over her head and she was just an amorphous blob.

It was the same as every morning had been for the last twenty years: I got up, shaved, took a shower (being careful not to use all the hot water). Gulped down a few bites of something; didn't matter what it was. All done as quietly as possible. After I got dressed, I looked back at Ann. She was still asleep and snoring. Twenty years ago, I would have woken her up to kiss her goodbye. Now there didn't seem to be much point.

It was a cold October morning and neither the car nor I liked it very much. The engine struggled while it turned over, but it was an old car and that was just to be expected. We couldn't afford to buy a new car, so I was stuck with one that was outdated ten years ago. I shifted it into gear and it started moving slowly. The cassette player had been broken for a while now, and I had to make do with the inane chatter of morning radio. From there, I parked at the usual commuter lot and took the bus into Providence.

Buses are unusual places. People thrown together for a short period of time tend to show their differences. Some, like myself, sit in stony silence, anxious for the trip to end. Others become loud and boisterous, insistent upon being noticed and heard. On any given day, I can learn about any number of private lives through one-sided cell phone conversations. Love, sex, hate—all through a phone. And the homeless are either frighteningly silent or willing to debate politics with anyone who dares to disagree with them. I close my eyes and try to decipher where the bus is by the turns and movements. I've gotten fairly good at it. I can pretty much tell where I am at any point on the ride from Warren to Providence. Sadly, this is often the highlight of my day.

Once the bus arrives at Kennedy Plaza, I avoid the traffic on my way to the Fleet Bank building. Once it was the Hospital Trust building. Before that, it used to be the Old Stone Bank building. I've come to realize that my life is marked by remembering how things *used* to be. Once inside, I sign in, take the elevator to the third floor, and punch my code into the keypad to open the door to the Dividends and Securities Department. I sit down at my desk, four rows down and two chairs to the left, and log into the computer. I nod a silent 'good morning' to my fellow prisoners and open up my work for the day.

My cubicle in hell is a clean one. All the files and printouts are in order in plastic holders on my desk. The desk drawers hold only what is needed. A few historical reports in cardboard covers take the bottom drawer. The second holds my employee handbook. Updated every year and never opened otherwise. The small top drawer holds the few stationery items I use: pens, paper clips, tape, scissors, staples, and a few candy bars for the afternoon lag. On the top of my desk is only my computer monitor, keyboard, mouse, a phone, and the plastic file holder. No photos. No doodads. No mementos. There's no rule against them. Flexman, who sits in the desk behind me, has framed pictures of his wife, his kids, a "world's greatest dad" award, a rock that he brought back from a beach in Hawaii, and a little plastic square that says "Jesus loves you, but I'm not Jesus." I used to have a picture of Ann on my desk, but that was a long time ago.

I suppose 'cubicle' is the wrong way to describe our situation. A 'cubicle' suggests walls that separate every work station. We have no walls. There are rows of desks, set in pairs. From where I sat, I could see across the room in every direction. There were maybe twenty rows and six columns of desks. I never bothered to count them all. To the right, near the front of the room, were the two manager's offices. They were the normal type of office one sees in a bank. Nothing particularly special, but they were made that way so that the inhabitants could be interchangeable. In the fifteen years since I'd been in that department, there had been five different people in those offices. It would take quite an effort for me to recall all their names.

The current manager was Tim Sympkof, who clearly saw the department as only a quick stop onto something better. He rarely bothered to talk to any of us and spent most of his days in his office, listening to one of those digital radios. The only time Sympkof came out of his office was if any of the executives came into the room, and that almost never happened. Most of the time, Sympkof left the running of the department to his assistant manager, Harry Helger, who'd probably been with the bank since the first account was opened. Harry was nice but essentially useless. He'd managed to keep his job by not making anyone mad and, basically, no one wanted his job anyway.

Through the years, the number of the people in the department varied. When I first started, nearly every desk was full. Now, with the economic 'downturn,' only about half the desks were being used. The work hadn't decreased, only the number of people to do it.

My job was handling dividends. I tracked securities and verified who was holding what and how much they were due. It was tedious and laborious and mind-numbing. If anyone ever says that they love accounting, then you know you are dealing with a madman. No one loves accounting any more than anyone loves cleaning out toilets, but it's something that needs to be done and it drives every aspect of the economy. Still, you'll never see a television commercial bragging about how exciting it is to be an accountant. There are no television shows about accountants solving crimes. Even truck driver school commercials look more exciting.

When I started, we still did everything by hand. Slowly, everything changed over to computers with new programs and e-mail and the like. I'd always been good with such things, so I picked them up pretty easily, which is probably how I managed to hold onto my job. All our computers were connected to the mainframe and we had access to e-mail and Internet, but we were constantly monitored. I could get around the spyware the bank put in but never bothered to. There wasn't much I wanted to spend my time looking at anyway. Flexman was different, though; so one afternoon I set up his computer so he could surf the Web as much as he wanted without anyone knowing. I mainly did it so he'd stop talking to me so much. But after I did that, he came to me with any computer problems . . . and he always seemed to be having problems.

"Hey, Doug," he whispered to me, "my computer's doing it again."

I turned and looked at him and he pointed at his monitor.

Sighing, I stood up and went and looked. The screen had several pornographic sites open. "I told you to be careful what you looked at."

Flexman laughed. He was a big man and his smile could take up half his face. The fact that he was black never made much difference to me. Black, white, Asian, whatever. We're all just as pointless.

The computer was locked. Somewhere there was a virus trying to get through.

"I'm going to have to shut this down. You're going to lose any work you had."

He moved aside and I pressed the right buttons in the right order and the screen went black. Five seconds later, the Microsoft Windows logo came up. I bypassed the log-in and opened the programs. "There," I said, "you should be all right now."

"You da man, Doug! You got, like, a gift with computers. Why don't you go into programming or something?"

"Oh, yeah, right. Go into the only other field that's as boring as accounting? No, thanks!"

As I looked up from Flexman's monitor, I could see there was a girl pushing a cart in the middle of the room. She was one of the 'runners': people who 'run' things from department to department that can't be sent via e-mail. There aren't as many of them as there used to be. She was thin, and young. Maybe twenty-two at the most. Her hair was straight, shoulder-length, dark with a streak of bright red dyed in the front. Her lips, and breasts, were full and I could have sworn she was looking at me. She threw a package in her cart and left the room.

"Who's that?" Flexman said.

I went back to my seat. "Just some runner," I said, "she'll probably quit by the end of the month like they all do." Punching my keyboard, I got back to work looking at the endless series of numbers.

At lunchtime, I logged off my computer and headed to the cafeteria. Fleet was one of the few places I knew that still had a cafeteria for their employees, and almost everyone used it. Situated on the fourth floor, it took up a large area and was designed with large windows that looked out over Kennedy Plaza. The place was always crowded and table space was usually at a premium. I sat down in my usual place: table for two, near the back wall, in a corner away from the windows. Around me, the tables filled and people came and went. It was like high school all over again. The tellers ate with the tellers, the managers ate with the managers, departments grouped together, and there was not an executive in sight. They ate in their private dining room upstairs on the tenth floor with their own kitchen staff. I'd heard that the food there was much better than what we were given here.

I took out my lunch and started to eat. It was plain turkey on white bread. No lettuce, tomato, or mayo. A small bag of chips with a bottle of water and some baby carrots finished the meal. I never brought anything to read. I'd never be able to concentrate with all the noise around me, and I hated to start reading something knowing that I was on a time limit. Never was one for reading newspapers either.

"This seat taken?"

It took a second before I realized that someone was speaking to me. That never happened.

I looked up and it was the 'runner' from before. She had a tray with something that pretended to be a hamburger but was probably more akin to a circle of cardboard. It was covered in cheese, lettuce, onions, pickles, and some oddly colored sauce. A tray of nachos was the side order and looked to have just about everything on it possible.

She was smiling, and I could see that her nose had been pierced.

"Hello? Can I sit here? There's no other seat available."

I could see several seats empty behind her.

"Um . . . sure. If you like."

"Thanks! Been a fucking long day already."

She sat down and immediately began to eat. There was a certain amount of animalistic joy in the way she attacked her hamburger. "I'm Maya, by the way."

I nodded. "I'm Doug. Doug Marsden."

She was wearing a thin shirt with mid-length sleeves. It was warm out, so they had the air conditioning on full-blast. I could tell that she wasn't wearing a bra, as two points started to rise up under her shirt. There was a hint of tattoos on her arm.

"So what do you do here, Doug?"

"Me? I . . . I work in Dividends and Securities."

She smiled. Her top lip turned up slightly. "Crap, that must be boring. How do you stand it?"

I nodded. "Well, you know, it's a job."

She scoffed. "I think I'd put a needle through my eye if I had to do that all day long."

As she ate, I looked at her more closely. Her hair was dyed black except for the streak of red in front. I couldn't tell if the red was her real hair color or not. Her ears were each pierced several times, and I unexpectedly caught myself wondering what else was pierced. Her eyes were green and her skin was soft and pink. Although not unhealthy, I doubted that she spent a lot of time in the sun. I think she caught me staring but didn't say anything.

"And what do you do, Maya?"

"I just started in the mail department. I'm a runner, you know. It keeps me busy. But I'm really a musician!"

"Oh?" I asked.

"Yeah, got a few things up on YouTube, y'know? All my own songs and everything. Look me up under 'Mayakeyes.' I'm looking to get something going."

I made a mental note for later and finished eating my sandwich.

Maya polished off her burger and started on her nachos.

"You don't talk much, do you, Doug?" she asked.

I looked up, startled at the question.

"Uh, no, not too much."

"That's all right. I like the strong, silent type."

She put her hand on mine. There was still cheese sauce on her fingers and I could feel it oozing between mine.

Near the windows, I could see a bunch of people from the mail room eating their lunch. There were several empty chairs.

"Are you sure you don't want to sit with your friends from your department?"

Maya looked over. "What? Them?" She scoffed and turned back to me. "Nah, they're boring. Insignificant assholes, the bunch of them. They're just too fucking stupid to realize it. But I've got a feeling about you, Doug, I think you *get* it. I can see it in your eyes."

She lifted her hand up, tracing her finger along the edge of my hand, and stood up. Maya stuck her finger in her mouth and sucked off the cheese. "Gotta run. Same time tomorrow, Doug?"

Without waiting for an answer, she turned and walked over to the trash and emptied her tray. She looked back at me and waved as she walked out of the room.

I sat there, feeling vaguely unsatisfied with the remainder of my lunch.

For the rest of the day, I struggled to concentrate on my work. I found myself looking up every time someone came into the room.

On the bus home, I miscalculated my position three times.

As I walked through the door, my phone beeped at me annoyingly. Ann had sent a text saying that she had to go to a church meeting tonight and I'd be on my own for dinner. I threw a frozen pizza in the microwave and ate it in front of a television that I wasn't watching anyway.

I sat down at the computer and tried to remember what Maya had said. I went to YouTube and typed in "Mayakeys," but nothing came up. I was sure that I'd remembered it correctly, but maybe my spelling was off. Tentatively, I typed in "Mayakeyes" and waited.

Four videos came up. Two just had the words "Maya Keyes," which told me virtually nothing. The other two looked to be home-made videos. One, I think, was in someone's basement somewhere, while the other one looked to be filmed outside.

I clicked on the basement one and sound exploded out of the computer speakers—loud, screeching sounds that could only be described as music by someone who had never heard any music before. I remembered punk music from when I was a kid, but this was beyond even that. Maya—I think it was Maya—was screaming and yelling and chanting, and I couldn't make out any words she said. It didn't even sound like English. I heard words like "Ktooloo" and "Daygon," but I couldn't say that they were even words. Maya, for her part, just jumped around the basement, screeching and gyrating as if she was having a seizure. I wondered if Fleet Human Resources knew about this. Maya was the only one in the video, and I couldn't tell if she was the one who filmed it as well.

The outside video looked as if it had been shot in a forest somewhere. There was a fire that Maya was dancing around, and it was apparently shot through one of those night goggles, because everything was in green as on those fake 'ghost-hunting' shows. The song started a little slower. I could hear an electric guitar, and then some synthesized drums came in. It was a strong, driving beat that gained in intensity as the song went on. I still couldn't tell a lot of what she was singing, but at least she wasn't screaming. I thought it was a love song, but then the beat got harder and more insistent and her voice got harsher and raspier. When she got to the chorus, she began singing about having sex with something called "my Deep One," which I couldn't figure out. Then she started thrashing back and forth, growling and howling and even, I thought, foaming at the mouth. I shut the computer off.

When Ann got home, I sat and listened to her tell me all about her day at the middle school where she taught and the church meeting. I had learned long ago how to listen to just enough to get by in case she quizzed me later. It was an endless litany of people I'd never meet and would never care about. When she asked how my day was, I just said it was a usual day. She looked at me, shrugged, and went back to her book.

That night, I had unusual dreams. I don't tend to dream too much and, when I do, they're not very remarkable. In this dream, I was wandering through a forest and it was dark. Somewhere there was something waiting for me and I was afraid that I was going to be late. Rushing forward, I came to a clearing where Maya stood, naked. I came to her and held her, but there was something off. She was not

the one who was waiting. There was something else . . . something beyond the trees that was waiting for me. I felt, rather than heard, it coming closer, closer—and then, suddenly, it was gone. I couldn't catch it,
whatever it was, and it had gotten away from me. I felt a sense of loss
and failure such as I had never felt before. In the dream, I sat down in
the clearing and cried, alone.

For the first time in years, I did not greet the morning with anger.

My regular routine was no different. I rode the same bus into work
and tried to concentrate on my mental game with myself, but some id-
iot two seats back wouldn't stop talking. Apparently someone had
gone crazy in Newport last night and wiped out his family with a knife.
Others joined in talking about how there'd been a lot of sirens in the
East Bay last night, and one woman whose brother worked at the
emergency room at Rhode Island Hospital said that they'd had a rash
of crazy, violent patients last night. I sat and tried to follow the progress of the bus in my mind. None of that had anything to do with me.

The morning passed quietly. Flexman spent most of his time on
the local news websites and kept trying to get me interested in what he
was reading. I just let him talk and, eventually, he quieted down. I kept
my eyes open, but Maya never entered the room.

At lunchtime, I took my lunch and, not knowing why I did it, sat
in a new seat, near the windows. It felt uncomfortable, being in the
light and in the center of people. I could sense that they felt it too, as if
I had intruded on their territory. Lunch today was a ham sandwich on
rye, dry. I was just about to bite into it when Maya plopped down next
to me; chicken parm sitting on her plate.

"Whew!" she said. "Didn't think I'd find you, Doug. What are you
doing sitting over here?"

"Just thought it'd be a change."

She playfully frowned on me. "Change? You? Please! I bet you haven't even bought new clothes in years."

It was true. I hadn't.

"I . . . I, uh, watched your YouTube videos."

Her eyes widened and she smiled. At that instant, knowing that I
had caused that smile was the greatest feeling in the world to me.

"You did? No fucking way! What did you think?"

"They're . . . they're different. You have a very distinctive style."

"You really think so? I can't tell you what it means to hear you say that!"

And she leaned forward and hugged me. Her breasts pushed into my arm, and I felt a pleasant warmth growing within me.

Some of the people around us took notice.

"I didn't really understand some of the words, though."

"Really? That's OK. The more you listen to them, the clearer they get."

My mind raced for something to say to keep the conversation going. "Where do you get your inspiration from?"

She laughed.

"Lovecraft, of course."

I looked at her. I had no idea what she was talking about.

My confusion must have been written on my face, because she answered before I even had to ask the obvious question.

"You know! Dude who lived in Providence in the 1930s? Wrote all those horror stories?"

"I . . . I don't know who you mean. I don't read much fiction."

"Are you fucking serious? How long you live in Rhode Island?"

I broke eye contact and looked back at my sandwich. "All my life, pretty much."

"And you don't fucking know Lovecraft? Maybe I was wrong about you, Doug."

"What do you mean?"

"I thought you understood. I thought you knew how the world was. I thought you and me connected."

I was stunned and my mouth hung open.

"Maya, I just met you yesterday! How could you know me?"

She looked at me, hard. Then she laughed. "I was only fucking with you, Doug! I know you, all right. Here."

She reached into her bag and pulled out a paperback. It was tattered and showed signs of having been read many times. The title read *The Best of H. P. Lovecraft: Bloodcurdling Tales of Horror and the Macabre,* and the cover was a colorless grey thing of what looked like different scenes in a kind of montage.

"Read this. You'll be amazed, trust me."

I had a flashback to movies about hippies trying to get the straight kids to try drugs, telling them that "it'll blow your *mind*, man!"

Maya took out a pen. "I'll underline some of the stories you should read first. These are the *best* ones." She spent a few seconds writing in the book and then handed it to me.

I muttered a "thanks" and went back to my lunch.

"Don't disappoint me, Doug! I know that you'll love this stuff."

"I won't—I promise!" And suddenly it occurred to me that it had become very important to me that I not disappoint Maya.

She went back to her lunch, which had an extraordinary amount of cheese on it.

"There's a lotta stuff out there, Doug. You shouldn't close yourself off to it."

"What do you mean?"

"You know, different experiences, different feelings. You need to open yourself up to them. Allow yourself to let them come through you. What are your plans for this weekend?"

"Um, no real plans. I have some yard work to do. There's always something to fix around the house."

Maya shook her head.

"Come over to my place. You'll have more fun than mowing the fucking lawn."

I held up my left hand.

"Maya, I'm married. See?" I wiggled the ring on my finger.

She gave me a 'yeah, right' look.

"No, you're not, Doug. You know you're not."

She stood up and grabbed the book back. She quickly wrote something else in it. "Here's my number. I'll be waiting for your call."

Maya leaned close and whispered in my ear. "I can show you things you always wanted to see, Doug, what the world really means and how it tastes." She licked my ear and I could feel that her tongue was pierced too.

As Maya walked out of the cafeteria, I could feel many pairs of eyes watching me, but I didn't care. I was watching her ass and desperately wanted to touch it.

Back at my desk, I did something I never thought I would do: I refitted my computer so that I could surf the Internet without the tracking programs seeing. I set off to learn as much about H. P. Lovecraft as I could and, by the end of the day, I had learned quite a bit.

To my surprise, there were actually a good many websites devoted to Lovecraft. From them I got an education on the man who was born in Providence in 1890 and would die there in 1937. I read about his unusual childhood, his relationship with his mother, and his writing career. His work was revolutionary, transforming not only horror but science fiction. Some critics considered him the twentieth-century version of Poe, and he had lived most of his life in my home state and I never knew.

I felt a poke from behind.

"Yo, Doug, what you doing?" Flexman asked.

"Just a little extra reading. You know how it is."

Flexman laughed. "All right, my man! Didn't know you had it in ya!"

I gave him a thumbs-up and went back to reading.

The more I read, the more I felt closer to Lovecraft. He didn't have a lot of happiness or success in his life and felt that he was separated from humanity. It came across in his philosophy. He felt that man and all his worries and concerns were meaningless.

Once in college, when I'd studied philosophy and literature before I met Ann and it was decided I'd become an accountant, I was in an ethics class and the professor asked everyone to think about what their personal philosophy was and how it impacted their lives. After much thought, I decided that I had no personal philosophy. I'd never been religious, never been in the military. If anything, I was a nihilist. I didn't care about anything. Nothing was important, least of all me.

That night, I read several of the shorter stories. Ann was surprised to see me reading but didn't say anything about it. While imaginative, I couldn't really understand the point of some of the tales and they didn't seem to line up to what I had read online about Lovecraft's philosophy. I'd never really been one for fiction. No imagination, I suppose.

I put the book down and went to sleep.

That night I had the dream again, but it felt different. I was back in the clearing and naked Maya was holding my hand, pointing toward something further away in the trees. Whatever it was, it was waiting for me and it was important that I find it.

I tried to move, but my legs were heavy and weak. I was tied to the earth, which clutched at me and tried to pull me down. I screamed to Maya to help, but she turned and walked away. On her naked back I could see a large tattoo. I couldn't tell what it was, but it was greenish and was a humanoid figure with tentacles on its face and wings on its back. As she walked, I could swear that the wings moved.

The ground swallowed me whole and I screamed.

The next morning, Ann 'reminded' me that she was going to the yearly meeting of her church group. I'd forgotten. If, that is, she had even told me to begin with. Every year, her church group got together with the other church groups in the state and had meetings and elections and such. I remember taking Ann to one a long time ago and being bored while I waited for her to get out. Since then, she'd arranged her own transportation and would usually stay over at whatever hotel was hosting the thing. If the timing of the meeting was strangely coincidental, I didn't notice it.

Less than an hour after she left, I was holding Maya's paperback in my hand, staring at the page with her phone number on it. Many years had passed since a girl gave me her phone number. I just had to find the courage to call. In the end, I compromised. Instead of calling, I sent her a text. Not even a minute later, I got her response: "Come over. I'm waiting." The second text was her address on Barnes Street on the East Side of Providence.

The place was easy to find. It was an older building, probably built around the turn of the century or so. I had no idea what architectural style it was, but it looked primarily Victorian. I only knew that it was old. It was a three-story tenement and had been split into two sides. The first-floor apartments had three panel windows, the kind that bulged out and you could make a nice window seat there. Maya's apartment was on the left side, third floor. I pressed the button and she came running down.

"Doug!" she squealed. "You came! Wasn't sure you would."

I looked at her. Maya's body was tight and young. She was wearing a kind of tank top that pressed her breasts up and together. She had tattoos on her arms. She had on a pair of the shortest shorts I'd ever seen and her legs were long and toned. She hugged me and, before I knew what was happening, kissed me on the lips, hard. Her tongue darted into my mouth and I could feel it seeking me. I moved my tongue and touched hers and felt myself getting hard.

"C'mon inside!" she said and took my hand.

We climbed the stairs and she led me into her apartment. It was a small place. One bedroom with a living room that connected to an open kitchen with a small table. A bathroom was between the bedroom and living room. The entire place was filled with stuff. There were books everywhere. A huge bookshelf was packed with DVDs and CDs. There were some movie posters on the wall, but I didn't recognize any of the movies. They had titles like *Re-Animator* and *Dunwich Horror* and weren't in English. There was a small synthesizer keyboard in the corner, and various other musical equipment was scattered about. A sofa was against one wall and it looked as if it had seen better days. A large TV was facing the sofa, and it was playing something I'd never seen before.

"So whaddaya think?"

"It's very nice. Cozy." I replied.

She laughed. "No, it's not. It's a fucking closet, but that's not why I took the place."

When I didn't respond, she replied, "The address? Hello? Lovecraft lived here!"

I looked around again. "He did?"

Maya scoffed. "Not in this apartment! He had the big one downstairs with his aunt. This was where he lived when he left his wife in New York and came back to Providence. Some of his best work was written here . . . can't you feel it?"

All I felt was uncomfortable. Maybe I had made a mistake. I wasn't really sure why I had come here anyway, and it seemed more uncertain with each minute.

"You, uh, you really seem to be into Lovecraft."

"Are you fucking kidding me? I live for it! Look at this!" She pointed to a tattoo on her right arm. I bent closer to get a better look. It was a black and white portrait of Lovecraft tattooed on her arm with various Gothic beasts around him. It was impressive.

She flopped down on the couch and patted the seat next to her. I sat down where she had indicated and could smell her body. It wasn't sweet and full of perfume: it was earthy and strong. "What are you watching?" I asked.

"It's *Dagon*," she replied. "One of Stuart Gordon's Lovecraft films. This one's pretty good even if it has more to do with 'The Shadow over Innsmouth' than fucking 'Dagon.'"

I looked at the screen. A woman was being suspended in chains over some sort of pit. She was naked and covered in what looked like oil. Someone, the 'hero,' I guess, was trying to save her. He didn't do a very good job.

"This is what Lovecraft is all about," Maya said. "There's all these gods that live outside our world that used to rule here and want to do so again. They're fighting to break through and come back. It's a constant fight to keep them out."

"Really?" That wasn't what I had gotten out of my reading. "You're sure that's what Lovecraft meant?"

"Lovecraft's about the *outside* trying to get in."

Maya moved closer to me, and I felt her weight pressing on my arm. She began to rub my chest and open the buttons on my shirt. Her hand slipped inside and moved in circles as her fingers lightly touched my nipple. I looked at her and saw the most intense look on her face. The kind of look, I imagine, that a wild animal has as it starts to devour its prey. She started to lick my neck.

"I . . . I don't think this is a good idea. Maybe I should go."

I made to get up and she pushed me back down.

"You don't want to go, Doug," she said into my ear. "You want to stay right here. You *need* to stay right here."

Maya unbuckled my belt and zipped the fly down. She reached inside and grabbed me and rubbed her hand up and down. I couldn't resist any longer and grabbed her face and kissed her. This time, my tongue was the one searching for hers. I reached down and grabbed her breast and squeezed. Her nipple grew hard, and I could tell that it was also pierced. Maya broke away and quickly took her shirt off and threw it away. She was beautiful. Her breasts were large and firm. The nipples were hard and erect and her areolas were large and swollen. With a quick motion, she ripped my pants off and moved between my legs.

My eyes were closed as she took me in her mouth and sucked. I ran my fingers through her hair, bringing her head up and down. The piercing in her tongue flicked over the tip of my penis. Before I finished, I looked down at her. On her back there was the same tattoo from my dream; the green monster with an octopus face and wings. As she moved back and forth, I could swear that the wings were flying.

Later, lying on the couch (we had not even made it to the bed), I felt her ass and traced little circles on it. We'd been talking about Lovecraft, of course, and I'd been saying how I understood his philosophy. Maya, for the most part, wasn't getting what I was trying to say.

"You don't really believe that, do you?"

"Yes," I said, "I do. Nothing really matters. We're all insignificant."

"No, you don't believe that."

"Why do you say that?"

She leaned up on one arm and looked at me. Her face was beautifully intense.

"Because if you did, then nothing would matter to you. No rules, no laws, no morality. You'd do whatever you fucking wanted because none of it makes a difference. Good, bad, indifferent. They'd all be the same."

"I do what I want."

Maya laughed. "Bull-fucking-shit! You don't do *anything* you want! You work a job you hate. You're stuck with a woman you don't love. You follow every fucking rule and regulation you have thrown at you."

I was getting mad. "I came here, didn't I?"

She smiled. "Yeah, you did. But who fucked who, Doug?" Her lips curled into a smirk.

"You wanna show me you really don't give a fuck about anyone or anything, Doug?" She reached over to a table next to the couch and felt around for something. "Take one of these."

Maya held out her hand. Lying on her palm were two black pills. I'd never seen anything so black. Each one had a large N on it in white.

"What are they?"

She waved her finger at me. "Uh-uh. No questions. Just take it."

"I'm on medications. I can't just take anything—"

Maya jumped off the couch. "Fuck it. I knew you weren't the right one."

I grabbed her arm and pulled her toward me.

"Give it to me." I said. She put the pill between her teeth and leaned toward me. Our lips met and she pushed the pill into my mouth. I cold-swallowed it. She popped the other pill into her mouth and swallowed. I grabbed her ass and pushed her down on me. "Now we'll see," I whispered in her ear, "who's doing the fucking."

Time ceased to have any meaning. It was just a concept. A concept that I, in my ultimate power, was rejecting. I'd never taken drugs before in my life. I remembered all the things I'd read and heard about acid trips and highs, but this didn't feel anything like that. It was like being in a dream but being fully awake.

I felt rather than saw Maya beside me. We were in the clearing but we were also in her apartment, limbs intertwined and thrusting. I was here but I was also there. My mind was split and I could move and function in both places at the same time. Off in the distance, something was coming for me.

In the here, I was looking in Maya's face as her eyes rolled up inside her head.

In the there, she took my hand and beckoned me further to the other side of the clearing.

In the here, my hands were roughly rubbing her breasts as her veins became brighter and shone through her skin.

In the there, I stepped outside the opposite edge of the clearing and heard something coming closer.

In the here, Maya's breath became short and ragged.

In the there, something moved toward me without moving.

In the here, she sang and chanted with the voice of something inhuman and *outside*.

In the there, something moved through the wood of the trees and shifted and ululated as it came forward like a mist.

In the here, I licked the sweat from between her breasts and tasted blood.

In the there, something crawled toward me and in its center was chaos.

In the here, Maya wept and laughed.

In the there, something opened my mind and stepped inside and I allowed it to.

In the here, my hands went to Maya's back and I felt leathery wings.

In the there, the voice spoke to me and I finally understood what it meant.

In the here, I felt myself ripping Maya apart.

In the there, I knew my insignificance and saw its truth.

When I awoke, Maya was in pieces on the floor. A bloodstained butcher knife was in my hand. I looked at her and felt only envy. I took a shower, got dressed, and left. If anyone had heard anything, I didn't notice it. In my pocket were about two dozen of the black pills.

Maya was right. I hadn't really understood. I had been foolish and innocent in my blindness. What I had thought was insignificance hadn't even begun to touch the truth. The chaos had shown me when it came into my mind. Nothing of man mattered. None of the history, none of the accomplishments, the wars, the heartbreak, none of it made any difference. The cosmos was awash with creatures whose footsteps eclipsed our civilizations in length and indifference. Laws, rules, and morality were mere trappings man clothed himself in while he desperately tried to convince himself that he mattered at all. Now I understood it all and what it truly meant to be insignificant. Nothing was important, which was liberating and damning all at the same time.

That's what Lovecraft had meant. The 'gods' and 'monsters' were just window dressing, something for the 'earth-centric' minded ones to latch on to. When you finally understood it all, you knew that there was no reason for anything. There were no 'gods' waiting to reclaim the earth. There was only the universe, spiraling onward, unknowing, uncaring, indifferent to man, who puffed up his chest like a little puppy barking at a garbage truck.

When I got home, I moved a chair to face the front door. I got a large knife from the kitchen and sat down to wait for Ann. Time no longer had any hold on me. I sat in the chair, swallowed black pills, and waited. When I was finished with Ann, I'd get on the bus and go to work and show them how insignificant they were. I'd show everyone how insignificant they all were and make them look into my face and see and know that they had never been important, they had never mattered. None of it ever had.

Hellhounds on the Trail

On May 1st, 1941, Robert Easton walked into the Louisiana swamp. He never came out.

*   *   *

It was early in April 1941 when Alan Lomax summoned Robert Easton to his office at the Library of Congress. Easton had been there before, of course, as one of Lomax's field recorders, but the assignments had gotten fewer lately and it had become impossible not to notice that most of the staff that remained were working on cataloguing and not out in the field where they should be. Not that Easton had been one of Lomax's top agents anyway. Easton had a habit of saying the wrong thing at the wrong time and failing to show deference or respect on some subjects. Still, in many ways Easton was tenacious and had managed to get recordings of several musicians who had refused to cooperate before. His methods were sometimes questionable but usually effective.

But Easton had not expected to find the normally energetic and motivated Lomax to be so deflated. As usual, Lomax's office was covered with papers and books and maps and records and aluminum and acetate discs. If there was an order to the chaos, only Lomax understood it.

"Sit down, Bob," Lomax said with an unbelievable dourness. It was a warm spring day outside, but it felt like the middle of winter inside the office.

Easton waited patiently for Lomax to begin. The six-foot-tall man was only thirty-six years old but had done more to preserve America's musical heritage than anyone ever had before. Because of Lomax, much that would have been lost to the mists of time had been preserved. But things were different now.

"The winds are changing, Bob," Lomax said as he almost fell into his chair with a sigh.

Easton lit a cigarette and took a deep drag even as Lomax eyed him with disapproval. "What do you mean, Alan?"

Lomax turned half away from Easton and the cigarette smoke to look out the window. It was a good view with the Lincoln Memorial away in the distance.

"I've got friends in Congress who tell me that we will be losing our funding."

Easton nodded. "I'm not surprised. I never could understand how you got politicians to fund this thing in the first place. How much longer do we have?"

Lomax stood up and stared out of the window. He put his hands in his pockets.

"A year at the most. In that time, we have to wrap up as much as possible. I've got most of the units working on the indexing and paperwork. They'll have their hands full for most of that time. But . . . there are a few projects that I've been putting off that we're going to finish while we still can."

"You mean Son House?" Easton said excitedly. The legendary blues musician had been one of the great holes in Lomax's collection. He'd gotten most of the greats like Johnson and Muddy Waters, but Son House had always escaped him. It was as if the man had vanished off the face of the earth.

Lomax turned around and faced Easton. "Yes, that's one of them. We've finally got a few good leads on him and we *will* get him recorded if it's the last thing I do."

"Great! When do I leave?"

Lomax shook his head. "No, that's not what I called you in for. I'm going after House myself and I'll get him. I've got something else in mind for you."

There was a file on the desk that looked older than all the others. Lomax picked it up and handed it to Easton, who casually leafed through it. There was a short, handwritten report along with a drawn map and an old picture of a small group of black men sitting on the porch of a feed store.

"This is something I've been holding for a while now. I've never dared to send anyone else after it."

"What is it?" Easton asked. Already Easton felt that he was being pawned off with a 'lame duck' case while Lomax chased his white whale.

"I made some notes. They're in the file."

Lomax sat down and looked at Easton. The intensity of his stare made Easton uneasy.

"This music was something I'd never heard before. I only heard a bit of it and that only briefly, but I've never been able to forget it. Sometimes, when I wake up in the middle of the night, I can still hear it. I didn't follow up on it then, but I want to now while we still have the chance. I wrote down what I remember as well as a contact name."

Lomax stood up and signaled the end of the meeting. The two men shook hands, but as Easton opened the door to leave, Lomax added, "Bob, be careful of the contact."

Easton smirked. "Why?"

"Because he spent the last five years in Parchman Farm."

"What's that? A cotton farm?"

Lomax scoffed. "Prison. He was in for nearly beating a man to death with his fists."

*   *   *

That night, Easton looked over the file.

The few pages of handwritten notes he now knew were from Lomax. The map was a crude attempt at directions to something, although Easton couldn't make much sense of it. The picture was meaningless.

Easton sat back and read Lomax's report.

"It was back in 1935 when it happened. I was helping my father, who was the first to record the rural musicians. We were working mostly out of Mississippi then. One night, when I was standing outside a juke because it was too dangerous for me, a white man, to go inside, a black man came up to me.

"We started talking about the music. Robert Nighthawk was playing that night, and his music sounded wilder than usual. I could see a group of men standing nearby, watching us while they drank.

"'Why you here, white boy?' he asked me.

"'I'm from the Library of Congress in Washington. I'm trying to record this music before it disappears. It's for history. We want to preserve the music and the heritage.'

"'I know that's why your daddy's here. Why are *you* here?'

"I smiled. 'Because I like the music.'

"He laughed at that, and it made me feel a little better for my safety. I still didn't dare to go inside the juke though.

"'And I want to know where it comes from. It's so primal. So . . . so primitive. There's been nothing like it before.'

"He smiled. 'Shit,' he said, 'this ain't nothing. You want some *real* music, you come to Louisiana sometime. We got music there that makes this sound like angels singing. Music like . . .'

"He started doing something which I hesitate to call singing. It was a mix of music and notes and grunts and animal songs. Its cadence was like nothing I'd ever heard before, and it seemed that he managed to create his own chorus. Some blues musicians can make one guitar sound like an orchestra. That's what he was doing with his voice.

"At the sound, the men standing nearby became alarmed and one motioned to my new friend, who instantly stopped singing. He nodded acceptingly and turned back to me.

"Quietly, he said, 'You wanna hear more, come find me at Reed's Feed in Lockport off 308. Name's Willie Brown.'"

"About a month later, I made a detour to Louisiana. When I found Reed's Feed, I was told that Willie Brown had been arrested the week before for almost beating a man to death. Beyond that, I could learn nothing more. No one wanted to tell me anything about Brown or his music. On a whim, I took a picture of the feed store, always hoping to go back some day, but I never did. I have never found anything like that sound Willie Brown made outside that juke back in '34."

Easton looked at the photo again. There were three men standing on the porch in front of a store, whose sign could barely be deciphered as 'Reed's Feed.' The men were all black and, from their look, very unhappy farmers. Two were older men, while one was probably in his mid-thirties. All were looking at the camera, and the picture taker, with obvious hatred and contempt. The more Easton stared, the more he thought that there was something behind the men, standing in the shadows, but he could not make it out. It was like a smudge in the photograph itself.

The map was Lomax's rough drawing of the location of Reed's Feed, with some road marks such as route numbers and arrows pointing to various towns. Easton had an uncomfortable feeling that the roads were probably all unpaved.

Easton was feeling more than ever that Lomax had sent him off on a wild goose chase. After all, he had no performer's names, no lists of jukes, not even a sample of the music. But, he reasoned, he might be able to salvage something out of it. Easton had always felt that the collection was weak in Cajun music so maybe he would just make a token effort to find this 'root music' Lomax wanted and spend the rest of his time recording some zydeco. Besides, something about that photograph made him uneasy.

*   *   *

Three days later found Easton in Louisiana with his recording gear stowed safely in his car. The gear was heavy and cumbersome and, in truth, really needed two men to handle properly. But, as Easton well knew, one man could handle it if needed and if he had enough experience. It was best set up in a room somewhere, preferably a hotel room that could be adjusted for acoustics and furniture removed if necessary. There were times, however, when Easton had recorded performers in their own kitchens, but the quality was not the best. Recording in a juke, or an outside concert, was the worst and to be avoided if at all possible. There was a smaller unit that could be carried over the shoulder with a strap, but the microphone was limited in such cases so Easton preferred not to use it if he didn't have to.

The beginning of his investigation was exactly as fruitless as Easton had expected. No one in New Orleans had admitted to knowing anything about Willie Brown (though many had snickered when asked), Reed's Feed, or any music outside of zydeco. Easton had spent a few days recording some minor zydeco musicians, but even their music seemed uninspired and limp. Word spread quickly that a man from the Library of Congress was in the city looking to record musicians, and soon Easton was subjected to all manner of performers of various and dubious quality. There was even one very earnest young man who claimed loudly that he was Robert Johnson, but whose guitar playing was more akin to that of a cat screeching in heat.

One performer, noticing Easton's lack of interest, boldly asked, "Just what the hell music you looking for, fella?"

Unsure, Easton shook his head and could only respond in a meek, timid voice, "I'll know when I hear it."

Several times Easton drove out alone along Route 308, looking for the elusive feed store, but could not find it. Lomax's map was worse than useless. Whatever Lomax's talents, mapmaking was not one of them. Easton could not remember a time when he'd been more frustrated. He had been ready to give up when he stopped at a Texaco station along the more populous Route 1 in Raceland. There, a young white boy who was trying his best to emulate Texaco's famed 'man with a star' motto busily filled Easton's gas tank and washed the car windows.

On a lark, Easton asked, "You wouldn't happen to know where I can find 'Reed's Feed' on 308, would you?"

The youth looked at him oddly.

"Why the hell would you want to go there?" he asked.

"I was told to look up an old friend there. Just where on 308 is it?"

The youth went back to washing the front window of the car, but his motions were less eager and accommodating. "Can't be much of a friend if'n you don't know where it is. Besides, it ain't on 308. It's on 306, but I wouldn't recommend you go there either, mister."

"Why's that?" Easton asked. His irritation level was continuing to rise.

Finishing the window cleaning, the youth with the name patch "Billy" sewn onto the nice new uniform put the gas hose back into the pump, even though the tank wasn't full yet, and said, "Let's just say you're a little 'pale' for them folk. That's $2.50, mister."

Easton drove back up Route 90 toward New Orleans. Shortly after passing through the Dufrene Ponds, he spotted a small marker for Route 306 off the main road. It was easy to see how he'd missed it before, as it was virtually overgrown with vegetation from a hanging tree. Easton took a right and began driving down 306.

Almost instantly, it was as if Easton had taken a turn into another place and time. The road was poorly paved, with deep potholes and sections that had lost pavement altogether. The trees were lush and overgrown as if they had never known an axe or the intrusion of man. Occasionally, a dirt road would break off with a worn, beaten mailbox the only sign that something human lived down there. No houses were viewable from the road, and it felt as if Easton had been swallowed whole by Jonah's whale.

The old Packard was beginning to protest against the bad road conditions when a turn opened into a clear space with a decrepit building flush against the forest on two sides. A few ancient Ford pickups were parked outside, and the sign above the door could barely be read as "Reed's Feed." A few men were sitting outside on the porch and eyed Easton angrily as he pulled in and parked.

Before he exited his car, Easton considered just driving away, but he had come this far. And, after all, he was just a researcher. Surely no one would feel a need to hurt a researcher, would they?

"Morning, folks," Easton said as he walked cautiously up to the feed store. "I'm looking for a Willie Brown. Anyone know him?"

The stony faces broke out in laughter as they shook their heads and pointed.

"I don't understand. What's so funny?"

An older man from in back of the group moved forward. Between a big smile, he replied, "Son, looking for a man named Willie Brown in these parts is like looking for John Smith up in New York City. What you want him for?"

"I was sent here by Alan Lomax. We work for the Library of Congress and we're recording rural musicians."

The group collectively shook their heads.

"Just another white man making money off our music," said one of the other men.

Easton stepped closer. "Now that's not true. We're not selling these recordings. We're making them in order to preserve this music before it dies out. A hundred years from now most of this music will be gone. Certainly the men and women who make it will be."

"What you want us for then?" said another, younger man. "Heard tell you already got most of the bluesmen in Mississippi."

As he got closer, Easton could tell that this was a strange mixture of men. There were about seven in all. Three were younger men, while four were obviously farmhands of some kind. They all deferred to the older man, who had not spoken since asking his first question.

Easton paused to wipe his forehead. The Louisiana heat was getting to him and the air seemed to waver between him and the men, like a smudge. On the far side of the building, the trees moved as if they were suffering a breeze, but there was no wind to be found that afternoon.

"About six years or so ago, Alan Lomax talked to Willie Brown outside of a juke in Mississippi. Robert Nighthawk was playing that night. Mr. Brown told Mr. Lomax that if he wanted to hear some 'real' music, then he was to come here, to Reed's Feed, and ask for Willie Brown."

The men stopped talking, and only the older man continued to look at Easton. Finally, he smiled again and laughed in a way that would have made Lomax very uneasy if he had heard it.

"Shit, yeah," the old man said, "I remember him. He was afraid to go inside the juke. Thought he was a smart man for that."

Easton walked up and held out his hand in greeting. "So you're Willie Brown? It's good to meet you, Mr. Brown."

Brown looked at the hand as if it might be hiding a gun or knife but finally shook it firmly. Easton knew that few white men in the South would willingly shake a black man's hand and that this gesture often helped to smooth over tensions.

"He came here looking for you about a month after you talked, but you weren't here."

The other men laughed at this.

"Yeah, that's one way of saying it. I was doing time up on the Farm. Went up about a week after we talked. So what you here for anyway?"

"Well, Mr. Lomax said that you sang him a bit of a tune that was like nothing he'd heard before. I came to hear more and record it if you're agreeable."

As one, the other men got up and moved away. A few drifted back into the store while others just walked off and disappeared into the trees off the road.

"What you wanna do that for? That music ain't for you."

Easton was nonplussed. Although he had faced such opposition before, generally playing to someone's sense of importance by placing them in the Library of Congress tended to overcome it.

"Mr. Brown, from what Mr. Lomax told me, this is a completely different form of music than we've ever heard before. Now, I know that this music is a part of your heritage and your people, but do you really want to see it disappear?"

"This music will never disappear. It has been made since man first crawled out of the ocean and will be made until such time as the earth is wiped clean. There's no need to 'preserve' it on a piece of vinyl. We preserve it ourselves. Now, mebbe what you need to do is get back in your nice car there and go back to recording drunk guitarists at jukes. This music we don't share."

Brown turned around and made to go back inside the feed store when Easton impulsively cried out, "I'll pay you $100!"

He regretted it the second he said it. Lomax would be furious, for one thing. The LoC was not in the habit of paying for recordings, and it would take up most of what money Easton had left. He'd have to wire Lomax for an advance just to get home.

But something told him that the music would be worth it.

Brown stopped and eyed Easton. Over the years, Easton had gotten used to having his measure taken by suspicious folk, but this was more intense. After a few seconds, Brown spoke.

"Be here at one A.M. tomorrow morning. Mebbe I be here, mebbe I won't. If I am, I'll take you to the music, but only one time and not in a hotel room. This'll be out in the woods. So you come on by, little white boy, if'n you got the balls."

*   *   *

The drive back to New Orleans was uneventful, but Easton felt that there was something wrong about himself. As if there were a bug or smell clinging to him that he could not see or reach.

For the rest of the night, Easton debated what to do.

He could call Lomax, of course, but was sure that Lomax would tell him to go no matter what. Lomax was like one of those people who run toward a disaster like a hurricane or a tornado just to take a picture. He could deny the whole thing ever happened. Just tell Lomax that he couldn't find Brown and no one else would talk to him. Given the flimsy leads that Lomax had given him, it'd be an easy sell.

And it wasn't as if Easton was any kind of crusader or anything. This wasn't his cause, it was Lomax's. It was more of a job than anything else. Still, there was something to be said for being the one to capture a recording of something entirely 'new.' This might even be something that trailed back to roots of African music and that, possibly, would mean Easton would be remembered for doing *something* with his life.

Was it worth it then? $100 and risking his life? By midnight, Easton was packing the portable unit and checking the battery. He slipped a steak knife into his pocket. He was surprised to find out just how vain and ambitious he truly was.

*   *   *

It was close to 1 A.M. when Easton pulled the Packard into the parking lot outside of Reed's Feed. There were about ten other cars already there; that surprised him, so he ended up parking almost on the side of the road, which would be something he would be very grateful for later.

Easton got out of his car and took out the portable recorder. He looked around, but all the cars were empty. The feed store was closed and dark. The more he looked at it in the dark, the more it appeared to be some sort of child's toy, constructed out of oddly sized toothpicks.

"Mr. Brown?" Easton whispered. "Are you here?"

A darker shadow detached itself from the porch and moved forward.

"Well, well, well," Brown said, "I would've bet my teeth that you wouldn't show, boy. Guess you really want that music after all."

It surprised Easton how much he wanted that music now.

He walked up to Brown on the porch. The man was dressed in worn work clothes that seemed as dark as his skin.

"Is it going to be inside then?"

Brown chuckled. "Shit, no. This ain't 'inside' music. You gots to make it outside, under the stars. Listen. Can't you hear it?"

Easton stood still and strained. He could barely hear *something*, but he couldn't tell what it was. It didn't have notes or instruments. It was like a primal pulse. As if the stars were beating out a rhythm nearby.

"You got the money?" Brown asked.

Easton pulled out an envelope and shoved it into Brown's hand. "I expect a good recording for my money."

Brown smiled. "Oh, you'll get your recording, all right. Come on."

Without another word, Brown turned and walked off the porch into the forest. For a second, Easton thought that he was running off, leaving Easton with an empty wallet and no recording; but Brown was standing at the edge of the trees, waiting.

"Now you stay close to me, you hear? No sound, no movement."

"I don't understand. Aren't we going to a festival or something?"

Brown laughed again. "Oh, hell, yes. Yes, we are."

They plunged into the forest.

*   *   *

Two days later, Easton was in his hotel room, furiously scribbling in his ledger.

The previous pages had contained nothing but entries for expenses and dates and receipts. Easton had always been particularly precise with his expense reports, but now his writing was crazed and frenzied. He continually looked back over his shoulder, as if expecting something to be there watching him.

In the corner of the room sat the portable recorder. Two aluminum discs lay nearby.

Easton was sweating profusely but not from the oppressive Louisiana heat.

"I've tried to destroy them," he wrote feverishly, "but I can't. They won't let me. I can't bear the thought of their being ruined. When I am done here, I will mail them to my sister in Springfield. She is of old Yankee stock, and that may save her. But I hope that she will never listen to them.

"I think I killed Brown, but I don't know. My knife is missing and I have blood on me, but I'm not sure whose blood it is.

"I am losing myself. The music is overtaking me, but it's not really music. Not in the way we know music. It fills me up, leaving nothing of myself inside.

"I hope I did kill Brown. He deserved it, as he would have surely killed me. I know he meant to give me to that thing that danced in the circle. The sound keeps filling my mind, pushing all other thoughts out. I can barely hold onto myself.

"Brown had brought me into the forest to hear the music. After about a half-mile, we entered swampland and the ground became wet and squishy. I could hear the pulse of the rhythm calling and, as we grew closer, I began to pick out voices and instruments in the mix.

"Lomax was right. It is like nothing on this planet and nothing made by man. It is older than this universe and passed down like some unholy heritage. It came from *outside*. Lomax only heard the barest minimum of it but could sense its energy. That's why he could never forget it.

"I tried to turn back then, but Brown refused to let me. This was what I had come for, he said, and he was going to make sure I got my money's worth. I could see flames flickering in the distance, in the deep of the swamp.

"As we got closer, I could see shapes leaping about around the fires while the music grew louder and louder. Brown cautioned me to go no further, and I set the portable recorder on the most stable ground I could find. I put a cylinder in the recorder and hooked up the portable microphone and, finally, for the first time, focused on the music.

"It was like a chant and a hymn and a song of supplication all at once. The lyrics were incomprehensible and the cadences followed an odd rhythm that seemed vaguely familiar. With a jolt of fear, I realized that it followed the 'call, response' form of old blues songs but was stronger, rougher, as if the blues music had spawned from it. The instruments were primitive drums made with what looked uncomfortably like leather skin and long white flutes of an odd shape which I now realize were human thigh and arm bones.

"A throng of naked men and women danced back and forth in an orgiastic spasm. As they moved, their features became less and less defined until they were nothing but blurs vibrating to the music. Some type of four-legged animals darted between them, and they looked as if they were hounds made out of angles that overlapped one another as they ran with an impossible speed and purpose.

"But it was the things that were playing the flutes that were the worst. They were some sort of amorphous creatures that undulated to the beat of the music. The sounds they made could not be made by any musician alive. They had no eyes or faces.

"I have to choose my words carefully now.

"Something began to rise in the center of the circle. It was large and grew fuller with each second. Its wings spread up to the sky, and the chorus screamed one word over and over again which I could not decipher. Something reached over the tops of the trees and called back in response.

"The music grew louder and louder, and suddenly I realized that it was being echoed by Brown beside me. Before I could stop him, Brown screamed out to the group. Most did not stop, but a few things did. Brown grabbed me and tried to pull me forward.

"I think that was when I stabbed him . . . I don't remember how many times.

"He finally loosened his grip and I tore myself away. I could hear other things coming through the wet ground of the marsh. Something moved in front of the moon, blocking the light. I looked back and screamed.

"I think I went a little mad then.

"Next thing I knew I was in my car and driving away as fast as possible. I was afraid to look in the mirror. I didn't even realize that the recorder was in the back seat until I got back here in the hotel.

"I ran inside and locked the door and sat against it in the dark, waiting for something to come.

"I've been waiting all day. I know that they won't be coming for me because they know I'll return to them. I can't sleep. Every time I close my eyes, I hear the music again. I told myself that I was only checking the discs for quality, but I knew that I really had to hear them again. The sound enveloped me. My sight changed and I was flying through the cosmos on strange wings or swimming through the deepest depths of the ocean amidst millions of others of horribly limbed creatures and I was terrified and thrilled at the same time.

"Just as I shut the disc off quickly, I saw a motion from the upper corner of the room's walls. It was as if something was peeking through the angle and evaluating me. Part of me wanted to rip out the corners while another part wanted to create more angles to look through.

"I can't stop hearing it. The sound pushes everything else out of my mind. I feel it pulling me back and I want to go hear them again. I want to dance among them and become one with the blur and feel the hellhounds dart between my feet.

"I'm packing everything up and sending it to my sister with instructions not to open, play, or admit any of this exists. If I cannot destroy it, I will bury it. I will silence the song."

"There is no quiet anymore. Only the music exists."

*   *   *

Excerpt of an article from *The Huffington Post*, posted on the internet on August 18th, 2008:

"Library of Congress celebrates unexpected discovery!

"A recent auction of the estate of the late Mrs. Florence Covington of Springfield, Massachusetts, yielded an unexpected treasure. A collection of mint-condition aluminum discs and a portable recording device circa 1938 was purchased by the noted antiquarian Timothy M. Goebel, who donated the material to the Library of Congress. It is believed that the recorder was used by Mrs. Covington's brother, Robert Easton, who worked with Alan Lomax during the 1930s in recording the 'root' and 'folk' music of the South. Easton disappeared in 1941, and these are believed to be his final recordings. Plans are being made to release the material to the public as well as to digitize the recordings, which will be distributed free over the Internet."

The Land of Lonesomeness

April 16, 1918

It had rained for most of the night before and, when the sun finally rose, the clouds were still heavy with impending downpours. Slowly, a hole opened in the clouds and a single shaft of golden sunlight broke through and brought the battlefield into sharper relief. No one moved. It was possible, from my position, to see the dead lying between the lines. Most lay where they had fallen, with limbs and heads and bodies making a grim seascape along the fields. I could see in their hills and valleys the oceans of my youth, turning dull and grey before a coming storm or hurricane. If you looked long enough, you could swear that they made waves that peaked and dived with the wind.

I sat in the mud and tried vainly to get some sleep. The German artillery had increased in ferocity and there was not a man among us who did not feel that he was bracing for an onslaught on our lines. No one said it, but we all felt it coming. We had held Mont Kemmel on the French line for weeks now, but I had long ago given up trying to understand why the British Army felt this mound of earth was so important. The Great War, begun among cheers and vainglorious boasting, had become a massacre over inches of useless, blood-engorged dirt.

The men of the 84th Battery of the Royal Field Artillery all wore the same look of hopeless resignation. We could keep going until we were told to stop or else just fall over dead at our posts. Whether death came by way of sniper bullet, artillery shell, or sheer hopelessness made little difference.

Only one face showed any type of life, and that was Lt. Arthur Worth. For that reason alone, no one else ever even spoke to Worth. His spirit was more than any of us could bear. It seemed unlikely, but I was probably the same as Worth four years ago when my wife, Bessie, and I made the mad escape from France back to England at the out-break of war. I sent her to live with my mother and sister in Borth even though I knew that there was no affection between them. My decision had been made and, even at my advanced age of thirty-six, I was determined to join the British Army and do my part.

With my second mate's certificate, I could have joined the Navy, but I had vowed never again to serve upon a ship in any capacity. Even the channel crossings put me in a foul mood as I watched the crew run back and forth on deck. Every second at sea brought back the memo-ries of that decade of my life, and I would call no man "captain" again so long as I lived.

I had no idea where Worth had come from. He vaguely mentioned a youth in Cornwall and a childhood around ships but, when seeing that I would not hear a word about the sea, he never spoke about it again. Worth had joined the 84th a little over a week ago while I was briefly laid up in the hospital unit. An enemy shell had exploded near me and, while I was not seriously injured, it had knocked me briefly unconscious and delirious. When I awoke, I was told that, in my stu-por, I had begun shouting that the Great Redoubt was being attacked by the Watchers and that I had to get back to my observation post in the upper levels or else humanity was doomed.

It took some time to convince the doctors that my remarks were nothing more than a brief memory of my old novel, *The Night Land,* and that I was in full possession of my faculties. They showed nearly as much interest in the plot of the novel as readers had back in 1912 when it was published. Its commercial failure had essentially ended my serious imaginative writing. Although unsatisfying to write, bland ad-venture tales sold far more easily, and I had a new wife and hopefully a family to provide for in the future.

When I returned to the 84th, Worth made me welcome and often sat with me during the long night watches. Although young and clue-less, he loved to hear me tell my stories. I would recite them late into the night, for I had rarely forgotten a word I'd ever written despite the nearly fatal head concussion I had suffered back in 1916 while training new RFA recruits on Salisbury Plain. Even when I was interrupted, Worth would remember exactly where I had left off.

As I spoke, I recalled the events behind every tale and their inspiration. The days and nights, so far away now, spent working away at my typewriter as I tried to capture my imagination on paper. The endless rejections as my work came back again and again until the day when the dam finally burst and first one and then another and then another story sold. The hopes that rose with the publication of each of my four novels, which would be eventually dashed as the low sales figures would slowly trickle back to the publishers. In a way, the war had come at an opportune time for me and I abandoned my writing career for that of a soldier.

But there were times when my stories refused to let me go.

I have seen them. Out there, on the fields, rising from the dead bodies. Those 'Ghost Pirates' of mine walk amongst the corpses. I don't know what it is they are looking for, but they search endlessly for something that hides from them. Occasionally a low moan floats over the ground, but I cannot tell if it is them or the dead that is calling. Several times I have caught them staring at me. Across the dead, we glare at each other, daring the other to make a move. I have sat this way for hours, feeling their fingers reach across and tug at my mind. Once I caught myself bringing my revolver up close to my head. Unaware, I was about to fire when my senses returned. Since that point, I keep my ammunition in a separate pocket.

These fields were once green and alive with flowers and birds. Now only corpses are planted here and the only singing comes from the mortar shells as they descend upon us. Their high-pitched screeches echoed across the fields in an unnatural mechanic choir punctuated by the explosions. The sounds of our artillery were different and with a lower timbre, so the shelling would become a strange symphony of fighting voices.

Worth had stopped over to see me and brought a warning. He had seen the units preparing the guns for movement. We were either preparing for a push or a defence. There seemed to be little difference between the two. I walked to the rear where the draught horses were quartered, but each step I took was like sinking into a soft sponge which took almost all my strength to step through.

"It's just like the ship in your story, Hope," Worth said to me with a smile on his face as he ran off again. In truth, he was right. Once I had written a story where a ship had become lost at sea and, through the mixture of chemicals in its hold and the centuries of elements upon it, had become alive. The seamen who found the ship were attacked by it as by an invading germ. Their boots were ripped off by the soft mass that was the ship's flesh. Only a few escaped alive. This death ground had become the same as that ship's deck. The parallels were disturbing.

Around midday, the Germans attacked with a sudden ferocity. Their guns began with a devastating barrage on our front line, making our soldiers retreat quickly while their fellows were blasted to bits. The order came to withdraw, and I led our men onto our horses as we shifted the guns to the pullback position. The horses strained as the guns sank in the mud, and I had to order several foot soldiers to push the wheels forward. The German army ran up quickly when its shelling subsided and pushed its line forward.

In a matter of minutes, the ground that we had fought and died to defend for most of 1918 fell back to the Hun.

We had to move the guns quickly into position, and the artillery teams were there waiting. There was barely any time to take the measurements before they fired their barrages into the German troops. The shelling slowed their advance but did not stop it. That task fell to the British Army, which, after retreating, set up a new line further in back of Mont Kemmel.

For hours, the air was filled with the high-pitched screeches of the shells and the screams of the men and machines exploding. The men enforced their positions and we moved the horses further back. I spent as much time as I could with my own horse, Monarch, cleaning and feeding him. This was my third horse since being in France. Most could only take so much of the sounds of the shells and the screams and the dying. I could look them in the eye and see when they were about to break. It's one of the skills that had made me effective as a lieutenant in the RFA. My lifetime with horses had come into good use but, lately, I had seen the same looks in the eyes of the soldiers around me. So much so that there were only a few men who did not have that look, and Worth was one of them.

I sought him out during dinner and found him, once again, alone and not eating.

I admonished him for not keeping up his strength. More than anyone, I knew the importance of eating to one's overall fitness. Without another word, I set to and quickly ate my own dinner as he stared at me in disbelief.

"How can you eat such food?" He asked. "It's disgusting."

I laughed and told him that this food was a luxury compared to what I had eaten in my youth at sea. I'd dined on slabs of hardtack that crawled with maggots and flies. Often the officers would bet on which of the starving seamen would break down first and eat from the open barrel. With pride, I remembered striding defiantly to the barrel, breaking off a large piece of tack, and biting down to the cheers of the cabin boys and sneers of the officers. The vomiting and bowel distress afterward had been worth it.

That night, I told Worth the tales of my own hunting ground, the Sargasso Sea. I told him of the ships caught helplessly in the grip of the seaweed-choked sea and the monstrous creatures that lived there. The story of the survivors of the *Homebird,* which had been one of my early successes, touched him deeply. "Did they ever escape?" he asked hopefully.

I looked in his eyes and saw the real meaning of his question. Instead of the truth I told him that their escape was a story that I had simply not written yet but would someday. But, in truth, there was no escape from the Sargasso. The rescue I had written in my novel about the 'boats of the *Glen Carrig*' had a false ending—one tacked on because my editor had requested an uplifting conclusion that would please readers. It hadn't seemed to make any difference in the sales.

Like those helpless, doomed characters, so were we marching towards an inevitable end. I knew in my heart that those fictional characters on my stranded ships would eventually succumb to the sea monsters around them or starvation. That was why I never wrote the final chapter. It was too much to deal with characters who, for all their efforts or enthusiasm or hopes, would never escape.

There were Watchers out there, in the dark, just waiting beyond the firing line.

Later that day, the commanding officer gathered us all together. We were a ragtag group, standing in the mud and the blood, patched together with bandages and grit. The line would be retreating in the night, he said, but we needed to set up a forward observation post on the base of Mont Kemmel. He could barely look us in the eye because he knew what he was asking of us. Volunteers were needed, he explained; he would not order any man to take the risk. It would surely mean death for any who stayed.

I volunteered immediately, although I had no idea why.

The C.O. nodded gratefully at me and paused. Finally Northrup also volunteered and we set out to prepare. I'd known little of Northrup and spoken to him less. He was a strong, strapping lad when he joined the 84th. Now he was shrunken and his clothes hung on him as on a child's doll. His eyes were dull and, though he would follow any order you gave him, the rest of his mind had walked away in the hope of coming back out someday when the sun shone again and there were birds singing in the air instead of bombs.

April 18th

The 84th has retreated further back from the line. We watched them leave with a sense of stern resignation. Under darkness, we moved forward and set up our post. Northrup said nothing and I lost interest in speaking to him. I put him in charge of sending our messages back to the company and tried to get some sleep.

When I awoke, a grey dawn had already broken and I was surprised to find Worth sitting by my side. "You didn't think I'd leave you here with that great sausage, did you? That'd be a fate worse than death!"

I laughed, and he asked me to tell him one of my Carnacki stories. I'd always enjoyed writing them and still couldn't understand why they didn't sell better. It would be a long, painful day, so I told him the story of the hideous 'Hog' from the outer spheres, which I always considered to be my best Carnacki yarn even if I couldn't sell it anywhere.

As I told him of the battle between Carnacki and the 'Hog,' I described the oppressive atmosphere that bore down upon the Ghost-Finder and the way it tried to influence him to create his own undoing. Worth asked if it was the same atmosphere as the one we felt there, dug into Mont Kemmel like ticks on a dog. I replied simply that it was the same atmosphere as I have felt all my life, whether in Ireland, on the deck of a ship sailing around the Horn, on a stage in Blackburn as I faced down the greatest escape-artist of all time, at a typewriter wrestling with my inability to express in words what I dreamed in my mind or here, on a battlefield that had lost all meaning. I carried it with me always.

The Germans made another advance with a volley of artillery later that day. The rest of the night was spent hiding low from the bursts and the singing bombs. We sent back several messages that alerted the 84th with no idea if they were ever received. Through the night we tried to sleep as much as possible, but little rest was claimed.

I feel old and that is not something I have ever felt. I look at Northrup and I feel our lives draining away from us. Only Worth remains upbeat. Sometimes his nature keeps me going but at other times I swear I could kill him.

April 19th

The barrage has been endless. I do not know how we have not been killed already. By the afternoon, a haze falls over the battlefield and all we can see are vague shapes moving back and forth. Northrup has been busy sending messages back to the 84th and I find myself praying that we will receive withdrawal orders soon, but the C.O. has been silent.

I have no more words. Worth asks for more, but I have none to give him.

My sight is riveted to the grey shapes coming closer in the mist and haze. The Ghost Pirates are there, running back and forth, stopping, running, crouching, and crawling. Their eyes penetrate me. I cannot tell if they are stalking me or beckoning me to join them.

Then, in the dim background, behind the grey shapes and booming crashes, I see it moving forward like a mountain walking. I have seen it before in my mind and in my dreams, but now it stumbles towards me.

I see the Watching Thing of the North-West from my land of future night eclipsing the dull circle of the sun. It strides forward. The sounds of the exploding bombs echo his footsteps. I try to tell Northrup, but he sees nothing.

I cry out for Worth to bear witness, and then Northrup finally speaks. There is no Worth, he says; who am I talking to? But Worth is there beside him, smiling. I point at him but, again, Northrup sees nothing. "You've gone mad again," Northrup says. "You've been this way since you took that blow to your head. Talking to yourself. Telling tales. I tell you there is nothing there!"

I look back at the battlefield and see the Watcher even closer this time. So close that I can see its huge maw opening and closing to the sounds of battle. "It's coming!" I scream and Worth moves away, apologising. He had only come for the stories, you see, and didn't want to see the end. Suddenly, as if he had moved behind a curtain, Worth is gone and Northrup is pulling on my sleeve.

We have to leave, he says, withdrawal or not. It's too dangerous as the German shelling comes ever closer and closer. I begin gathering up our gear when I hear the Watcher's voice speaking to me. It comes in a high-pitched shriek. I look back in a terrified peace as I see the great mouth screeching at me. The sound of the bombs comes closer. I stand still, arms outstretched. Northrup grabs at me, but I do not move. The Watcher speaks me out of existence.

[*On April 19th, 1918, William Hope Hodgson and another officer sustained a direct hit from German artillery. They were blown to pieces.*]

Passing Spirits

For H.P.L.

"... Cthulhu never existed. Azathoth never existed. Nyarlathotep, Shub-Niggurath, Yog-Sothoth, none of them. I made them all up."

I was sitting in H. P. Lovecraft's small study, listening to him rant. It was 1936. In barely under a year he would be dead of stomach cancer. I felt a need to try to tell him this. To let him know that the pain in his abdomen was not just 'gas' but a serious medical problem that he should seek treatment for immediately. When I tried to explain that I knew all about those types of things, he refused to listen and went on ranting.

"But you know what is the worst thing about all this?" he continued in his nasal voice. "This is what I'll be remembered for ... if I'm remembered by anyone. For making up a pantheon of monster-gods. Basically, for stealing from Dunsany."

I tried to explain that that wasn't the truth, that he had added much more to it than just the idea of a cosmic mythology; but he wouldn't listen. It was very strange and not at all the type of conversation I had envisioned having. I wouldn't say that the man was bitter, but he certainly wasn't happy about a lot of things.

Looking at him, I felt that there were so many things I should be saying, but I didn't. My time was too short for that and the memory was already fading.

When I awoke, I was in my apartment and there was a ribbon of spit on the pillow next to me. I checked it for blood, but it was clear. My head throbbed as usual and I felt the familiar dull ache behind my eyes. I crawled out of bed and turned the TV on as I dressed. CNN was going on about some flareup in the Middle East (I had long ago stopped caring about such things—there was always a flareup somewhere or other), and I flipped it over to "Scooby-Doo" on the Cartoon Network. It was one of my favorites from the first year (the best year before they got into all that guest star nonsense and then brought in Scrappy-Doo—who the hell ever thought that was a good idea?) with the laughing space ghost that had the glowing skull head. I remember how that scared the piss out of me as a kid. A lot of things scared me back then, before I learned that the only real scary thing in life was stuff like cancer and brain tumors. There weren't any gods or monsters. Not in the real world. Here we had sickness and disease instead of vampires and ghosts.

I brushed my teeth and took my medicine. Looking at the clock, I had about an hour to get to work, so I knew I'd have enough time. I sat down and watched the rest of the show, waiting for that great 'Scooby-Doo' ending where they unmask the villain. I always loved that.

At work, I tried to pretend that I cared about what I was doing, but it didn't really matter. I was just another clerk in just another bookstore. Nothing special. Nothing unique. I had 'Help Desk' duty, which everyone knew was the worst. Listening to blue-haired old ladies trying to describe what they wanted. "I don't know the name but I saw it on Oprah. It had a green cover."

The other clerks tried not to look at me too closely. My hair had grown back, more or less, but there's still something about a cancer patient that sets you off from everyone else. Maybe it's a smell or some invisible 'early-warning' system, but no one looks at you the same way afterward. That didn't bother me too much. Most of them weren't worth knowing anyway; weird, trendy people of questionable sexuality. I'd never had much in common with them, nor they with me.

Lovecraft's ghost followed me through the Reference section while I guided a customer who was pointing out books with errors in them. I hate it when someone does that.

"The tumor's getting larger," intoned Dr. Lyons with all the seriousness of a hanging judge. He held up two cat scans. "As you can see from the earlier one, it was only about the size of a grape. Now it's getting close to a plum."

I'd never eaten a plum, so had no idea about its size. I figured that it wasn't a good comparison.

"So none of the treatments have done anything?"

Dr. Lyons sighed. "No. The radiation treatments barely seemed to slow its growth. Since we stopped doing those, it's gotten bigger. The medication doesn't seem to be working either. Surgery, although not recommended, is still an option."

"You told me before that it was too dangerous."

"It is. But I don't really see any other way." He got up from behind his desk. "Michael, you have to understand that without surgery this is going to continue to grow."

Apparently I wasn't impressed enough by this.

"Michael, you will die without this operation."

I thought about this. Dying wasn't necessarily the worst thing. Chemo was certainly on an equal footing. Poverty was right up there too.

"How long?"

"If the tumor continues to grow at this rate, maybe four to six months, on the outside. But, Michael, they won't be comfortable months."

He went on to describe how, as the tumor grows, I would begin to lose brain functions. My speech and sight would be affected. My coordination would deteriorate, and I would start having hallucinations. In short, it would be a living death.

I thanked him and left. Dr. Lyons was confused and followed me out into the hall. He wanted to know why I didn't want to schedule the operation immediately. I looked at him.

"Because I can't afford it." I turned away. He didn't stop me.

Robert E. Howard made a writing career out of stories of strong, rugged men who tamed their worlds and bent others to their will. It was a universe of barbarians with strong sword arms and evil sorcerers who plotted magic schemes of conquest. Not once do I recall an REH character dying of cancer or an illness. Of course, that probably would have been too personal a thing considering how his mother died.

"Don't forget," Lovecraft said, "Two-Gun Bob killed himself."

"Yeah, well, there's plenty of ways to do that. Sometimes doing nothing works just as well." I replied.

There had been an article in the paper not too long ago about a doctor doing work on cancer treatment. It wasn't one of those peach-pit things, but it was an herbal remedy—supposedly some type of combination of herbs and diets. I'd read a lot of those books, including the one by Norman Cousins. Sometimes they seemed to work, most times they didn't. I'd never had the discipline to see them all through but, considering the alternatives, I didn't have a lot of choices.

At work, I looked up the doctor's book. To my surprise, we actually had a copy. As I glanced through it, it looked more like a cookbook than anything else. The medicine was a blend of herbs and vitamins (supposedly available at any health food store), and there was a special diet that focused on macrobiotics and avoided things like meat and oils. It seemed to be typical stuff, but the doctor's photo had a kind and gentle face, so I bought it. I enjoyed making my manager nervous when she rang it up. It was obvious why I was buying it, but no one dared to mention it.

"You know," Lovecraft said to me in a horrified whisper, "someone once said that my Shub-Niggurath was a representation of sexual disease. Can you believe that?"

I heard this at least once a day. It was one of the things that really bothered him given his upbringing and personality.

"Yeah, I can believe it," I replied. My manager didn't even look at me. She had gotten used to me talking like this.

On the way home, I bought the herbs listed in the book at the local health food store. I didn't recognize most of the names, and the clerk wasn't much help either. Several of the ingredients weren't there, so I had to substitute. The clerk thought that the other herbs and vitamins were just as good; even though I didn't believe him, I didn't have anything else to go on.

I stopped at a local restaurant and had a big steak meal with a plateful of french fries. My farewell to meat. I avoided the seafood platter out of deference to Lovecraft, who, as always, kept looking around and exclaiming, "Gad, how these birds do eat!"

At home later, I read through the book some more. The doctor believed that the steady use of his herb/vitamin combination, along with the diet, was able to curb the growth of cancer. In a few instances he described, the cancer had disappeared completely. I laid the pill bottles on the counter. I mixed the herbs together. There were clear specifications on what to take, how much, and when. I took the first dose and followed it with Dr. Lyons's medication. It had a long clinical name that I couldn't pronounce, but it was "the latest in cancer treatment." Couldn't hurt to keep taking it: I'd paid for it, after all, and it hadn't been cheap. The cost of being poor and sick in America.

There wasn't much on TV that night. The cable channels were all boring, so I put on an old *Night Stalker* tape and read for a while. Out of habit, I picked up *The Dunwich Horror* and started reading "The Shadow over Innsmouth" again. It had always been one of my favorites, but Lovecraft wouldn't give me any peace.

"Disease, disease, disease. That's all they keep talking about. According to some critics, everything I wrote came from a fear of disease, either sexual or mental. Why couldn't it just be a story? Why did it have to be *about* something?"

"You think that's bad," I replied, "you should read Hodgson. Now there's a man who had a real problem with disease."

That piqued his interest, and he settled down with a volume of Hodgson's short stories. One of the small-press books, of course; I would never have been able to afford a first edition, and he wasn't reprinted often.

Lovecraft read quickly and quietly. Reading was one of the few things that kept him calm. Every so often he would chuckle to himself or make a satisfied sound after reading a particularly good section.

In this way, I eventually fell asleep.

I was walking through the streets of Innsmouth. Past the Esoteric Order of Dagon church (with its sinister shadow in the basement), along the streets of houses that, though habitable, showed no signs of life. I walked by the supermarket and waved to the stock clerk who, as usual, bore a striking resemblance to Frank Belknap Long. (I hoped he'd had an easier life than the real Long.) Zadok Allen was wandering about, of course, and we exchanged laughs and old stories.

"Well, ya know, death's funny. It comes when ya don't call and never answers when ya do!" Zadok laughed without the trademark Yankee accent.

Lovecraft the narrator came lumbering down the street from the supermarket, and Zadok staggered off to meet him, practicing his Yankee-speak as he walked. They had an appointment to keep.

I sat on the beach and looked out at Devil's Reef. It was an ugly thing—a piece of rock jutting out of the water. Beyond it, I knew, the ocean floor fell away and the Deep Ones swam not far beyond.

Several fishermen with the 'Innsmouth look' stopped by and encouraged me to swim out. "G'wan," they said, "why not?"

Why not, indeed? I took off my clothes (never self-conscious in dreams . . . I had never had the 'waking up in school naked' dream) and entered the water. Though I had done it a few times before, I'd never swum out very far. This time felt different. The water was warmer, heavier than before and it enveloped me like nothing I had ever felt. I swam out to the rock and climbed on top of it.

From there, I could see Zadok and Lovecraft talking on the beach as Zadok gave his little speech. And then it struck me. Every other time I'd been here, I had only seen and experienced what Lovecraft had written in the story. I'd never been out to Devil's Reef before and, remembering the story, neither had the narrator. Oh sure, he described planning on going to Devil's Reef with his cousin and diving off the deep end, but it wasn't an actual place visited in the story. Yet I was there. I could feel the rough stone beneath my fingers and, looking over the other end, could swear that I could see other things beneath the surface, beckoning to me.

Slowly, I dipped into the water and followed.

When I woke up this time, there was blood on the pillow. That wasn't good. I touched my nose and my fingers came away bloody. Suddenly, my head was shoved into an invisible vise and I collapsed back into my pillow, barely able to keep from screaming.

In his chair, stroking an invisible cat that wasn't there but was anyway, Lovecraft sat silently.

After a few minutes, the pain subsided and I was able to sit up. The front of my undershirt was covered in blood. This hadn't been the first attack, but it was definitely the worst.

"Dr. Lyons said it would only get worse," Lovecraft added unnecessarily.

I ignored him and went to clean myself up.

Sometime later, I made myself some breakfast. I didn't have any of the macrobiotic stuff the book doctor recommended, so I made do with eggs and bacon. I'd give up the bad stuff later, although I had begun to think that there wasn't any point in giving anything up and that I should just surrender to excesses. Spend the last months of my life carousing from one bar to another, drinking too much, eating bad food, sleeping with anonymous women (assuming I could find any who were willing), and giving myself up to the extremes.

Lovecraft looked disapprovingly at me.

"I know," I said, "you'd probably prefer if I just sat there quietly and suffered the way you did while I eat a can of cold beans and some crackers."

"You could do worse," he said, but I didn't see how.

"I could do a lot better," I said and started mentally counting up the money in my bank account. Just enough for a real large splurge or six months of diminishing capacity. Yeah. Life's great.

"What about the dream?" Lovecraft asked.

I looked at him. I'd grown used to him asking questions at the most inappropriate time for a spirit who shouldn't even be here ("Why are you haunting me anyway? What did I do to you?"), but this was unexpected.

"What dream?"

He looked at me. I knew perfectly well what he meant, and he had this habit of looking at me a certain way when I was avoiding a subject. I expected him to hand me a business card someday with "H. P. Lovecraft, Conscience" printed on it. Jiminy Cricket had nothing on him.

"It was a dream, that's all."

He just glared at me. "Here," he finally said, "read this. It might help you understand." He threw a copy of Hodgson's *The Ghost Pirates* at me. I still hadn't figured out how he was able to manipulate objects, but my head was hurting too much to wonder about it.

I looked at the book. "I read it already."

"Read it again. You obviously didn't get the connection." He went back and starting petting the cat again. It was an all-black kitten whose name, if you dared to mention it in today's PC climate, could get you into a lot of trouble. "All the pigeons come home to roost," I thought.

I took the herb/vitamin potion and chased it with one of Dr. Lyons's Miracle Cure. "Good for what ails ya!" I got dressed and left for work. On the way, I found the Hodgson buried deep into my coat pocket. He put it there. I put it there. Didn't matter. It was there anyway.

When I got to work, I saw Keziah Mason in the occult section, chuckling to herself as she read one of the New Age witchcraft books. She certainly didn't look like the young, trendy/sexy girls that are witches in today's movies and TV shows. Brown Jenkin was curling around her feet, looking up at her from time to time with a very hungry shine in his eyes. This was something new. Usually it's just Lovecraft, now other characters were coming to visit.

Poe lived virtually his entire life in poverty. He died in a gutter in Baltimore. That tells you something right there. He never lived to see his work gain the fame it deserved. Neither did Lovecraft. Neither did Howard. Is there a pattern here?

The last clear thing I remember from that afternoon at work was waiting on Nyarlathotep. I suppose it was only inevitable. With Keziah and Jenkin about, the Dark Man couldn't be far away. I was running the register when he came up. He put a couple of self-help books on the counter (two of those *I'm Okay, You're Okay* self-affirmation kind of things) and started fumbling for his wallet. This struck me as kind of funny, as I couldn't imagine Nyarlathotep having a wallet. I wondered what would be inside it. Would he have a driver's license? From where? Kadath maybe? Snapshots of Keziah and Azathoth? Who did he want contacted in case of an emergency? And what was the wallet made out of? I started laughing, which made him look up at me. The man was dark. I don't mean just your normal black man. Nyarlathotep was the antithesis of light. Then he smiled and I could smell his breath. It wasn't the stagnating breath of decay as I'd been expecting. It was sweet and cloying. It made you think of hot summer nights when the heat sticks to your skin and you can peel your sweat away in layers. My eyes closed and I went away.

I was in the Miskatonic Library with Lovecraft and Henry Armitage. We were looking at the dead thing that lay on the floor where the guard dog had killed it. The upper body was strange enough, but it was below the torso that "sheer phantasy began." Wilbur Whateley had died in his attempt to steal the *Necronomicon*. "Why didn't he just buy a copy from a book dealer off eBay or something?" I said. Armitage glared at me.

The game was afoot and I was standing in the open fields of Dunwich. Before me was the farmhouse of the Fryes, the poor, doomed Fryes. It was 3 A.M., but I could see everything as if it were high noon. Even from a distance I could hear their terrified conversation on the phone party line. I saw the trees near the house bend apart as the invisible thing came closer. I had expected it to be something like Godzilla rampaging through downtown Tokyo. That's what happens when you're a child of the media and you grow up watching a genre that consumes itself with such gusto.

I heard the splintering of wood and looked up to see the top of the farmhouse cave in at the middle. The screams were horrible. Within seconds, the house was gone and the thing continued walking through the forest. "The Elmer Fryes had been erased from Dunwich."

I made my way up to Sentinel Hill where the final confrontation would take place. I had walked this route before with Lovecraft/Armitage, but this time felt different. I could feel the wind on my face. My body had form and substance where before it was only dust and mist. Sometimes I was Rice. Sometimes I was Morgan. And once, just once, there was a brief time when I could have sworn I was Armitage and I was spraying the spawn of Azathoth with the powder.

Above me there was the usual half-face squirming in torment, except this time it stopped. It looked straight at me, ignoring the other two. "And what do you think you're looking at?" it said before it went back to its part and obligingly disappeared. I almost expected it to say "I'm gonna keep my eye on you" before it left, but it didn't. Afterwards we went back to the circle of terrified townsfolk and Armitage went into his speech. "Watch the skies!" I mouthed behind him. "Watch the skies!" The townspeople looked at me as if perhaps the wrong thing had been sprayed with the powder on the hill.

I regretted not seeing Old Wizard Whateley this trip. He was always a lot of fun to talk to, particularly if you got a few drinks into him.

When I awoke, I was in a hospital bed.

I'd been in them before, of course, so this was no really strange thing to me, but it still wasn't a good sign. There was a strong coppery taste in my mouth. I knew that wasn't a good sign either. My finger was hooked up to one of those machines, and I could hear the heartbeat monitor behind me, happily beeping away. (I've always wondered why they put those things just out of your sight. As if watching your heartbeat might make it stop.) I felt weak and worn out. My clothes were gone and I was in the hospital gown. Lovecraft was sitting in the chair near by.

"Can you believe what they've done to my city?" he asked when he saw I was finally awake. "They tore up the bridge. Tore up that historic bridge to make room for more traffic and make the downtown more *scenic.*" He pronounced scenic with an extra flourish of sarcasm.

"Where am I?" My bed was encircled by one of those curtains but, due to the lack of noise, I could tell I wasn't in an emergency ward. It was still somewhat light out, so I knew it was daytime, but I didn't know what day.

"You're in Rhode Island Hospital. It's attached to Jane Brown, you know. I went and looked in at the room where I died. There's a nurses' station there now. Everything changes."

I pulled the cord and buzzed for the nurse.

A large woman in a white uniform came a few minutes later. She explained that I had been unconscious for the last few days after I'd come into the emergency room by ambulance. "You've had an attack," she said, and Dr. Lyons had me admitted. She'd alert him that I was awake and left the room after giving me some more medication. "Painkillers," she said, but she didn't bother to tell me what kind.

Inspector Legrasse walked by my door and waved at Lovecraft. He was dragging along some half-crazed swamp dweller behind him.

A little while later, Dr. Lyons came in, but he looked an awful lot like Jeffrey Coombs from *Re-Animator*.

"Mike," he said.

"Dr. Lyons," I replied in my best Jack Webb voice. "Where's Bill Gannon? I heard he got arrested for wife beating."

He looked at me as if I were some sort of test bug. "What?"

"Nothing. A lame attempt at pop culture humor. What am I doing here?"

Dr. Lyons pulled up a chair. "You had an attack."

"What kind of an attack?"

He sat there for a moment, searching for the right words. "You were at work. Do you remember that?"

I nodded yes.

"You were waiting on a customer. He was a black gentleman. In the middle of the transaction you began screaming and yelling for him to leave you alone. In fact, I'm told that you actually said that the man should 'take his old witch away and stop haunting you.' Sound familiar?"

"No. Not at all. I really did that?"

"I'm afraid so. A few of your co-workers tried to get you to calm down, but you went into a spasm and blacked out. You've been here for two days."

I tried to concentrate on what he was saying, but all I could see were those weird dimensional things from *From Beyond* circling his head.

"What happened?"

"The tumor is growing. It's pressing on the part of your brain that covers motor functions and memory. I don't know what's happening to it. It almost seems as if something is making it grow faster." He paused for a moment. "Michael, you're experiencing hallucinations."

"Oh?"

"It's not unusual, given the tumor's location. But I admit that I didn't think this would happen so quickly."

Dr. Lyons/Herbert West stood up so he would appear more impressive.

"Michael, you need to have the operation."

"We've gone over that before."

"I know. You don't have the money or insurance. But we'll find a way, Michael. You've got to do this."

I looked at him. It was easier to just go along.

"Okay. Sure."

"Good. I've got you set up for the operation in two days. We'll keep you here and keep an eye on you until then. Okay?"

I nodded.

"All right. Just rest easy. I'll be back later."

After he left, I lay there for about ten minutes. Then I got up, got dressed, and left. Lovecraft followed me out. No one stopped me. It seemed that no one took any notice of me, and I wondered if they saw me at all or if it was just the way things are in Rhode Island.

I took the bus home.

There was only one message on my machine. It was from my boss.

"Michael . . . um, I'm sorry to have to say this but we're going to have to let you go. I hope you understand. We just can't have any more scenes like today. I know you have problems but, legally, we can't afford the risk. Sorry. We'll mail you your last paycheck. Um . . . so you don't really need to come back. Okay? Hope everything works out for you. Bye."

I took an extra dose of the herb/vitamin potion and lay down in bed.

"So now what are you going to do?" asked Lovecraft.

I didn't say anything.

Lovecraft was standing near the window. There wasn't much of a view to see. He had on one of his father's old suits. It fit him pretty well but was still a little loose in the shoulders. I wasn't sure if it was one of the suits that got stolen while he was in New York.

"You know," I finally said, "I've read both of the biographies. Joshi and de Camp's."

He grimaced.

"At least Joshi took the time to try and understand the era," he responded. "De Camp lived through some of it and he still couldn't understand how it affected me."

"They never said much about your death. About how you felt as you lay there in that bed at Jane Brown."

He turned to look at me. For some reason, his lantern jaw looked more solid. I could almost swear that his chin was reflecting the light.

"Go to sleep, Michael." It was the first time I had heard him refer to me by name.

I went to sleep.

Professor Wilmarth/Lovecraft was talking about the black stone. Akeley had sent it through the mail and it had disappeared. I took out the stone from Machen's "Novel of the Black Seal" and showed it to him. He was interested but disappointed. "Yes, but it's not quite what we're looking for." He played the record for me, and I listened to that strange otherworldly voice.

"To Nyarlathotep, Mighty Messenger, must all things be told. And He shall put on the semblance of men, the waxen mask and the robe that hides, and come down from the world of Seven Suns to mock. . . ."

It was not surprising that it was my voice speaking on the record. Wilmarth/Lovecraft took no notice.

Suddenly, we jumped forward and I was in Akeley's cabin. Wilmarth/Lovecraft was talking to Akeley, who was sitting in the opposite chair and covered in his huge robe. Akeley was describing Yuggoth with its great cities of black stone. After a while, Wilmarth/Lovecraft went to bed and I took his place.

"So," Akeley said in that queer, disjointed voice, "what are you looking for?"

"Not much," I answered. "It's just that I've always wondered—a lot of us have wondered—who are you really? Under that mask. Who are you? Are you one of the Fungi? Are you Nyarlathotep?"

"Why don't you see for yourself?"

I reached over and took off the mask. It was Lovecraft. "Of course," he said, "who else would it be?"

I never developed a taste for Clark Ashton Smith. I knew he was a good writer, but something about his work never clicked with me. Lovecraft, Howard, and Smith were touted as *Weird Tales*'s "Three Musketeers." And yet it was often said that Seabury Quinn was more popular with the readers than any of them. Lovecraft never got a cover. Guess Margaret Brundage just couldn't bring herself to paint

Cthulhu and, after all, there were no half-naked damsels in distress in Lovecraft. Maybe he would have been more successful if there had been.

The next few days passed strangely.

I don't need to say that I didn't show up for the operation. Dr. Lyons called once, demanding to know where I was and why I didn't come in. He didn't call again. In fact, nobody called after a while. I got to the point where I had to pick up the phone and check it regularly to make sure it was still working.

I stopped doing that when a thick, guttural voice came on the empty line and said, "YOU FOOL, WARREN IS DEAD!"

The dreams went back and forth then. Sometimes I'd have them when I was sleeping. Sometimes I'd have them when I was awake. I'd be walking down Thayer Street and suddenly I'd be walking down a street in Arkham, heading for the Witch House.

Were they real? Was anything real at this point? I remember all those stories where everyone knows that the dreams are real except for the dreamer. In *Pet Semetary,* the main character (whose name escapes me but he was played by Dale Midkiff in the movie which wasn't a bad adaptation—King had suffered far worse) goes for a midnight walk with the spirit of the dead student. The student leads him down the path to the Pet Semetary and then tells him not to go beyond the wall. He might as well have put a big neon sign saying, "This way to the Wendigo's Zombie grounds." When he wakes up, he's stunned to find his feet covered with mud and sticks. When I read that, I wasn't overcome with fear. Of course the dream was real. Aren't they always? My first thought was, "Damn, that's gonna be hard to clean up."

The dreams. Eventually the dreams are the only things that are real. In the dreams there's no cancer, only monsters, gods, demons, ghouls, and things you can grab and hold with your hands. Something you can fight and batter into submission. Ever try to grab a cancer?

I stopped eating after a while. Didn't know why I was bothering anyway. Everything tasted the same and had that metallic, coppery taste to it. Lovecraft approved of that. We talked a long time about things, and only occasionally would something creep through the woods or the walls. I kept taking the herb/vitamin potion along with Dr. Lyons's medication until it ran out. The Hounds of Tindalos ran through every once in a while but stopped coming when I ran out of food to give them. The cats of Ulthar never bothered to come at all, preferring to stay on the moon until everything was over.

"Am I dying?" I asked Lovecraft.

"Maybe. Who knows? What is death? Don't ask me."

"But you're dead."

"I am?"

I finally found the section in *The Ghost Pirates* that Lovecraft was talking about.

The good ship had been plagued by the appearance of ghost pirates who are making away with the sailors. There were ghost ships following them through the mist. The narrator tries to explain what's happening:

> "Well, if we were in what I might call a healthy atmosphere, they would be quite beyond our power to see or feel, or anything. And the same with them; but the more we're like this, the more real and actual they could grow to us. See? That is, the more we should become able to appreciate their form of materialness. That's all. I can't make it any clearer."

I was spending more time away. I couldn't remember what day it was or what month. The cable was shut off eventually, which was okay because the electricity followed shortly after. I lay in bed, fumbling through my mind. Things and places wandered through me until, eventually, I found myself spending less and less time in that small room in Rhode Island. When I was there, my head was one large hurt. I had begun to think of my brain as a big black stain. If I could lift my head and look in the mirror, I felt sure that my eyes would be completely black.

Lovecraft accompanied me most of the time, but sometimes I was alone walking through the worlds. I was solid, with form and substance. Here I was thin and ghostly. The people there welcomed me. They grabbed my hand, slapped me on the back, and brought me along. Here, only Lovecraft stayed at my side and, eventually, I woke up and even he wasn't there anymore. He had moved beyond, and to see him I'd have to let myself drift away.

I didn't float off the way you hear in those near-death shows. I fell away from myself, sinking through the earth. I was going beyond and following old Joe Slater to that strange place that was a star far away which shone upon Olathoë aeons ago.

The ground below me became a solid deck of a ship. I felt it move through the water as we raced forward into the strange and forbidding sea where an island had suddenly appeared.

Asenath looked at me through Edward Derby's eyes. I sent three bullets into her brain.

I reached for the smooth surface of polished glass.

I thrilled to the sound of Erich Zann's music as the deaf-mute man called to something outside the window.

I tore through Capt. Norrys's body while the sounds of the rats ran off in the distance.

I unfurled the photo at the corner of Pickman's painting.

I cringed in Nahum Gardner's farmhouse as the colour sprang free.

I . . . I . . . I . . . had become . . . fiction.

Acknowledgments

"The Adventure of the Prometheus Calculation" is previously unpublished.

"Casting Fractals," first published in *Black Wings V*, edited by S. T. Joshi (PS Publishing, 2016).

"'The Dreamer in Fire': Notes on Robert Winslow's 'Sutter's Corners,'" first published in *Grimoire* No. 1 (1993).

"The Gathering Daemonica," first published in *Dark Corridor #3* (2009).

"'Good Morning, Innsmouth!'" is previously unpublished.

"He Whose Feet Trod the Lost Aeons" is previously unpublished.

"Hellhounds on the Trail," first published in *Shadows of the Past: Arkham Horror Book Club Anthology, Volume I,* edited by Frederic Norton (NEHW Press, 2014).

"Homecoming," first published in *New Tales of the Old Ones*, edited by Michael C. Dick (KnightWatch Press, 2013).

"'How Does That Make You Feel?'" is previously unpublished.

"The Land of Lonesomeness," first published in the *Weird Fiction Review* No. 5 (November 2014).

"My Brother's Keeper," first published in *Wicked Tales: The Journal of the New England Horror Writers, Volume 3* (2015).

"Passing Spirits," first published in *Black Wings*, edited by S. T. Joshi (PS Publishing, 2010).

"Showtime," first published in *Dark Corridor* No. 1 (2007).

"Static," first published in *Machina Mortis: Steampunk'd Tales of Terror, Volume 1*, edited by Sam Gafford (KnightWatch Press, 2013).

"Sunspots" is previously unpublished.

"Weltschmerz," first published in *Black Wings III*, edited by S. T. Joshi (PS Publishing, 2014).

"What Was That?" is previously unpublished.

www.ingramcontent.com/pod-product-compliance
Lightning Source LLC
Chambersburg PA
CBHW061441030726
47503CB00005B/1516